Henry Muselle's Treasure

A Search For Lost French Gold

Henry Muselle's Treasure

A Search For Lost French Gold

Roger A. Bartley

Copyright © March 2003 by Roger A. Bartley
First Edition

Without limiting the rights under copyright reserved above,
no part of this publication may be reproduced, stored in or
introduced into a retrieval system, or transmitted, in any form or
by any means (electronic, mechanical, photocopying, recording,
or otherwise), without the prior written permission of both
the copyright owner and the publisher of this book.

Published by Aventine Press, LLC
45 East Flower Street, Ste. 236
Chula Vista, CA 91910-7631, USA

www.aventinepress.com

ISBN: 1-59330-022-0

Printed in the United States of America

ALL RIGHTS RESERVED

For my three sons Todd, Corey and Daniel, the adventures we have shared together and the treasures we have found.

For my grandchildren Kyrsten, Christopher, Alex and all those yet to come. May you find the right questions.

Chapter One

Henry Muselle's Journal
Late Thursday Night, April 13

It's three AM and I'm awake - again. This sleeplessness has to stop. When I relax and my mind begins to clear, all I can think about is the treasure. It's been nine generations since my ancestor hid it. That one day, two hundred and fifty years ago my life changed. I wasn't born. I wasn't even a twinkle in anyone's eye. And yet, it influenced my life as much or more than anything in my own lifetime. I didn't ask to be related to someone associated with a treasure. It is not my fault my family is obsessed with clearing up the mystery. Now, I am the one charged with finding it - whether I want to or not. After all this time and all the searching, it should be simple to find - but it's not.

The trail leads to a farm outside of this town - Minerva. I've been teaching history here for seven months. It's not a bad place for an American history teacher to be marooned. There certainly is plenty of history here.

The village sprang up in the early 1800's, as did many towns in the area. Its political savvy and its location, far enough from industrial centers to be comfortable, brought it roads, canals, railroads, and industries. Nestled in the glacial hills of Northeastern Ohio, it was named for the Greek Goddess of Wisdom, Goddess of War, or the first white child born in the village depending on which story you want to believe.

As I peruse the volumes in the local historical society, looking for answers to my own quest, I have found the village to be full of treasures. No one will ever know the number of patents and inventions, which originated in Minerva. Steel railroad cars, electric fuse panels, snow plows, street vacuums, and turbine blades made from a single metal crystal are some of the things which quietly make the world better. Treasures like a Secretary of Defense, brothers who played in the World Series and a famous judge's wife all fade from memory. I think Minerva's principal treasure is its families. They raise good kids here.

There is talk of a new project in town, which I fear may change the complexion of this rural haven. I hear a new road is coming near the village. There is a lot of talk about it, but I'm not sure the denizens realize the impact the highway might have on their lifestyle.

History and highways certainly aren't helping me find the treasure. Mention of the "lost French gold," as the Minerva folk care to refer to it, brings strange reactions. I get the feeling the local people don't care about my search. I'm an outsider. They seem to have a treasure agenda of their own. Will any of them help me with my problem? Fat chance. I don't know whether they think I'm an academic type when I ask about the treasure, or if they just think I'm crazy for being so intensely interested.

Maybe I am crazy!

I keep dreaming. They're not normal dreams; they're strange recurring dreams. I feel a part of them and remember each one vividly when I awaken. Maybe that's why I can't sleep. I don't know if it is because of the stress of teaching or my increased inquiry into the existence of the treasure that is causing them.

They are occurring more frequently. I had one of those dreams tonight. This one was similar to all the rest. It took place in a Native American village. I think it is Delaware, possibly Iroquois, around the mid 18th century. The landscape of the dreams leads me to believe they take place in this area, the headwaters of the Tuscarawas River, as both tribes resided here at one time or another.

At this point, I believe I have met most of the people in the village. Two of them stand out. One is the chief. He is easily distinguishable by his dress and mannerism. He walks around the village in a double tailed headdress made of eagle feathers. It is hard to imagine eagles in Ohio. But then it is also impossible to imagine these hills teaming with virgin forests full of elk.

The chief inspects all aspects of village life. He seems to enjoy stopping to give instruction to everyone who hesitates in their task. He is definitely the leader of the village, and in his leadership role, he remains the great teacher.

The most interesting character in the village is a young brave who tends to stir the others into a frenzy. He is tall, slender and bronzed from the sun. He is muscular and has long black hair. He is good with a bow and arrow, and has excellent stalking and hunting skills. He speaks and acts before he thinks. He is constantly trying to get others to do his bidding. He is certainly vying for a position in the village, possibly chief, although that is many, many years away.

My most vivid vision of him has him standing next to the campfire raising the skull of a bull by the horns above his head during a religious ceremony. His horned headdress mimicking the silhouette of the bull, his taut muscles reflecting the flickering campfire, he stands rigidly as the medicine man recites the liturgy of the ancient ritual.

He looks out for me on our adventures and is a constant protector of mine in the tribe. I call him Guardian.

In these dreams, I feel that I am an alien looking on as the Native Americans go about their daily business.

I am accepted by them, but am always aware that I am not one of them. It is as if a giant window has opened and I am permitted to visit a time long since past.

Tonight, the chief gathered the children around the campfire to tell them a story. Guardian and I stood on the perimeter of the group and listened silently as the chief began his tale.

Even in my dream, he spoke in his native tongue. It was evident, however, that the tale he told was of great importance to the future of his people and to me. He made gestures of someone feverishly digging and then of rifle fire and death. He told not a tale of Indian death, but of foreigners - invaders of their homeland fighting among themselves. As he concluded, he took a leather pouch from his belt. He slowly opened and pulled a gold coin from its depths. The children scurried forward to see. As they knelt before the chief he explained the significance of the coin. Slowly, the children leaned forward and he slung the pouch in a wide arc spilling the treasure on the heads of the youth. They scrambled to get their fair share of the chief's bounty.

Guardian motioned to me in a dream sign language I have learned to understand, that the treasure the chief spilled was not his, but mine.

As I awakened, I realized Guardian will help me find the lost French gold. But he is a dream - an apparition. How can he help? I need someone here in reality to help me search. It is my foreordination- my destiny.

I have nine generations of research in my attic. Why can't I solve this puzzle? Why can't I figure this out? Why is it so elusive? Why won't it let itself be found?

I can't imagine what the dream means. I just know the dreams are becoming more frequent. Nightmares, that's what they are.

Someone has to help me. Someone must come forward with the answer. Someone must help me find an answer to my dilemma - or I will go stark raving mad!

Chapter Two

The Science Fair
Friday, April 14

A science fair is no place for a history teacher, Henry thought as he handed Ralph and Martha Saling a program and directed them to the corner of the gymnasium where the judges were gathering. It was not the way he had wanted to spend his Friday afternoon, but Mrs. Talkington needed help, and Henry was never one to say no.

Mrs. Talkington was a great science teacher. She taught at Minerva High School nearly eight years. She made sure her students had the basics, but she also insisted that science be practical. "I want my students to take what they learn in class today and use it at home, tonight," she once told a local newspaper.

The students believed Mrs. Talkington had been a teacher forever. Her drab dresses and high heels were the fashion statement of the high school. She wore her coal black hair in a bun on the top of her head. Rumor had it; if she let her hair down her brains would fall out. She ruled her classroom with an iron fist. She had no discipline problems, as her green eyes could pierce a hole clear through a person, and she was credited with creating a disproportionate number of professional scientists. Mrs. Talkington's students won many state ribbons. She received several grants for her teaching prowess. The science program at the high school was one of the school district's crowning jewels.

The annual Science Fair was a big deal in Minerva. The high school gym was filled with rows of tables upon which cardboard display panels acted as backdrops to a myriad of exhibits produced by young scientists from the junior and senior high schools. A stroll down the aisles took Henry past foaming volcanoes, hamsters desperately trying to find their way out of mazes, flowering and withering petunias, dissected cats and guinea pigs, electronic gadgets galore, motors, televisions, computers, test tubes, beakers and even a wind tunnel for testing the aerodynamics of model rockets.

Business and community leaders vied not only for the invitation to judge the Fair, but especially for the opportunity to evaluate the senior science projects. It was a privilege to send the best and brightest to the state competition and have one's picture with the winners appear in the local newspaper. Minerva was still enough of a small town that to hear someone say, "I saw your picture in The Leader," was sufficient to inflate even the humblest person's pride.

Henry, however, had an ulterior motive for wanting to be there. Even at the Science Fair, Henry was treasure hunting. He took every opportunity to be around a different clique of Minerva society. Each niche, each breed, in fact each family had a different twist on his treasure. He would eavesdrop on conversations, and if the opportunity arose, he would extract another bit of information about the treasure. Stealthily, he was compiling a new generation of data about a centuries old mystery. The judges at today's Science Fair, he hoped, would provide him with a target rich environment. He watched as Mrs. Talkington gave the judges their assignments.

Henry surveyed the menagerie of individuals gathered in the gym this day. Towering above everyone else was Dr. James Dorman, a tall, slender, gracefully aging former college professor. His gray hair was always neatly combed. It was his electric blue eyes that gave away his excitement in the moment. Everyone, including Henry, was aware of his reputation as an accomplished scholar. He could integrate what seemed to be opposing technologies in a heartbeat. He was constantly modifying, inventing and creating new gadgets and gizmos. For many years, he taught Physics at a local college. One former student remarked, "Taking a physics course from Dr. Dorman is like taking a Bible course from God!" He could explain the structure of the atom to junior high students or discuss the mechanics of time travel with fellow physicists. He loved theoretical challenges, as well as he loved challenging high school scientists on their hypotheses.

Talking with Dr. Dorman was Philip Bobinger, President and CEO of First National Bank of Minerva. He was a frequent science fair judge. Henry figured, this year Phillip would be looking over his shoulder, as his daughter was involved with a project that had been the buzz of the school for weeks.

Henry recognized Joe Gunther, another frequent judge. He was the head of the local EPA office. He was dressed in a business suit. His black hair and dark eyes made him look like a Secret Service Agent. He enjoyed working with the students. This year, Henry knew there was a special project, which caught Joe's eye.

Howard Rutledge was there again this year. To look at him, Henry had figured he was just a dumb old farmer, but he knew Howard's wisdom of the soil had turned an otherwise useless piece of ground into one of the most successful farms in the area. Students were never sure what questions might come from good old Howard. His performances at the science fair were legendary.

Ralph and Martha Saling were there representing the area family farmers. Ralph routinely judged the soil experiments. Martha took any assignment given her. Henry knew this was a bittersweet year for them, as the new road would dissect the farm forcing them to give it up after five generations.

Mrs. T had explained to Henry that having Fred Johnson of Johnson Construction, the firm in charge of building the road as a judge would complicate matters. Fortunately Fred's right hand man and peacemaker, George Huntsinger, was also there. Ralph and Fred had had words in the past. Mrs. Talkington was hoping that a public forum geared to youth would keep the two of them on their best behavior.

Henry watched as Mrs. T arranged everyone like a groom placing horses into the starting gate. Ralph, Philip and

George would judge the junior high physical science projects. Fred, John Jones and Howard would take care of high school biology. Dr. Dorman, Martha and Joe were assigned high school physical science.

The three groups began moving between the tables to their assigned projects. "I've got it! I've got it!" echoed through the gym. The sounds of Sherman's entire army marching through Georgia, the guns of the Allied armada on D-Day, and the footsteps of Tarzan's elephant army came thundering down the hallway. It could only be one person – Todd Evans.

"I've got it! I've got it! I've got it!" he yelled as he swept across the room and headed for Mrs. Talkington. He carried a glass jar in his hand.

Henry grabbed Todd's arm to slow him down and bring the situation under control. "Got what?" he asked, a little more than perturbed at the disruption.

Todd turned to Henry with his sparkling blue eyes. "I've got the sample which will prove we have a major pollution problem."

"Let's see," Henry demanded.

"Here it is, fresh from Ralph Saling's farm: water with bacteria so large you can see them with the naked eye!" He held up a quart jar with a swirling black cloud inside. Thousands of tiny tailed objects churned the water. Henry grabbed a magnifying glass from a nearby table for a closer look. "Tadpoles!" Henry exclaimed.

"What?"

"Tadpoles. Baby frogs. You've brought back a sample with a thousand tadpoles in it. Where did you get it?"

"From Saling's spring. He said that's where the water came from that fed the house. Corey said he wanted it from the source."

"But tadpoles? Didn't you think about straining the water so you didn't capture them?" Henry asked.

"Look, we want to prove there's pollution in our water. After I walked through that field . . . "

"Did you clean your shoes off before you came in the school?" Mother Henry asked.

"No, but they're clean," Todd responded, inspecting the soles, "sort of . . . Anyway," he continued, "with all this manure and all the years that field was a pasture, I figured it had to be loaded with nitrates. And since nitrates cause things to blow up, like in TNT - tri-nitrate-toluene, it didn't surprise me to see these huge bacteria."

"Todd, your logic never ceases to amaze me," Henry said, shaking his head. "And by the way, it's tri-*nitro*-toluene. Did you hear anything as you walked up to the spring - anything like a splash?"

"Well, yeah," he replied sheepishly, not knowing where this line of questioning was going.

"Did you wonder what it was?"

"I thought I'd kicked a rock in the spring."

"Did you see a rock?"

"No."

"Could it have been the mother or father frog hiding under the edge of the spring?" Henry was very persuasive.

"Well, yeah," Todd said hesitantly.

"Todd, you can't jump to conclusions," scolded Henry. "You have to examine the situation completely. You're trying to solve a mystery. If you don't get all the clues, you're going to come to the wrong conclusion. Do you have any other samples?"

"Yeah, I got them all. I thought this was the most important; so I brought it to the Fair."

"Well, take it over to your booth, Corey, Dan and Michelle are waiting for you," said Henry. "And hurry, the judges have already begun."

Todd hung his head and obediently took his jar of pollution to his team's display. Henry knew this outburst was typically Todd. He was a bundle of energy. His red hair and freckles made him a poster child of American mischief. When Webster needed to define "precocious," he described Todd. Everything was a production with Todd. He was small for his age, almost the runt of his litter. His stature made him the target of all manner of childhood pranks. He came from a well-to-do family. Being given everything, he never had to want for much. Because of that, his classmates looked down upon him. He compensated by overachieving and trying to prove that he could do things on his own. Todd Evans was a student who always had to be in the limelight.

Henry had Todd in History class. He had heard that Todd was a good student through his freshman year. He had been polite and respectful. Then came the divorce. He changed to the class clown and was now bordering on being the class troublemaker. He went from a smart kid near the top of his class to an unruly, almost unmanageable child. His life of luxury had become a life of hardship.

His mother, who had only worked as a wife and mother, was forced to get the only jobs for which she was qualified. Her infrequent alimony and child support checks forced her to find a job where she could make the most money with flexible hours. She waited tables at Little Forest Inn. However, it wasn't long until her situation forced her into working later hours. Her youthful figure and dazzling red hair sat well with the clientele.

Henry had been told that many a shift was concluded at the bar with a grateful guy listening to her woes and lubricating her sorrows with the best Scotch in the house. He figured it was probably not unusual for Todd to get ready to leave for school and find his disheveled mother asleep on the couch not knowing how or when she had gotten home, or what had transpired after she clocked out. Henry suspected Todd did not appreciate the stories his friends relayed from their parents.

Todd and Henry constantly clashed, but Henry was one of the few teachers at the high school who could calm him enough to begin to get through to him. *What a waste of a perfectly good kid*, Henry thought. *He's walking a very thin line. I wish there was some way I could keep him from going over the edge.* Henry had heard stories of the ruined project. He only hoped that Todd's shenanigans would not cause the whole group to fail. He cringed as the high-powered group of

Dorman, Saling and Gunther approached the table where the ill-fated experiment lay.

* * *

Henry knew everyone in Science class had to do a Science Fair project. Corey Wagner, Daniel Jones and Michelle Bobinger chose the question, "Is there pollution in the sources of drinking water in Minerva?" It was not an unusual topic to choose. It was as ordinary as "What detergent cleans the best?" and "Who has the hardest water?" Henry thought nothing of the project as he overheard early reports of its progress from his students.

During his short time in the village, water had not been a hot topic in Minerva. When news reports cited the higher than normal cancer rate and unusual birth defects, health officials had calmly reported that nothing was out of the ordinary. After the PCB contaminated ground was buried behind the local aircraft plant north of town and the old dump east of town was placed on the Superfund list, Henry sensed people were going on as if nothing was wrong. But at Minerva High School, these events were not going unnoticed. Early in his tenure, Henry spotted a group of super sleuths who had one eye on the football field and the other eye in the newspapers. This was no ordinary group of seventeen and eighteen year-olds. They had petitioned Village Council to have the best sled-riding hill in town closed to car traffic during major snowstorms. They led the drive to establish a recycling center in the community by piling their recycled newspapers and cans next to the Police Station. They were frequent attendees at Council meetings, and Henry had heard it rumored they wanted to combine their ages so they could collectively run for office.

Henry was not surprised when they decided to discover the source of the pollution problems. He could envision them finding pollution that the experts couldn't find. He watched them take a while to get heading in the same direction. They had agreed they wanted to find pollution, but they couldn't decide exactly what to test for or how to continue once they had found this unnamed pollution. It was Corey Wagner who had finally set their course. Henry could tell he was concerned when Mrs. T assigned Todd Evans to the group when no other entourage would have him.

Even though this was the first public presentation of the student's results, Henry had already heard from overenthusiastic parents about the boggled project with the intriguing conclusion.

Henry gave up his position at the door and moved closer to the project so he could hear the judges' comments.

* * *

Henry knew this was the moment of truth. Nearly half a year's planning and execution were coming to fruition. Corey planned it as such a simple experiment. Collect water samples from around the community. Plot the location of the samples on a map. Test them for a variety of pollutants. If pollution appeared in a number of samples, trace them through the aquifer back to their source. Then, present the results at the science fair and win the prize. Piece of cake . . . easy A . . . until Todd joined the team.

It was evident to Henry that Corey was the brains of the group. He never said much in class, but when he did open his mouth it was profound. He sat quietly in class acing tests and ruining the curve. Nothing about Corey was usual. He was too smart, too tall and too skinny. His wire rimmed glasses and unruly dishwater blond hair gave credence to his professorial persona. In his aquamarine eyes, he carried the excitement of youth and the inquisitiveness of Galileo.

Todd, on the other hand, was the other hand. He was as much the opposite of Corey as an opposite could be. Maybe that was why he and Todd had become such good friends. But this pollution experiment was pushing their friendship to the brink.

Daniel Jones, a short and spunky senior with unruly blond hair, brought the judges sheet to the table. He was the legs of the operation. All anyone had to do was ask, and Dan was there. He seemed to love to help people. When there was a boy kind of thing going on, Dan was right in the middle of things. Dan's deep brown eyes looked almost black, and seemed to reflect a wonderment at Creation. Henry sensed Dan had been honored to be asked to be a part of the auspicious group searching for unfound pollution.

Michelle Bobinger was standing at the table arranging test tubes and conferring with Corey about the presentation. Henry knew the experiment was not her priority. Michelle's flowing blond hair reached to her hips. It was said that girls grew long hair to draw attention away from another deficiency. Physically, she had no deficiencies. Todd had accused her of growing her long hair to hide her blossoming womanhood. Her bright blue eyes and newly braceless teeth were betraying her efforts. Henry saw her as a leveling influence for the group. It was unusual for senior boys to have anything to do with a girl, academically. But, Michelle had proved time and time again, from the baseball field to the creek that she could hold her own with any boy. Henry felt the experiment showcased Michelle at her finest. She could see to it he designed an experiment they all could understand, keep Todd from calling the FBI, and make sure there was no Daniel mischief in their project while still being just one of the guys.

It was apparent to Henry with the science fair nearly over and the school year approaching an end, her thoughts were focusing on finishing school and having a great summer with Todd - whether he knew it or not.

Henry watched as the judges arrived at the display and inspected its various components. Joe Gunther seemed curious about the equipment and chemicals they had used. Martha investigated the map and the location of the samples they had collected. Dr. Dorman studied the report and the plethora of data it contained.

"Well Corey, it looks like you were in charge," Dr. Dorman started, putting their report back on the table. "Tell me about your experiment and this magnificent map."

"Our drinking water comes from deep within the ground," Corey began. "So pollutants, no matter what kind, work their way through tiny air holes in the soil. As the pollutants move deeper and deeper, more holes become filled with water. The depth where all the holes are filled with water is called the water table. Ground water is the word used to describe the zone below the water table.

"Layers of material that can hold a lot of groundwater and let it pass freely are called an aquifer. Aquifers can be many miles long and many feet thick. Wells can be drilled into them, and water easily pumped out of them. Once pollution enters an aquifer, it easily spreads throughout it."

What intrigued Henry the most about this project was Corey's deep understanding of the problem. Corey had realized that critical to identifying pollution was the location of the source of the sample. He wanted each sample pinpointed to where it was drawn. To accomplish his final goal, Corey had covered one wall of his workroom with topographical maps. It had taken nine maps in all, each one being two feet wide and three feet long. He had cut the adjoining borders and taped them together making a map six feet wide and nine feet tall. A portion of the test area wrapped around the ceiling. If he got too close, Corey walked on part of Carroll County.

Corey had placed a red dot on the map where each home was located. A green dot was placed at the water source. Most dots were next to each other, except in Minerva where the city well was nearly a mile from the source home. Corey had transferred the data to a smaller scale map, which hung from the front of the display table. As far as Henry was concerned, the map was the focal point of the experiment.

"What we had hoped to find," Corey continued, "was pollution in a variety of samples, then trace it on the map to its source."

"According to your report, you didn't find the pollution you thought you would," Gunther chimed in with all of the authority of his EPA.

An uneasy hush fell over the group. The "somebody better say something" look went from Corey to Dan to Michelle to

Todd and back to Corey. "Well, not exactly," Corey began to explain, when the voice of impending disaster echoed throughout the gym.

* * *

"We found gold," Todd announced matter-of-factly. The silence turned into a groan. This was it. This was the revelation that had Minerva tittering. Corey and his friends had discussed it earlier and hoped they could get by without a mention of it, but Todd just fixed that.

"Gold?" said Gunther, "Do explain."

"I realized that under the noble leadership of Mr. Wagner, we failed in our attempt to discover pollution," Todd flamboyantly proclaimed, his blue eyes flashing in the amber halogen lighting of the gym. "Being the astute chemist I am, I came to our rescue with some new innovative tests of my own. Observe . . . "

Todd replicated his misdeed as Corey, Dan and Michelle watched the events, which threatened their very existence as credible scientists. Mrs. Talkington had repeatedly stressed that any deviation from the original project would mean failure in the class and no chance to advance to the district or state science fairs.

Todd reached under the table and retrieved two containers. In his right hand was an old brown glass bottle. The label was so dirty it was almost unreadable. Its cork shrank beyond usefulness years ago and the bottle's liquid contents had crystallized around the edges to maintain the seal. In his left hand was a half pint can. Its label was no better than the bottle's.

"What's that?" asked Martha.

"Gentlemen . . . and lady," Todd began, "we've done it by the book thus far, now it's time to do it Einstein's and Edison's way - true experimentation."

"You're crazy," said Corey. Todd sensed he was searching for an escape route.

"You be careful with that stuff," Michelle warned. Todd motioned her away. She was always too cautious.

"I will. I will," said Todd. With all the flare of the Great Zambini he demanded, "Bring me the untreated samples."

Michelle and Dan dutifully set a rack of six test tubes before him. Todd put on rubber gloves and gingerly worked the cork on the bottle. The crystals cracked and popped. It sounded as if the top of the bottle would break off at any minute. Slowly, he pulled the cork out and the room was filled with the pungent aroma of bitter almonds.

Dan complained, "That's gross." Todd ignored him. Todd held the bottle high in the air as if presenting it to some Science god.

"Tell the judges what that is, right now," demanded Michelle, hoping to salvage something from their efforts.

"Hydrocyanic acid - Cyanide," Todd said with the authority of ancient chemist. He lowered the bottle to safety.

"Where did you get cyanide?" Martha wanted to know.

"Since my career as a respectable student is over, I must now confess before God and our esteemed judges that is it purloined from the bowels of the chemistry supply room, overlooked by decades of lab assistants, feared by scores of chemistry teachers as a potential chemical agent which could be used by disgruntled students to bring about their untimely demise."

"You stole it from the lab?" Martha pressed him for a straight answer.

"Rescued ma'am. It was sitting in that dark corner of the cabinet, so pathetic and lonely, having been neglected since before the Age of Aquarius when student rights superseded student responsibility. I felt it was my duty to demonstrate to the world that high school students can use deadly chemicals in a responsible way."

Todd paused to check the response of his audience. Even though he knew he was now center stage, he realized he was walking a tightrope and any misstep could be disastrous to the entire group.

Martha seemed to accept the explanation with the gullibility only a mother can enjoy. Dr. Dorman appeared intrigued with Todd's ingenuity, and eagerly awaited results that would match his bravado. Gunther scowled as he skeptically watched the hotshot handling the environmentally sensitive material.

With that, Todd placed an eyedropper into the bottle. He took his loaded weapon and held it above the first test tube.

Plink . . . Plink . . . Plink. Nothing happened. Now on to the second.

Plink . . . Plink . . . Plink. There was a little cloud for just a second, and then it was gone. He continued adding the cyanide as precisely as he had ever done anything. Every now and then, there was a little cloud, but then it would go away. In the later samples, a couple of test tubes clouded up and then stayed cloudy. When Todd had tried this in their basement laboratory, Corey, the consummate scientist, had taken copious notes. Todd knew there was a danger in this new twist. If anything came of this new test, it might change the direction of the experiment - and that could be disastrous.

"And now, for the grand finale," announced Todd. He opened the can.

Dan coached him before the judges. "And what's that?"

"Zinc," declared Todd.

Michelle, playing her role as skeptic quizzed, "Now why should we add zinc?"

"Because this is the end of the experiment, we will add zinc because it is the last element in the periodic table," Todd stated with a wink in his eye.

"No it isn't," Corey corrected.

"It starts with 'z', it should be last," countered Todd.

Todd relaxed as the judges chuckled, apparently enjoying this extracurricular, impromptu experimentation.

"It's good enough for me," said Dan, "let's finish up, I'm tired."

The zinc needed encouragement from the sample spoon in the chemistry set, but slowly Todd raised the one-gram sample into the daylight. He dropped it into the last test tube.

He lifted the test tube high into the air and swirled its contents. The zinc disappeared.

Even though he knew the outcome, Todd could see that Corey was getting aggravated because he had worked very hard to make sure the experiment complied with the strictest scientific standards. Corey pushed his glasses back on his nose and took a deep breath.

Todd got a little grit in the bottom of the first and second tubes, but when he added the zinc to the third test tube, the cloudiest of all, the strangest thing happened. It cleared up. Then, as the torrent died down, tiny specks began settling to the bottom of the tube.

"Now that's pollution," said Todd.

Shiny, sparkling specks. Dr. Dorman came closer to look.

"Crud is what I'd call it," declared Dan.

"Metallic flakes. Gold! ?" Dorman pondered out loud.

"Couldn't be," Corey insisted.

"Just coincidence," Michelle said.

"It was something in the cyanide," said a still unbelieving Corey.

At the encouragement of the judges, Todd tested each of the tubes. In three of the tubes there was some type of sediment.

"I think there was a chemical reaction with something in the water, and this gold stuff was the result," Dan said trying to break the tension building in the judging group.

"We turned water into gold," cried Michelle. "I remember our science teacher talking about how scientists in the Middle Ages tried to do that."

"No, I think the gold stuff in the water is real gold," said Dr. Dorman.

"But how?" asked Todd. "I don't know of any gold mines in the area."

"Todd is right," Gunther interjected as he straightened his tie. He picked up a test tube and examined it closely. "However, you stumbled upon a process that began in South Africa before the turn of the century and revitalized the modern gold industry in Colorado.

"The Colorado gold rush began in 1858," Gunther continued. "The gold was found in veins which ran deep underground. As miners worked the edges or reached the end of veins, it became harder to separate the gold from surrounding rock. This scrap rock, still laden with gold, was used for road and railway beds leading to the gold camps.

"In 1890, miners in South Africa ran into sulfur bearing ore. They solved their problem by grinding the ore into a fine powder and treating it with cyanide."

The wheels were turning in Todd's head. Corey turned and walked to the edge of the booth. Todd could see Corey knew they were in trouble.

Gunther continued, "The slurry is agitated and zinc dust is added to precipitate the gold and other metals."

Todd probed again, "But is there a gold mine around Minerva?"

"No, Mr. Evans, the geography of our fair valley does not lend itself to gold," Dr. Dorman reemphasized.

Todd stood mesmerized by the test tubes. They discovered "pollution," but what kind of pollution was it? If it was gold, what was its origin? Todd stared silently at the test tube, as the flakes danced in the water like the fake snow in a snow globe. He could hear Dan breathing next to him. The judges, too, seemed fixated on the surprising results without saying a word.

Suddenly, the gymnasium exploded with comments about the group's results. Todd recoiled with the intensity of the reactions.

Howard was walking past the booth on his way to inspect the exposed bowels of another guinea pig when he paused for a moment and overheard the judges' final comments. "It's the 'Lost French Gold'," he shouted.

"Not that damned gold again, Rutledge," Gunther snapped as he spun around and came face to face with Rutledge. "Let it alone. Come along with us into the twenty-first century."

Todd watched another judge come forward to take Howard by the arm before he could respond to Gunther's pronouncement. "Come along Howard, this is a Science Fair, not a place to debate the authenticity of a local legend."

In the adjacent booth, George Huntsinger watching rays of static electricity jump from a steel ball and cause Ginny Gill's hair to stand straight up, yelled, "That old coot ought to go back to his farm where he can commune with the ghosts of dead Indians and French soldiers."

His fellow judge, Phil Bobinger the banker, chimed in, "Let him alone, George. If you had thirteen million dollars buried in your back yard, you'd be a believer, too."

Todd's neck nearly snapped as Fred Johnson's booming voice was heard from around the corner where he was witnessing a foaming volcano. "I don't know what's worse, believing in fairy tales, or letting bad science reinforce bad literature. Besides, coming from the Saling farm, I seriously doubt it's gold. Nothing at that dump is that valuable. We even considered passing it by with the road, but then the powers that be said to go straight through it. They considered it a civic improvement."

Ralph Saling left the static electricity experiment like he had been shot out of a gun. Mrs. Talkington heard the growing commotion and headed for Saling and Johnson before World War Three could break out. Both men converged in front of the water experiment. Todd was scared.

"Johnson, you wouldn't know anything valuable if it hit you in the face," Ralph screamed. "I don't believe these kids found gold, but give them a break. Just because you don't like me, don't take it out on them. And as for your road, you can stick it . . . "

"Now gentlemen," said Dr. Dorman, stepping between the two men. "This is supposed to be a learning experience for the children, not a contest between adults."

"I think it's wonderful that these young adults discovered, not pollution, but gold," added Gunther. "And the construction of the road is a moot point. That was all approved last year. It's out of our hands.

"Well, there might be a road going through it, but there's no gold on my property," said Martha, jumping into the fray.

By this time all of the judging had stopped and everyone was congregating in front of the pollution experiment's table. Todd gathered his friends at the back of the booth. This was no time for heroism. Todd vacillated between confronting these ranting adults or abandoning his friends and running for cover.

"But if there was gold, just think of everything that you could do with all that money," added Phil Bobinger.

"Is that all you can think about - money, Bobinger?" one of the other judges hollered going nose to nose with Phil. Todd felt Michelle lunge forward to rescue her father if a fight broke out. "A man's livelihood is at stake here. How's he supposed to make a living once his farm is gone."

Johnson advanced the idea, "But the state made a more than reasonable offer to the Salings. You might say they found their treasure already." Todd didn't like this man. He was mean and sarcastic. He hoped he'd never meet him alone.

"Treasure, I'll show you what you should treasure," said Ralph lunging at Johnson. Mrs. Talkington deflected his blow into the outstretched hand of Dr. Dorman who brought Ralph's hand to his side and escorted him away from the brewing trouble.

"Do you think we got an 'A'?" Todd asked Corey.

"I think we're lucky to get out of here with our lives," he responded.

Todd was relieved when Mr. Boggs, the principal, came into the gym and broke up the judges. He began restoring order and dismissing students as he calmed edgy nerves and collected score sheets.

"A couple of flakes of gold and the whole town goes nuts," Todd said.

"Well, act like you had nothing to do with it," Corey replied. "If you hadn't performed your dumb 'experiment', none of this would have happened."

"But if I hadn't performed my dumb 'experiment', we wouldn't be on the verge of a gold rush."

"Good point," said the talented scientist Corey.

* * *

Henry watched as the judges turned in their score sheets and moved into the auditorium for the awards ceremony. "I didn't believe that one person could cause so much chaos," Henry said to Dan and Michelle as they were leaving the gym.

"But that's why I think he's so cute," said Michelle. "Some day I want a chance to try and tame all of that energy."

"You're sick girl - really sick," was Dan's reply.

Henry could remember young love, but that was a long time ago. This had been an interesting afternoon. He had never seen the sides played out so distinctly as he had today. There were some real issues in this town, and the "lost French gold" seemed to be the hot button that triggered them all. What if they knew about him? What if they knew his story? Would he be hero or villain? The kids' experiment might be the key to getting closer to his answers, but only time would tell if the hope they found was real or a cheap imitation.

Chapter Three

Saturday, April 15

Fred Johnson was wrong. There were very few times he would admit to making a mistake, but he knew his outburst at the Science Fair was the biggest blunder he had made in a long time. He was in the middle of the biggest project in his career, and he didn't need to draw undue attention to it by spouting off at some rinky-dink high school science fair. There were still hard feelings all over town about which route the road finally took. The Science Fair was a prime example of how a mention of the road could draw battle lines.

There were three proposed routes, two to the north of Minerva and one to the south. Either of the northern routes would have benefited more smaller communities, and been a little costlier to build. The southern route was closer to Minerva, but initially had more environmental concerns.

For thirty years, people talked about building a four-lane highway from Canton to the Ohio River. It made it through Canton, but as it reached the rural areas, the political clout and road money stopped. Then the solons got smart. The people from Stark County began working with the people in Carroll and Columbiana Counties. Suddenly, politicians in the state capital of Columbus began to listen. It was a hard battle, but, finally, the peoples' voices were heard and the new road was being built - one five-mile stretch at a time.

Fred turned away from the map hanging on his wall and sorted through the papers on his desk. The map marked with dotted lines a corridor that ran from northwest of Minerva, south and then southeast of town. Inside the dotted lines were thick black lines, which ran over and through the names of the property owners in the path of the new Route 30.

It was almost time for Fred's meeting with his job supervisor, George Huntsinger. He was anxious for George's report because he felt the project was really beginning to pick up steam. Now that ground had been broken, the politicians wanted the road finished. There was too much political bloodshed along the way. Any delay in construction caused a potential backlash clear to Columbus. It required using political capital that could be spent on other things - like getting reelected.

To keep things moving, they built a completion bonus into the contract. If preliminary excavation reached the Ohio River by August 1, the contractor would receive ten million dollars. Every day before August 1 was worth an additional $100,000.

Johnson was there from the beginning of the road. Johnson Construction had waited a long time for this contract. His job was to break ground for the new highway. His heavy equipment blazed the trail for the road. He tore up cornfields, defoliated forests and demolished homes that stood in the way of progress. He was good at what he did, and his ability was about to make him a very wealthy person. He'd come too far. He'd bought too many politicians, paid off too many consultants to get to this point. Nothing, absolutely nothing would stop him from completing his highway.

Johnson had a fabulous office in a new building in the center of Canton. The new complex covered almost five city blocks. He called it the Golden Triangle. New State and Federal office buildings formed the corners of the base of the triangle. The Department of Transportation, Department of Natural Resources, Environmental Protection Agency and the Army Corp. of Engineers were some of the agencies that were given very lucrative leases by the Johnson Development Corporation. Between the two buildings was a six-story public parking deck accessible from any floor of either building.

At the point of the triangle was the eight-story Johnson Center. Federal and State employees walked through covered walkways into the concourse area of the Johnson Center to get to the enclosed all-weather employee garage. There were no complaints about having to walk nearly a block to get to the parking deck. The concourse in the Johnson Center featured a restaurant, snack bar, newsstand, beauty parlor, barbershop, gift shop and flower shop. Once employees drove their cars into the garage, they left any inclement weather behind. There were two entrances into the garage. One led directly to the parking area, the other to an automated car wash and valet parking. Giant ventilator shafts removed exhaust fumes while circulating cool air in summer and warm air in winter. Gentle music welcomed them to work.

Coincidentally, Johnson Center offered many services which government employees and their business contacts found helpful. A travel agency with rental cars complemented the airport shuttle. The second floor offered one-bedroom efficiency business suites. The third floor was filled with conference rooms of all sizes. They were equipped with all manner of video and audio conference capabilities - most of which were, unfortunately, left out of the office buildings.

At the end of a hard day's work, government employees only had to get in their cars and begin to drive. An infrared toll system debited their parking account. A specially timed traffic light on Cherry Street let hundreds of cars stream out of the garage, over the bridge, and right onto the new Route 30 heading for home. Fred could sit at his mahogany desk and watch the cars from his penthouse office. Just beyond the horizon his men were pushing the road farther east toward his fortune.

But he preferred not to work in his fabulous office. Most days he could be found in a double wide trailer with his cadre of secretaries and engineers, never more than a couple of miles from his most advanced units. He knew every problem his men were having from the flat tire on the grader, to the substandard soil in the roadbed. He knew what the problem was, who caused it, when it was corrected and who fixed it. The men complained the closer they got to the Ohio River; the closer Fred's trailer got to the lead bulldozer.

Fred's office was no ordinary construction field office. He occupied the master bedroom in the trailer. He placed his desk so he could look out the bay window at the crews. On the other side of the room was a walk-in whirlpool tub illuminated by a skylight. The vaulted ceiling sported track lighting strategically spotlighting Johnson's many awards and citations.

What caught one's eye when you entered the room was the gigantic map on the back wall. Blown up nearly four times, there was no mistaking the path the road should take. Along the route were dots - red and green dots. The twenty red dots marked the monthly progress the contractor needed to make to complete the project on time. The green dots indicated where the contractor was now. They marked the trail from the start of the new highway (off the left corner of the map) to where construction was now nearly due south of town.

Fred peeled off another green dot and stuck it on the map. He wrote the date on it, April 15. It was a full two inches ahead of the red dot labeled May. "That's what we like to see," Fred said, leaning back in his chair, "two weeks ahead of schedule coming into spring. We're past Minerva, past the politicians and heading into God's country where no one can stop us now."

He'd waited his entire professional life to build a super highway. He was always passed over by the "big boys." He was too young when the interstates were built. He was too inexperienced to land the contracts when the "revitalization" took place in Canton. It looked as if Route 30 would be the last big building project of the century. The politicians were now listening to an electorate demanding a lean, mean government and threatening a tax revolt. Fred saw Route 30 as his last chance. He called in his markers, advanced a few careers and now it was about to pay off.

Henry Muselle's Treasure

Growing up, Fred never thought he'd have this chance. He was the second son and always reminded of it. Charlie Johnson was the first-born son of Edith and Bob Johnson. They owned a furniture store in Minerva and made a decent living. Charlie was smart and a good artist. Bob and Edith showered him with everything a boy could want. There was never quite enough to give Fred the same things.

When it came to college, Charlie was sent to the best architectural school in Ohio. Fred went to work for a local contractor to pay his own way through college. Charlie graduated with honors and immediately landed a job with Lander and Lander in Cleveland. His first assignment was to work on a new ballpark and sports arena complex. Two years later Fred graduated from Kent State University with a degree in civil engineering. He had enough practical experience to be a supervisor for the Ohio Department of Transportation.

Ironically, Charlie and Fred ended up working almost side by side. As the steel was being delivered for the new ballpark, Fred was down the street planning the strategy for the renovation of the Detroit Avenue Bridge across the Cuyahoga River.

When the ballpark opened, everyone in the country knew it as Jacob's Field - that is everyone but Edith and Bob. They referred to it as Charlie's Field. But there was never any mention of Fred's Bridge. Engineers from across the country called the bridge the greatest engineering feat of the 20th Century. Urban planners from around the world marveled at the minor inconvenience to Clevelanders during construction. Bob and Edith didn't notice.

Even when Fred showed them the plans for Johnson Center, they didn't notice. Charlie was going to Moscow to build their first shopping mall. Now it was the new Route 30. The new Route 30 would replace the old Route 30, which ran in front of Johnson's Furniture Store. The new Route 30 would bring commerce and new people to Minerva. They had to notice now. Fred already determined there was nothing that would stop him from completing the project. If he came upon a problem, he would find a solution. And no one, absolutely no one would buck his authority. Anyone who was not one hundred per cent behind the project and Fred Johnson could find another job.

It was 8:45. Fred knew Huntsinger was waiting in the outer office. Huntsinger was always early. Fred was ready now, but the meeting would begin at 9:00 sharp. This was Fred's meeting and everyone played by Fred's rules.

* * *

George didn't mind waiting for the stroke of nine because that was just one of Fred's games. But he sensed a deeper more sinister change, and he wasn't sure how to cope with it. There was a time in their relationship when Fred would listen to his suggestions. Now, it had to be Fred's way or not at all.

Huntsinger put down the fifth magazine he had looked at since he arrived. Not only was he not interested in any of the articles; it was difficult to read with no lights on in the office. You were not allowed to turn on lights in an area when you were not working, and George was not working - he was waiting.

The room where Huntsinger was sitting was nicknamed the "antechamber" by employees. Fred called it the waiting room. The foyer of the trailer was divided into several smaller rooms. One walked in and ran straight into the receptionist's desk. She routed people to the appropriate manager behind her and to the right and left. To her right were the restroom, the anteroom and Fred's office. It was rumored Fred could monitor who went to the restroom and how long they stayed. Most occupants of the trailer went outside to the portable latrines.

Huntsinger was not afraid of Johnson; in fact, they were good friends. George Huntsinger went to work for Fred Johnson shortly after he started his own business. They worked hand in hand through the hard times. As Johnson was passed over for contract after contract, Huntsinger noticed Fred beginning to change. He stayed loyal to

Johnson even when his duties began to include paying off inspectors. He looked the other way as Johnson bought off politicians. Now with Route 30 nearing completion, Huntsinger didn't know how much more he could take.

Suddenly, the door to Johnson's office flew open and the antechamber was filled with light and music from the office.

"Come in, George, and let's get this over with," Fred said. "I'd like to get in a round of golf before noon."

Johnson was a big man, six feet two and well over two hundred pounds. He had a booming bass voice and sharp hazel eyes which pierced like a knife when he was angry.

Huntsinger, on the other hand, was only five feet four and didn't weigh one hundred fifty pounds soaking wet. His coal black hair showed streaks of gray. To see them walking side by side on the job site brought comments of "Mutt and Jeff" and "David and Goliath." Regardless of size, there was never any mistaking who was the boss and who was the subordinate. Each assumed his role very well.

"Well, George, tell me how things are going. Randy said yesterday we were two weeks ahead of schedule," Johnson said, leaning way back in his chair and swinging around to admire his last green dot on the map. Now was not the time to be the bearer of bad news, but Huntsinger knew it came with the territory.

"Fred, we've got a little problem," Huntsinger said matter-of-factly. Maybe by confronting the problem head on, he could stem Fred's wrath.

Fred spun back around in his chair and leaned forward on the desk. "No, George, you have a problem. How many times do I have to tell you?"

George Huntsinger was Johnson's right hand man. He was the person who cracked the whip on the job site. He didn't confront the boss unless it was for real. "No, Fred, you've got to listen," Huntsinger retorted. "We've found a spring."

"A what?" Fred was confused; he just wanted the road done. "Well, just throw it out of the way and keep moving."

"Not that kind of spring." George was getting a little frustrated. "A spring!! A little hole in the ground that water comes out of. Right in the middle of the roadway. It's not on any hydrological map. It's not on any environmental study, but it's there - big as life."

Johnson did not hesitate in his reply. "Bury it." He slid a paper from one stack to another.

"You can't just bury it." Huntsinger got up and walked to the map. He pointed to the general location of the spring, trying to get Fred's attention. "That spring makes the surrounding area a wetlands. We'll have to call EPA and let them decide how we should proceed."

Johnson came out of his seat. "You'll do no such thing! The EPA will shut us down for years. Those bureaucrats will moan and whine while they decide what we have to do to protect one damn spring."

"I can't lie to the EPA," George complained. "The locals know about the spring. I'll go to jail."

Johnson sat back down in his chair and pondered for a minute. "Does anyone know you discovered the spring?"

"No," Huntsinger said, a little relieved the crisis might be over. "Don and I were out making our preliminary survey when he stepped in it."

"How far away was the equipment?"

Huntsinger could see a plan forming in Fred's head. "We should reach the spring in two days."

"Good. Then here's the drill." Johnson was now back in control. "Tomorrow, when there's no one around, break a track on the lead dozer. Then, on Monday morning, when you find it broken, give the men two days off until you get it fixed." Huntsinger didn't know whether he liked what was coming.

"On Wednesday, put the men on three shifts, work round the clock." Fred was making notes. George knew this was so he could tell later if his orders were followed. "That should put you at the spring Friday during the afternoon or midnight shift. By Saturday morning, the initial excavation will be done. You'll be able to tell if the spring is still leaking through. If it is, have Central haul you in three or four loads of sand and dry concrete. Saturate the area with it. Then cover it with new dirt and keep right on moving. The spring water will set up the concrete and give us a good solid base. By Monday, when the inspectors get back, you'll be past the trouble spot. Tuesday, go back to the regular shifts. If they ask questions, just tell 'em you were trying to get ahead so you could give the boys a long Memorial Day weekend." He emphatically dotted his last "i" and looked up, smiling at George.

George was not smiling. "But Fred, Central's not an approved sub-contractor for us."

"It's the weekend, and it's at night. Who'll know?" he asked.

"I don't know, Fred," said Huntsinger still looking at the map. "I think we ought to play it safe and call the EPA."

"Mr. Fernandez?" Fred asked with a slightly sarcastic tone.

"Well, sure," said Huntsinger, not catching on. "He's the agent overseeing the project."

Fred got up and walked to the map where George was standing. He lovingly put his arm around George. "You do that," he said. He walked to the left side of the map, which showed the beginning of the project. "By the way, I think I'll put in a call to my old college roommate, Bill. Did I ever tell you he went to work for the FBI? I'm sure he'd be interested to know why Mr. Fernandez's bank account was $20,000 richer." Fred turned around and looked at George. "And by the way, George, you certainly have been accumulating a lot of side accounts in a variety of obscure banks. You aren't skimming, are you?"

"OK, OK, I get the message," George relented. "Tomorrow, I break the dozer, Wednesday, three shifts, call Central." He picked up his papers and started for the door. "Sorry I bothered you, Fred."

"So am I, George. So am I. Keep up the good work and some day I may tell you where those bank accounts are."

Huntsinger was at the door. "Thanks, Fred, have a good round of golf."

"Now I will," Fred said. Huntsinger entered the antechamber. He had lost again.

* * *

Fred picked up the phone and looked again at the map. "Springs," he said. "Let the cows worry about them. I've got to call Mr. Boggs and see if I can't replace that ratty old scoreboard at the football field," he said, thinking out loud. "Our students shouldn't have to compete in such antiquated facilities. Maybe I could donate a new set of bleachers. That should unruffle some feathers.

"Besides, the jocks pull a lot more weight in this town that any spinster science teacher."

Chapter Four

Monday, April 17

Henry shaded in the corner of the box in his lesson planner labeled Monday, April 17. Today, he was supposed to teach about the American aristocracy in Virginia, but current events had changed the urgency for the knowledge of local Ohio history.

He had lived in Minerva a short time, but was still amazed at how quickly the news of the altercation at the Science Fair spread. He spent several hours roaming the aisles of the grocery store listening to the chatter of the women searching for the proper laundry detergent and the pomposity of the men in the coffee shop patiently waiting as the spouses gathered the weekly provisions. The gossip about the discovery of gold passed from one authority to another growing with the embellishments of each sage.

He arrived early at the barbershop and intently read three newspapers as the pundits debated the authenticity of the legend. Even at church, discussions as to the work of the hand of God in planning and developing a new road replaced scheduled Sunday school lessons.

Except for those parents whose children's semester of work had been vanquished to second and third place by the water experiment, no one questioned the bias of the judges in awarding top honors to Corey's group. Todd's part in the near riot was never mentioned.

Putting all of the hoopla aside, Henry had decided today would be the day he would enlighten a new generation with the story which had so captivated their home town for two and a half centuries. Even as the students began filing in for the day's lectures, he could hear them banter about the excitement created last Friday afternoon. Was it by coincidence or fate that the four students at the center of the controversy were in his audience? They were oriented toward science, not history. They were good students in every subject, but less enthusiastic in his class. Maybe it was because he was new to the system, and had not yet passed muster. Perhaps it was his intense feelings for the value of history that made him at times too enthusiastic. He was not sure, but today he was certain of one thing. Now was the time to tell the story. Today, they would not only listen, they would learn.

Henry could tell the kids' minds were not focused on history. He suspected they were reflecting on a mystery. Dan looked bored. Michelle was no better. She was shorting papers and looking through her algebra book as if she could not wait for class to be over. Todd was daydreaming, again. He was always in another world. Henry knew from reports from the guidance counselor and other teachers that Todd's world was much more exciting than the real world. He had told the counselors, there was no pain in his world. He always succeeded in his world. Most importantly "that man", as he called him, was not a part of his world, and "that man" could not hurt him or his mother again. Henry figured Todd didn't care there were no gold mines around Minerva. Todd didn't care that the "experts" said his results were a fluke. In Todd's world, he had found the gold.

Henry knew the gold would be the answer to all of Todd's problems. He would be rich. It would be better than winning the lottery. He would be President of The Todd Evans Mining Company. Minerva would have the Todd Evans Olympic Training Center complete with the Todd Evans Pool. Todd could easily be elected mayor or better yet to the Senate. He knew this gold find would make him the wealthiest man in America. He could run for President.

To this august audience, Henry began his lecture. "The French and Indian War," Henry said, as he ran his fingers through his thick curly hair blousing it beyond his ears and collar, "was one of several wars between France and England

Henry Muselle's Treasure

to determine control of their colonial empires. It was the American campaign of the Seven Years War and was fought by British troops. Prussian soldiers on Britain's behalf fought the European campaign.

"In 1754, the French began building a series of forts from the St. Lawrence River to the Mississippi. A young lieutenant colonel from Virginia, George Washington, was sent with about 200 men to defend a fort being built where the Allegheny and Monongahela Rivers met."

Henry watched Michelle doodling on her paper, drawing interconnecting lines. It could be a tree, or underground rivers of an aquifer.

"Washington learned, en route, that the British fort had been overrun by the French and renamed Fort Duquesne, now Pittsburgh. He marched to within forty miles of the fort and began building a fortress of his own which would later be called Fort Necessity. On May 28, 1754, he launched a surprise attack on an advance party from the fort killing the commander, nine others and making the rest prisoners."

Henry noticed Corey not paying attention. Maybe he was mulling over Todd's part of the experiment. Henry wondered since none of the other tests had produced such dramatic results, maybe it was gold.

Henry watched as one by one the students noticed, he was not talking with his usual dryness. It was important they knew today was different. He was not telling about the French and Indian War; he was the French and Indian War.

"On July 3, the whole French force moved against Washington. They besieged the fort with 700 men and forced his surrender. The French agreed to let Washington and his troops return to Virginia, if they agreed not to build another fort on the Ohio for a year."

Dan was staring out the window. Was he could imagining Washington riding passed on his white horse? Henry stopped talking. Dan looked up and found the bespectacled teacher staring right at him. The other students heard the silence and stopped doodling, reading and daydreaming to gaze at the peculiar stare.

"Good," Henry said and relaxed a bit, "now that I have your attention, I want to relate, as they say, the rest of the story. In all of American history there is no episode as overlooked as what I am about to relate. It is minuscule in the eyes of major historians, but the mystery's impact could be profound on Minerva."

He could tell the scientists were intrigued. They had never seen or heard him like this. He pulled a chair from the library table, turned it around backward and sat down. He usually never left the lectern to speak to the class. He wanted them to know, this was important. The students were on the edge of their seats. Henry leaned over the back of the chair and in a low soft voice began to tell his-story.

"It is 1755. Minerva wasn't even a dream. The land upon which she would stand was forest, disturbed only by the Indians who found its woods full of game, its streams loaded with fish. The valleys between the gentle sloping hills formed a natural corridor leading from the Tuscarawas Valley to Detroit. Traveling by horseback and on foot, the Indians moved from one fertile valley to the next. The route became known as The Great Trail.

"Following Washington's initial attack, tensions mounted between the two countries. A plan was devised for the English to attack the French stronghold at Fort Duquesne. The French used the fort as a staging area for operations in the Northwest Territory. Here they accumulated food, supplies and gold for their troops. The French amassed nearly $4 million of gold and silver at the fort to pay their troops in the field.

"In the summer of 1755, English General Edward Braddock set out with 2200 men to drive the French from the forks of the Ohio. He faced a French commander with less than three hundred men. Afraid of the inevitable defeat, the French commander loaded his treasure onto sixteen pack animals and sent it with an escort of ten men along the Great Trail to Fort Detroit. Braddock's assault was repelled, and only through the gallantry of a young George Washington did the British escape complete annihilation. But, the French gold never arrived at Fort Detroit.

"In 1829, a young man arrived in the small community of Minerva inquiring about the gold. He bore a letter written by his great-uncle, a French soldier. It read:

> We of the French Army were defending Fort Duquesne against the British. When it was known that the English were attacking in force, a detail of ten men and sixteen packhorses was selected to carry the French army's gold and silver away from the fort. I was chosen for the detail.
>
> Three days and a fortnight later, northwest by west from the fort on the Tuscarawas Trail, our advanced scout returned to our little column announcing a British column advancing upon us. The officer in charge of our detail ordered us to stop in our tracks and dig a hole in the ground. He posted a guard while the rest of us dug. The gold was unloaded from the horses and placed in a hole. Then the silver was lowered into the hole. On top of this we shoveled the dirt and covered it with branches.
>
> The first British firing began at this time. The digging shovels were put under a log on a hillside. No sooner was this done than the British were upon us. Eight were killed. Only Henry Muselle and myself were spared. The English had not noticed where we hid.
>
> We made the following marks of the area before we fled. The gold was buried in the center of a sort of square formed by four springs. About one half mile to the West of the hole in which the treasure was buried, we jammed an odd rock into the fork of a tree so that it would stay. Six hundred steps to the North of the hole are the shovels. As we left by the East, I carved a deer into a tree, which I judge to be one mile from the hole.
>
> Events following made it hazardous to return.

"Many attempts have been made to find the gold, but none have been successful," Henry concluded. He watched as the information floated through the air and slowly sank into the heads of his students. Gold never found. Buried near springs. Four million dollars! Dan looked at Michelle. Michelle looked at Corey. Corey looked at Todd. The bell rang.

"Mr. Evans, Ms. Bobinger, Mr. Wagner and Mr. Jones would you be so kind as to join me for lunch next period?" Henry shouted as they got up to leave. They nodded in agreement never imagining what the invitation could possibly involve.

* * *

It was an unusual lunch period. But then, it was an extraordinary day. Henry had to know the validity of the experiment. Were they really young scientists who had made a major discovery or immature high school students who bluffed their way through a project? He must know. He had taken their project to the next logical step, now it was up to them to do the same. Lunch was not a great time to get all of the answers he needed, but it was a good time to plant the seed of inquiry.

Several faculty members wandered through the tables looking for a place to sit. Most faculty ate in the faculty dining room. This was their midday break away from students. There were only a handful of teachers who wanted to eat with students. They said it gave them the opportunity to hear students' problems and concerns. Henry heard enough of that in class. Two teachers were assigned to eat with students, and Henry was not usually one of them. If a riot or food fight broke out, they were the administration's first line of defense. Today was Henry's day to eat with the students, but today he didn't mind.

The lunch line plodded along. The cooks were slower than usual getting food ready for serving. Everyone was taking too much time deciding what he or she wanted for lunch. Finally, the young treasure hunters got through the line and headed toward a table at the end of the cafeteria. The kids were deep in concentration talking about the experiment and its relationship to Henry's story when Henry asked, "Mind if I sit here?"

"No, go ahead," was Todd's reply as he continued to tell the group why they should try to find the gold.

Henry chuckled as they crouched over their food and whispered like a dog growling while guarding its quarry. They were unusually quiet for high school kids. They didn't want anyone to know about the experiment or the gold.

"So, you think you can find my treasure," Henry said. His comment took them so by surprise. Todd stopped in mid-sentence. Todd, Corey, Dan and Michelle turned as a unit and stared at Henry sitting at the end of the table. "Sorry," he blushed a little. "I didn't mean to startle you."

Henry was aware they knew very little about Mr. Muselle. Many of the teachers had been at Minerva High forever. Some of them were students there and came back after college to teach. One day Henry suddenly appeared in Minerva, and the next fall began teaching American History.

Henry lived and breathed American History. Class lasted forty minutes, but he only taught thirty minutes a period. The last ten minutes were devoted to reading from an Ohio author. His favorite writer was Zane Gray, and his favorite period was the eighteenth century. He was especially interested in the transition from Indian Territory to European settlements.

There was silence at the table for the longest time. It was evident none of the young scientists wanted to admit what they thought they found. And yet, Henry's treasure comment was causing them to nearly explode.

"Mr. Muselle," Dan was the first to get enough courage to speak, "what did you mean 'my treasure'?"

"Ah, so you were paying attention," Henry said, but he could tell, they were not amused. This was no time for jokes. They had serious treasure hunting to do.

"I still don't understand," Michelle said.

Henry began teaching again. "Do you remember who survived the attack?"

It finally hit Corey. "Henry Muselle," he shouted a little too loudly.

"That's right," Henry said. "That Henry Muselle was my grandfather nine generations ago."

"Cool," said Dan.

"His father was a Colonel in the French army, who was sent with his family to Quebec to help settle French territories in the New World. When Henry was seventeen, he enlisted in the army."

"He was my age," said Todd. "I was seventeen in May."

"He was a lot like you, Todd," Henry continued. "He was adventurous, always wondering about what was around the next corner. He was like Dan because he knew how to survive in the wilderness. He was inventive and always looking for new ways of doing things. There was a little Michelle in him, too." She blushed.

"He was skeptical of just about everything, but he used that skepticism to put himself on the right path. However, it was because he was most like Corey that he ended up on the expedition."

"What do you mean?" asked Corey. No one was eating now. The macaroni and cheese were hardening into a lumpy orange mortar, the Jell-O melting into green soup.

"Henry was intelligent and well organized. He could anticipate problems. So, his commander had trained him as a quartermaster. He was in charge of all the supplies."

Todd slapped Corey on the back. "Way to go, Cor!"

Henry continued, "When the French ran the British out of the fort on the Ohio, Henry was sent in to organize the new post, keep it supplied and build up provisions for an ever growing army on the frontier."

"Where did the gold come from?" asked Michelle.

"Part of it came from France and was meant to pay the troops. The rest of it came from the Indians."

"The Indians?" Henry could tell that Dan was spellbound.

"The French were befriending the Indians. They knew

that in any coming war with England they would be valuable allies. The Indians on the other hand were vying for power among themselves. Raiding parties would overrun opposing tribes' villages and take their valuables in order to bring them into submission. The valuables they did not want, the gold and silver, were traded to the French for guns and provisions. It didn't take long for it to add up."

"I guess not." Todd laughed with dollar signs in his eyes.

"When the French heard of the British move against the Fort, it was Henry's idea to move the gold. The rest is history."

Henry went right back to eating. He had told them enough - in fact too much. His struggle was overcoming him, again. It was the ever-present battle between finding the gold or running from it. Its discovery would free him from his familial curse, but he knew all too well, there had always been a terrible price to pay. He could pay it, but why should he involve these outsiders, these children, in something that they so innocently stumbled upon?

They could tell something was wrong. "Is that all?" asked Corey.

"That's it. I told the rest of the story in class," Henry said rather matter-of-factly. His sweaty brow was a giveaway that there was more to the story.

"They never found the gold?" Michelle asked.

"Never," Henry said, looking for a way to escape his minions and reconsider his next move.

"We think we've found it," boasted Todd.

"Oh sure, you and a thousand other people," Henry replied. "I saw your little magic show in the gym. Congratulations on finding pollution. That was what you found wasn't it?"

"Well, sir," Corey interjected, "we found something that looks like gold."

"Something that looks like gold, you say. But how do you know it's gold? How do you know it's my gold? Until this morning, you people hadn't heard of the Tuscarawas Treasure, and suddenly random samples from across the county are signs of a lost treasure? Get real. How can you be sure?"

He could tell, Todd was sure. "Mr. Muselle, we think the stuff in the test tubes is gold. After hearing your story in class, I'm convinced it is your gold. I think our methodology was good. I think we can find it. Will you help us?"

Corey, Dan and Michelle joined in agreement. "I'll need a little time," Corey said, "but I'm sure I can figure out a way to pinpoint the gold."

"I'll collect as many samples as we need," Dan volunteered.

"I'll keep accurate records so we won't be mislead," Michelle said.

Henry was moved by the sincerity of his students. To be so young and so consumed by a quest reminded him of himself not so many years before. But the danger - the curse, as it seemed. He knew the price his family had paid, how could he ask these youth to risk their futures for something that didn't concern them? Finally, he decided this was his fight. He concluded, for their own safety, they could not be involved.

"Kids, that gold was supposedly buried two and a half centuries ago. People have been searching for it for about a hundred and fifty years. I appreciate your wanting to help, but I'm afraid there is really nothing to search for. It's a legend . . . a hoax. You'd be better off searching for the real pollution you found. I'm sorry, I ever brought it up."

He pushed his chair back from the table and stood up. He turned and walked across the cafeteria. He placed his tray on the conveyer and walked out, never looking back. The students were stunned. They sat there for a moment digesting the bizarre occurrence. "That was strange," said Corey.

"He knows more than he's telling," Todd added.

Dan verbalized what Todd was thinking, "Why would someone that close to the gold story end up teaching history in Minerva and not be interested in finding the gold?"

"We can find it," Todd exclaimed. "We've got to find it. We'll show Mr. Muselle and everyone else we can find it."

"But how?" From behind them came a still small female voice. They all stopped, turned and looked at Michelle. She gave them her best "I'm sorry" smile.

Corey continued, "We'll meet in the war room after school. We'll decide where to go from here."

* * *

The bell rang and the doors of the cafeteria opened. Students flooded the hallway. Henry watched the group of treasure hunters break up as they were carried by a current of students down the corridors, precariously dodging locker doors and drinking fountains. In the middle of the flow were teachers sifting through the onslaught of students. They picked the gems and the jewels, the flotsam and jetsam, the flora and the fauna and directed them into the eddies of education.

Under the pressure of learning, some would bubble forth with a wellspring of knowledge to nurture the world and provide a better place for us all. Others would be washed back into the river of life to battle the turbulence and enjoy the quiet pools as they journeyed to the sea of eternity. Henry knew someplace, deep inside were all the answers. It was just a matter of being quiet enough to hear the right questions.

He watched the ebb and flow of the students the rest of the day. He listened to their comments - their gossip, dreams, hopes and desires. He remembered the first time his father sat him down and told him the story of Grandpa Henry and the Tuscarawas Treasure, as his family had called it. His father was so alive, so on fire trying to discover the gold and clear the family name.

All through school, Henry immersed himself in history and the sciences so that when he became a man, he could help in the search for the family treasure. Then it happened. That act, that day when his world came to an end. It was years before he could begin again. But now he had, and in these children he could envision a reenactment of his own situation, a fate he would wish on no one.

Down the long hallway he could see a sandy head bobbing along with the current of students. He didn't travel in groups like the others, but was a solitary figure being moved along by the flow rather than under his own direction.

He's a bottle, Henry thought. *He's carrying a message for someone, and they don't know it.* He watched Todd bump Dean as he passed his locker, and Dean summarily pushed him through a group of girls to the other side of the hall. *I wonder if he'll make it safely to shore where someone will open the bottle and read the message, or if he'll be dashed to splinters on the rocks?* Muselle's reverie continued.

As Todd neared his room, Muselle took him by the shoulder and steered him inside. "Can I speak with you for a minute, Mr. Evans?" he asked in his most compassionate tone.

"Sure," Todd agreed.

He motioned for Todd to sit in the front row. Henry sat at the desk next to him. There was an uncomfortable silence as Henry contemplated the proper way to approach the subject. "Do you have dreams, Todd?"

"Did I do something wrong?" Todd asked. Henry knew being called before a teacher was nothing new to him, but he recognized this line of questioning was out of the ordinary.

"No, I just wanted to talk to you about these last couple of days."

"I didn't do anything to Dean. He pushed me," Todd said defensively.

"I'm not talking about that."

"And I only did what Dr. Dorman asked me to do. I can't help it if those people don't get along."

"I know that, too."

Henry could see Todd did not understand his reason for being there. He lashed out at the one he assumed was attacking him.

Henry Muselle's Treasure

"If you want me to find your treasure, you can forget it. If you're not interested, I'm not going to waste my time looking for it. Besides, if I didn't find it, you'd probably blame all your family troubles on me."

"I did call you in here to talk about my treasure, but more importantly I called you in here to talk about your attitude."

"So what's wrong with my attitude?" Todd bristled.

"Todd, you've got to quit blaming everybody else for your troubles."

"I don't blame everybody else, and besides, why shouldn't I. I didn't ask for my life to be this way. You don't know what my life is like."

"Oh, I might," Henry remained calm. Maybe now he would discover the source of the battle raging within his star pupil.

"Yeah, like your father ran off with your Jr. High math teacher when you were in her class. Made me feel like a fool. Sometimes people grow apart, he told me. He grew apart all right. They moved to Cleveland where he's a big wheel in a cellular phone company, and she lounges around the pool and plays hoity-toity with his clients. Mom gets support checks when the attorney tells the judge that dad is in arrears. Why shouldn't I have an attitude?"

"I never know if mom's going to be sober enough in the morning to leave me lunch money. I go home after school and find a note about the tuna sandwich I can have for supper. If I need help with homework, I can call her at work, and if she's not serving some company party, she might have time to answer my question. If she can't, she tells me to go to the library and wait in line until one of the tutors is free and can help me. Most of the time, I don't bother with homework. It's easier to fake it."

"I noticed."

"*You've noticed*? Everybody *notices*, but nobody does anything about it. You and every other teacher single me out, criticizing me, telling me I should do better. Nobody understands what it is to raise yourself," Todd continued nearly in tears.

"I understand," Henry said, looking at Todd with the compassionate gaze of a loving father. He had seen that look before when his own father finished reading his bedtime story and tucked him in bed.

Todd still attacked this unrequested empathy. "How can you understand? You're an adult. You've got it made."

"Todd, my father died when I was twelve." There was a stunned silence. Henry waited for a moment for his comment to sink in.

"When I was a boy, good mothers didn't work outside the home, so after my father died my mother took in laundry. When we kids would leave for school, she'd leave and go clean houses until it was time for us to come home. Everybody at school knew my home situation, so my status dropped. I became an outsider. As the story of how my father died spread, I was avoided even more. I understand completely why you act the way you do."

Their eyes met in an understanding seldom achieved in education. The look went deeper into their respective souls than either had intended. Todd's eyes filled with tears. "Mr. Muselle, he destroyed my life. He's having a good time in Cleveland with someone who is old enough to be my sister, and he's left me to fend for myself. I don't have anyone to talk to. I don't have anyone to answer my questions about life and living. My grandma and grandpa won't come around anymore because they blame my mom for the divorce. How am I supposed to grow up and be somebody when there's no one to show me what to be?" Todd laid his head on the desk and sobbed uncontrollably.

"I know, Todd, I know," Henry said moving from behind the desk to the chair next to Todd. He rubbed his back in an attempt to comfort him.

Finally Todd lifted his head, his eyes red and swollen, his cheeks streaked with tears. "How did you do it? You seem to have survived?

Henry reached over and laid his hand upon Todd's clenched fists. "You have to have a dream, a vision, a quest."

Henry Muselle's Treasure

"I don't understand," said Todd pulling his hands back.

"Didn't you ever say, 'When I grow up, I wanna be President?'"

"I guess so."

"Did you mean it?"

"No, not really."

"Orville and Wilbur Wright said, 'We think men can fly.' Neil Armstrong said, 'I want to fly as high and as far as any man has ever flown.' Einstein said, 'I think there is more to the makeup of the universe than others see.' Pavarotti said, 'I can sing better than any other tenor in the world.' They all had dreams."

Todd wiped his nose on his sleeve. "I dream I spend one day in school without being yelled at."

Henry smiled and continued, "And that's the way dreams come true."

"What do you mean?" asked Todd.

"Once you've set your sights on a dream you have to do those little things that will put you on a path to accomplish your dream. You can't be the owner of a multi-gazillion dollar Internet company, if you don't know anything about computers. So, to have a goal that one day you have all of your homework done, and you don't do anything that would cause someone to yell at you is a good first step toward fulfilling your dream."

He could see Todd felt it was all too simple. "How do you do that if there's no one to tell you if you're on the right track?"

"Your heart will tell you," Henry continued. "All of the teachers, counselors and wise men cannot guide you toward your dream. In fact, historically, which is by the way my area of expertise, the greatest dreamers have been called fools by the wisest of their time. Your greatest help, that little voice that tells you you're on the right track, will come from the most unexpected places." He took Todd's hands again.

"Can I share something with you, and do you promise you won't tell any of the other kids?"

"OK," said Todd apprehensively.

"When I'm confused, and I don't know whether I'm on the right track to reach my goal, I have a dream about an Indian. I call him Guardian. In my dream, there is some clue that usually happens in the next day or two, which confirms I'm headed in the right direction."

"No way," said Todd, pulling back.

"Yep, in fact I've recorded all of the events leading toward my goal in these journals." Henry pulled a tattered spiral notebook from the top desk drawer. Todd took several minutes reading about the days of turmoil and struggle in Henry's search for the treasure.

"Mr. Muselle, what's your dream?"

Henry paused for a moment as he contemplated the proper response. Todd closed the journal and handed it back to Henry. Henry held it close to his chest as he answered. "My dream Todd, is to find something which will prove that the Henry Muselle who moved the gold to Fort Detroit did nothing wrong in the loss of the money."

"Wow," said Todd, "How you gonna do that?"

"I don't know," said Henry. "I just take one day at a time. Now Todd, what's your dream?"

"I don't know, Mr. Muselle," said Todd. He took Henry's hands, his own soaked from tears. In a voice crackling with emotion, he whispered, "Will you help me find one?"

The clanging of lockers in the hallway diminished as the tide of students left the building. The whoosh of the janitor's broom faded into adjoining hallways. The spring sun tucked itself into the treetops spreading its rays of new beginnings over the fields, forests, farms, factories and families of the northern Sandy Valley. On that crisp spring day, in a stuffy history classroom buried deep in the bowels of the high school, an old dream gave birth to a new dreamer.

Chapter Five

Corey and Todd were the first to arrive at the "war room," as they were now calling the workroom where the initial work on the science fair project had taken place. Corey walked past the rack of test tubes sitting on the counter. They seemed to snap to attention as their commander passed in review.

What a difference a day made. Just last Friday, it appeared to Corey that the experiment was over. Todd's shenanigans, although spectacular, seemed to be just one more in a series of attention getting events. Mr. Muselle's revelations gave credence to their initial hunch that the residue in some of the samples was gold. Now they had to turn a hunch into proof.

The friendship between Corey and Todd went back many years. They grew up across the street from each other. They were elementary school buddies.

Corey tried to warn Todd of his father's indiscretions after overhearing conversations between their two dads. He was a good listener as the messy divorce destroyed his best friend's family. Separated by the move mandated by the courts, the boys grew apart.

As they entered high school and Todd's new personality developed, Corey saw Todd's inclusion in the Science Fair project as a way to help out an old friend. He never anticipated Todd's exploits would jeopardize his well-planned experiment. His commitment, now, was to prove or disprove their discovery of gold. He had to do it for his own reputation. He had to do it to salvage the reputation of his friend.

Referring to his notes, Corey placed a yellow dot on the map for each sample where cyanide and zinc produced a reaction. Todd sat on the stool and watched. Corey stepped back from the map. "Well, that's it," he said.

"But there are only eight yellow dots on the map," Todd complained. "Shouldn't it be a bull's-eye?"

"That's all the samples where something precipitated," Corey replied.

"We found more gold than that," Todd insisted.

"No, Todd, we found precipitate, not gold," Corey corrected him.

"But, Mr. Boggs said that cyanide and zinc precipitate gold and there's gold buried near Minerva," Todd protested.

"And dinosaurs once ruled the earth," snapped Corey. "This is a pollution experiment. You wanted to find pollution; we found pollution. Gold or not, there's something in the water. You should be ecstatic."

"Well, I am . . . but I thought . . . pollution?"

"Look at this map," Corey continued. "All eight samples are south of town. They look like they run East and West, but they're spread over five or six miles. So, who knows what it is or where it's coming from?"

"Well, Einstein, what are you telling me," Todd said disgustedly.

"I'm telling you; I just don't know what to make of it."

Michelle and Dan walked through the war room door just in time to hear Corey's proclamation. Dan took off his coat and hung it on a hook on the wall. "Well, if you don't know what we've found, how are we mere mortals supposed to figure it out?" Dan asked. Corey knew that Dan believed from the beginning that the specks in the test tubes were gold. Mr. Muselle's story only confirmed to him the gold's existence.

Corey was rummaging behind one of the cabinets. "If you people just give me a minute, maybe we can figure this out. You're always so impatient. You want an answer right now, and I can't give you one that quickly."

"There it is," he said, pulling a large tablet from behind the cabinet. He reached under the workbench and retrieved

Henry Muselle's Treasure

a collapsible table easel. "Sit down and we'll see what we know and what we don't know."

Michelle obediently pulled the chairs in front of the workbench and made Dan and Todd sit down. Corey placed the tablet on the easel and began writing on it with a marker.

There was no question in Corey's mind that he would not become a research scientist. He was applying to small liberal arts colleges in order to get a broad based education upon which he could add additional degrees. He was not sure whether it would be biology, chemistry or physics based, but he knew he would make a major contribution to the environmental stability of the planet.

He divided the paper into two columns and labeled one side "Present" and the other "Future Actions." "First," he began, "have we completed our initial tests, and do they indicate there is a pollutant in the water?"

"I don't think so," Michelle answered like a girl still in class.

He wrote on the board "original experiment . . . future action . . . complete testing."

"Next," he continued, "we believed, if this was pollution, we could trace it through our samples to its source. Right?"

This was Todd's bailiwick. "Yeah, that is the purpose of this whole experiment."

"Does anything you see on this map help us solve that problem?"

"No," Todd realized.

"You know," Dan chimed in. "We never researched the water supply; where it comes from; where it goes."

"Water supply," Corey was writing, "future action . . . needs more research."

"Next, do we know the precipitate we got is gold?" he continued.

"Well?" Professor Corey asked.

"We'll have to find out how to do that," said Todd.

"Precipitate," Corey wrote, "future action . . . determine if gold."

"The samples with the precipitate are too spread out to really prove anything, aren't they?" Dan asked.

"If it weren't for the fact that they are all on the same side of the town, I'd say we hadn't really discovered anything," said Michelle.

"I still think it's coming from the French gold," Todd insisted.

"Well, the French gold is not a part of the original experiment, but proving a pollutant and its origin is," said Corey.

"Do you think we can prove it's the French gold?" asked Michelle.

"There's only one way to find out," said Corey. He wrote on the board, "French gold . . . future action . . . collect more samples.

"Here's what we'll do. Dan, you take sample 12, it's the western most and track west a half mile. Cover an area north and south a half mile, too. Bring back five samples."

"Michelle, you take East of sample 12 to sample 15. Use the same North-South pattern. Get five more samples.

"I'll take from sample 15 East to 17. Samples 18 and 19 fall in this area, and it seems to have the highest concentration. I'll get ten samples from here.

"Todd got sample 17. That's the farthest East we've gone. You do like Dan and go a half mile farther east and a mile north and south. Bring us ten samples. That way, we can see if it's beyond where we stopped last time.

"The sooner we get it collected, the sooner we can pinpoint the treasure. Do you all know your starting points?"

"I'm going to Oneida," said Dan.

"I'll start at Van Horn's," said Michelle.

"I'll be at Miller's," said Corey.

Todd hesitated, just a little. "And, I get to start at the cow patties at Saling's."

Dan and Todd took off from the war room as if they had been shot out of a gun. Michelle stayed to help Corey straighten up while she waited for her father to come pick her up.

"I really don't think it's gold," she said, isolating the suspicious samples and placing them in a safe spot.

"Why not?" asked Corey. "It all fits. The right chemicals . . . the right order. It could be gold."

But our experiment . . . I mean your experiment," Michelle continued, "was to determine if the aircraft plant, or any other industry in town was polluting the water. I wanted to be a part of your team because the way you figure things out, I knew we would get an A. But now this thing that Todd did . . . "

"You said it was OK if I let Mrs. T put him with us."

"But, you knew I liked him."

"That's not my problem."

"C'mon Corey, you know how smart and innovative he is. The 'bad Todd' is just an act. He uses these harebrained antics to hide his real feelings."

"Oh, dear, dear, dear," said Corey as he dropped the easel back in its storage spot. "Next you'll be telling me your real quest is to discover the key to his heart and unlock the treasure buried deep within."

Michelle didn't say anything. Corey turned to make sure she was all right. When the redness of back of her ear shone through the blond hair tucked behind it, Corey realized the droplets she was cleaning from the counter had not come from the test tubes. They continued to clean in silence until the doorbell rang. Corey's parents were still at work, so Corey answered the door. It was Sue Yant.

"Hi, Corey," the vivacious 45 year-old said. "I was hoping you would be here."

"Hi, Mrs. Yant. Michelle and I were just doing a little extra work on our science fair project.

"So how's the experiment going?" Corey was amazed that even she had heard about the project, but he wasn't completely surprised at her visit. Sue was President of the volleyball mother's club, and Corey knew she was always looking for ways to help any of the kids who might need it.

"Oh, pretty good," Corey said. "We decided we needed to test more samples."

"Didn't Dan Jones come to my house and get a sample for the project?

"Yes, he did. In fact, he just left here not ten minutes ago for more samples, and I'm sure your house was going to be one of his stops. I hope there's a way he can get it without you being home. We'd like to start our new testing right away."

"Sure, he can get it out of the side faucet. I think that's where the last one came from. What are you testing for?" she asked.

"The usual things - dissolved oxygen, fecal coliform, nitrogen - you know," Corey replied.

"Are you going to determine a water quality index?"

"Well, yes, but how do you know about the water quality index."

"My husband helped develop it. He was a hydrologist with the Muskingum Watershed Conservancy District. They worked with the Ohio EPA to define the tests to determine a water quality indexing system."

"He did what for whom?"

"He worked for the Conservancy District. They were originally just concerned with controlling flooding along the Muskingum River, but now they work with water quality issues in all the area that feeds the Muskingum. That's most of the Eastern sixth of the state.

"The watershed was instrumental in early methods of flood prediction. G. T. McCarthy devised a formula to help determine flood routing based on his experience in the Muskingum Valley. When the EPA looked for an area which was at the forefront of water quality issues, they came to the Muskingum Watershed."

"And what did your husband do?" Corey asked.

"He helped them sift through the multitude of tests that could be run on water and determined how important each was to good water quality. You'll never see his name mentioned in the literature, but if it wasn't for Tom Yant, you wouldn't be doing your experiment now."

"That's really great. You know, we've got all these samples, and we think we might have found something. But, we don't know how to track where the pollution might be coming from."

"You need a map," she said.

"We've got a map, but all it shows is where the samples are," he replied.

"No, a hydrological map," Sue said.

"A what?" Corey asked.

"A hydrological map which shows where the aquifers are and how they run."

"Where do I get one of those?"

"It just so happens, Tom left me with an abundance of maps. What do you need? Sandy Creek? Walhounding River? Tuscarawas River?"

"I think Sandy Creek will do it."

I had a hunch you might need one, so I threw a couple in the back seat of the car before I came over her. Let me go get it."

She went out to her car and returned with a tube marked Sandy Creek Watershed. Corey led her back to the war room where Michelle had cleared a place on the workroom table. She spread the map out on the table, and there in all its shades of blue laid the answers to many of their questions - light blue aquifers, pale blue underground rivers feeding streams with familiar names. Light red lines outlined the boundaries of familiar roads, giving badly needed reference points.

"This is terrific," Corey squealed. "Can I borrow it?"

"Borrow it? You can have it. That's one less I don't have to dust," Sue said.

"Great!"

Corey directed them as he, Sue and Michelle spent nearly an hour comparing points on the hydrological map with dots on his map. When they were finished yellow dots lay on top of blue pools of water. Corey could imagine many different scenarios to create the pattern, but nothing to point them in the direction of gold. The search ended with another ring of the doorbell.

"Michelle's dad is here," Corey said, not even bothering to look out a window. Corey left to go fetch Mr. Bobinger from the front door. Corey knew that Michelle was Phillip Bobinger's baby and whatever she needed, she got. He was a supportive father, no matter what the circumstances. Even though she could have gotten a driver's license a year ago, he was content to be her chauffeur.

Phil entered the workroom and was stunned by the maps and their dots.

"Pretty impressive, isn't it?" Sue asked.

"It certainly is," moving to where he could get a better view.

"We've only got eight confirmed samples, so we're not sure what we're seeing," said Corey.

"Well," Phil said as he became more oriented, "are you looking for pollution, or gold?"

"Pollution," said Corey.

"Gold," said Michelle.

'It looks like you two are no more unified than the rest of this town," Sue said, as she gathered her things.

"Dad, do you really believe the gold's still here?" Michelle asked.

"I don't know, Michelle. It was buried almost 250 years ago. A lot of people have lived here and looked for it," Phillip replied.

Corey knew Phillip fell into the camp of those in town who believed in the legend. For several years, Minerva promoted a "Lost French Gold Festival" and Phil was its chairperson in its earliest days. Although he had been supportive of their efforts in the project, when it came to his daughter's discovery of gold, he was less convinced.

"I remember, as a child, somebody found some gold coins buried near a tree stump out in McDaniel's field. The whole town went out and dug up his field. Somebody finally did some history and figured out they dug up the Poole brothers' bank. They decided that in 1755 the French didn't leave U. S. currency dated 1808.

"Good thinking," Michelle said. "If it's there, how much gold is there?" she asked.

"You've been reading my mind," he said. He reached into his suit coat pocket and pulled out a folded sheet of legal paper and handed it to Michelle.

"I've been trying to figure out where the gold is for years. I wondered how big an area we'd be looking for, so I put a few numbers on paper."

Michelle read the page. "There were sixteen pack horses and ten men. Assuming four of the pack horses were for provisions of the trip, that leaves twelve horses to carry the treasure. Assume that each horse carried two boxes three feet long, twelve inches high and twelve inches deep.

"They had to bury it in a hurry. If they buried them side by side and two deep, you'd need a hole twelve feet long, three feet wide and about thirty inches deep.

"You have ten men. One goes out as an advance scout. Three stand guard. Two unload the horses while four men dig their portion of the trench three feet by three feet by three feet. It wouldn't take very long.

"If each box contained one hundred pounds of gold, you'd have twenty-four hundred pounds or thirty-eight thousand four hundred ounces. At three hundred fifty dollars an ounce, that's thirteen million, four hundred forty thousand dollars worth of gold."

There was silence in the room.

Michelle finally asked, "Dad, do you think we're crazy trying to find the gold?"

"Do I buy a lottery ticket every week?" was the reply.

* * *

Fred crumpled his lottery ticket and threw it into the wastebasket. "Damn those things, anyway. I wasted two dollars on a chance for $16 million, and I didn't even have one number."

Papers blew out of his in-box and across his desk. He looked up to see the door to the anteroom open and Huntsinger standing in front of his desk.

"Don't you believe in knocking?" he snorted. "Close the door before everything blows away."

Huntsinger walked back to close the door. There was a trail of muddy footprints leading into the office.

"What do you mean coming in here with crud all over your shoes? Were you born in a barn?" snapped Johnson rising from his chair.

"I'm sorry Fred," said Huntsinger as he slipped out of his work boots. He left four muddy prints on Johnson's new office carpet.

"What's such an emergency that you couldn't call?" he asked pinning the notes back on his wall map.

"Fred, the EPA's here," George said.

Fred Johnson turned from the progress map. All the color drained from his face.

"Who is it, and do they suspect anything?"

"He says his name is Joe Gunther. He's Fernandez's boss."

Johnson dropped in his chair. Fred worked very hard to cultivate Enrico Fernandez. He had come from Puerto Rico and was employed by the EPA through a minority quota. He was sharp and knew his stuff, but was treated by his fellow workers as if he were an illegal immigrant. Fred knew Fernandez was caught in the web of bureaucracy. On one hand he was encouraged to side with the agency to promote its goals. On the other hand he was to expedite projects of high political importance. He had been easy prey for a fast talker like Johnson. All it took was a little interest in his family, a couple of little gifts at holidays, and Fernandez was hooked.

When Johnson began paying bigger money, Fernandez was able to realize the American dream. The new EPA report Fernandez wrote was a masterpiece. Johnson knew if he was paid handsomely enough he would not squeal. It was clear that Gunther, however, was another problem.

Joe Gunther had been with the EPA since its inception. Johnson realized that once he had been assigned to the water division, he found his true love. He protected the water supply with a passion and prosecuted violators with a vengeance. There was also no love lost between Johnson and Gunther. He had the potential of being a very large problem.

"Gunther said he wanted to see how we were coming along," Huntsinger continued. "Fortunately, with that broken dozer, no one was working today."

Johnson's hopes were renewed. "Then we're on schedule for this weekend and the spring?"

"Yes, I've got everything set up," Huntsinger replied. "But, Fred, this guy wasn't looking for that spring."

"He wasn't?" Johnson was a little amazed.

"No, Fred, he showed me Fernandez's report."

"The original?" There was true fear in Fred's voice.

"No, the new one."

Johnson smiled in relief. "Then everything's fine."

"But Fred, he made me take him clear to the end of the route. We walked through a lot of the fields."

Johnson knew by the tone of his voice this was exactly the situation Huntsinger did not want. Here he was lying to a very powerful government official about things he didn't want to have done in the first place.

"Did he say anything?" Johnson wanted to know.

"Yeah, he wanted to know if we ever built platforms to protect sensitive environmental areas from roads. I told him we did it all the time."

"Was he satisfied?" Johnson really wanted to know.

"I think so . . . I hope so." Huntsinger appeared frustrated. "Man, I don't like him snooping around," he said. He stood directly in front of Johnson's desk. Placing both hands on the desk, he leaned forward and looked Johnson right in the eyes. "Do you realize what we're doing? We're going to rip through that valley tearing up swamps, springs and bogs. I guess I can overlook the lives we're destroying; the state is the bully on that one. But, Fred, look what we're doing to the land. Worst of all, what are we doing to the water. You've made me destroy things I was always told to respect. I don't know how much longer I can do this."

Johnson was on his feet. They were nose to nose. "Let's get one thing straight, Mr. George Huntsinger. I don't give a hoot about swamps or springs or bogs. Those funky old farmers can catch water in a rain barrel, carry it from the stream or buy it from me, but they'll not stop me from completing this road."

"Fred, I don't know what was in that original report, but it was enough to send the road by another route. I'm afraid the spring at Jackson's is just the beginning. Let's tell Gunther about it and let the chips fall where they may."

Fred was amazed. George had never stood up to him like that before. It was now a game of chicken. They glared at one another, as they had never done in their long friendship. Who would flinch first?

"How does the sound of steel doors slamming grab you?" Fred said never losing eye contact. He leaned toward George to make his next point. "Because if you don't continue to tear up that tidy little valley, that's all you'll hear."

Huntsinger flinched first, knocking over a dolphin paperweight. "OK, I'll go on," Huntsinger relented. "But if Gunther asks too many questions, I'm coming to get you."

"You do that," Johnson retorted.

Huntsinger started for the door.

"You be past that spring and back on schedule by Monday."

Huntsinger looked at the muddy footprints.

"Do you want me to have Myrtle come in and clean this up?"

"No, leave it. It'll remind me of the mess you have things in."

Johnson turned back to the map. Huntsinger stopped at the door and turned as if to try to convince Johnson to change his stand.

"That little so and so almost ruined me." He caressed the last dot on the map. "When I make it here," Johnson mused,

"I collect $10 million dollars. Plus a hundred thousand a day for every day we're early, and we're already ten days ahead of schedule. I know we'll pick up another week along the way. If I can figure out a way not to build a platform for those four springs, we could pick up another two weeks. That would make an even thirteen million."

Huntsinger approached Johnson as he stuck a blue pushpin in the map at Saling's farm.

"There," he said, "is the key to my treasure. It's my thirteen million dollar farm."

Fred felt Huntsinger's presence in front of the desk. Fred turned around. "Something more you have to say? Any worries about Gunther or Fernandez?"

"No Fred, I guess not," George said, his eyes dropping to the floor. We'll talk about it later." Huntsinger turned around, walked out of the room and quietly shut the door.

Chapter Six

Henry Muselle's Journal
Wednesday, Seventh Period

Does my fate now lie in the hands of high school students? How are they going to accomplish what hasn't been done in two and a half centuries? Find gold from a few flakes? Impossible! Mrs. Talkington and Mr. Boggs feel that their hypothesis is sound. I can't imagine that they have enough data to track down the source of the gold. The information I have is more historical and archeological. They are taking the scientific approach. I don't know how I can ever juxtapose my material onto theirs.

I don't know why I let every little piece of new information get me so excited. All of them have led down dead ends before. Why should this one be any different?

I had another dream last night. I dreamed that Guardian was walking in the woods when he came upon a trapper's camp. It was apparent the trapper had been ambushed. His tent was destroyed. There were bloody signs of a struggle all around the camp. His attackers made off with his furs, but it appeared they spared his life and he escaped - although wounded.

In a tree on the outskirts of the camp, he had tied a bear bag in a limb about twelve feet off the ground. The purpose of the bag was to place food items and valuables high enough off the ground so that bears could not get into it. The tree was nearly surrounded with briars. There were no low lying branches to grasp to begin the climb up the tree, but somehow the trapper had managed to climb the tree and secure the bag to the limb.

As Guardian devised a plan to rescue the bag, his children friends came into the camp. One of them said that he could climb the tree. Guardian used all manner of persuasion to convince him he could not do it. He warned of the briars and the dangers of a fall from the high limb.

Not dissuaded, the young brave walked to the tree. He moved a young poplar tree to one side and placed his foot on a knot just a foot and a half off the ground. He pushed himself up and placed his other foot in a crevice on the far side of the tree. He grabbed the bottom of a low branch and pulled himself around the tree to another foothold. In this manner, he walked upward around the tree until he reached the branch where the bag was tied. He loosened the knot and let the bag fall into Guardian's hands.

In the leather pouch were not only the rations for the day, but coins and a map showing the escape route to be used by the trapper in an emergency. It was a message left behind so that anyone who would find it could follow the trail and rescue him.

As Guardian pondered the message, one of the children told him that he should not have discouraged them. They said that children learn they are not able to accomplish some goals because they are demoralized in their quest by adults.

Dreams! I still don't understand dreams.

Chapter Seven

Corey didn't leave anything to chance. He planned his route carefully. He'd battle farm animals and junkyard dogs, if he had to. He knew that when his quest was finished, he'd have ten good samples and a direct path to the gold - if it were gold.

He called each of his prospective sample donors ahead of time. It was a convenient way to avoid people. He could collect his samples and without the interference of human contact. He wanted water from sources as opposed to tap water that was contaminated by water softeners and old lead pipes. As he rode his bike to Miller's, his mind raced ahead. He saw himself in the admissions department of M.I.T. receiving the news he would be given a full scholarship to the university. He envisioned graduation and being greeted by a representative of Dow-Corning offering him a job.

He rounded the sharp turn on Brush Road and imagined he was entering the drive of the research complex. As he passed the cows in the field, he spoke to them as if they were his coworkers heading for the lab. He rode up the driveway to the Miller farm. The white pillars in front of the house were more reminiscent of a Southern plantation than an Ohio farmhouse.

As he parked his bike out front and retrieved the jar for the sample, he pretended he was getting his prepared remarks for his acceptance speech of the Nobel Prize. Corey dreamed grand dreams, but he was certain they would be reality if he just worked hard enough.

The Miller's had a separate well house where the water was distributed to the house and the barn. There was a separate faucet that was used for drawing test samples and other odd jobs around the building.

Corey quickly drew his sample and sealed the jar. He went back to the bike, secured it in his saddlebag and headed off down the road. Next stop was Howlett's. It would be a quick stop because they had a spring.

He was excited about the experiment - gold or not. He knew that variations in the water quality index could be another pointer to the gold. It was as important to him to have a successful conclusion to the experiment, as it was to find any buried treasure. Maybe this would make the other kids like him. Dan, Todd and Michelle learned a long time ago about the neat kid behind the nerd. They knew how witty and funny Corey was. But most of the other kids in school only saw the brainiac. They teased him about how much he studied. The more awards he won, the harder they laughed. They more they laughed, the more he studied.

He pulled in Howlett's drive and walked the bike up the steep hill past the potholes. He propped the bike against the side of the springhouse. He took his sample jar and went into the building. The smell inside was incredible - cool, damp and fragrant with the odors of treasures washed from deep within the earth. Corey paused for a minute and watched the water trickle from the rocks. He plunged the jar beneath the surface of the water and pulled it up sharply so it did not strike the bottom of the spring. After the water settled down, Corey stared into the abyss. He counted the smooth rocks in the bottom of the spring and watched the plants swaying in the current. Out of curiosity, he stuck his hand in the spring and submerged it clear to his elbow. He pulled it back out and dried off his arm. He watched the water settle again and noted its almost silvery sheen.

It was a good place to pause and reflect, so to speak. He liked the smell and the isolation. He could see in the water the science fair awards' ceremony. He was receiving the best in show for the water experiment. The water falling on the rocks sounded like the applause of his classmates. The sound of an approaching tractor broke his reverie. He'd have to hurry before John got to the barn. He didn't have time for the questions. There were samples to collect. There was an experiment to finish.

* * *

It was a long ride to the Saling's. Todd was not looking forward to the walk through the field to collect another sample. Todd hated the cowpath. His last trip to Saling's farm he'd ruined his best pair of tennis shoes. He got a demerit in gym class and spent the whole period in the shower scraping the tread of his shoe. Now the shoes had shrunk and were brittle - all in the name of science.

Corey really made him angry sometimes. Todd agreed they needed more samples, but he didn't think they needed thirty more - especially if Todd had to collect ten of them. Maybe Corey thought Todd should collect that many because this whole mess was Todd's fault. You would think Corey would be willing to pursue the gold angle of the experiment. But no, Corey had to do everything by the book. So, instead of hunting for gold, Todd had to risk life, limb and tennis shoes to find some unknown pollutant.

Todd was still contemplating his talk with Mr. Muselle. He liked the idea of having a dream. He had dreamed before, but it had always been make believe. To dream that he could find the lost French gold seemed almost too big a dream to start with. He realized, with Mr. Muselle's confession, its discovery would affect many more people than just him. If it were true and if he could in some way find the treasure, it might be the solution to many of his problems. It was all too unreal, too incredible to contemplate. He was a high school Senior. He knew he could not single-handedly find the gold. He knew all along his actions had been wrong. He knew he had hurt many of the people who had tried to help him since the divorce.

Maybe a dream was the answer. For now, there were samples to collect. The Saling farm was just over the hill.

He'd try to be more careful. He'd hurt his friends before. He didn't want to do it again.

* * *

Ralph placed the rocker on the farmhouse porch and sat down to await Todd's arrival. He sipped his cup of after dinner coffee as he soaked up the sweet spring air. The locals described Ralph Saling's farmhouse as a "big ol' farmhouse." It was white with original green shutters still serving a purpose in winter. It had a grand porch that went around two sides of the house. A porch swing hung at one end. During the summer, cane rockers, settees and easy chairs were generously positioned to invite family and neighbors to "sit a spell and visit."

He modernized the "visiting" aspect of the porch by placing a picnic table and propane grill on the side porch. When coupled with the horseshoe pit to one side, the volleyball net in the front yard, and home plate in the other side yard, the porch provided a vista from which to watch children and grandchildren enjoy the fruits of family growing up in the country.

He spent most of his time working the farm and had very little time for things like high school football and basketball games, but he liked kids. He was always helpful to kids, and he wished his kids came around a little more often.

This little piece of Heaven ran east and west bordered on the north and south by a ridge of gentle, rolling hills. The hills nearly met at either end of the valley forming a little pocket in which the Salings had hidden for a hundred and twenty-five years. The valley was as much a part of Ralph as the Salings were a part of the valley. Ralph Saling was born in the farmhouse in which he lived. His family settled the farm in the 1850's. The first settlers on the land were the Salings. He was the fifth generation to work the land. The land was good to him and his family. It provided food. It provided income. It was the school where he taught his family the facts of life. Nothing would pry him from it. The farm was more than a piece of property. It was an attitude. There was never any question what Ralph would do when he grew up - he would farm. He loved the farm and all it entailed. He didn't mind the long hours or the little vacation.

What made the Saling valley so special were the springs. There were not one, or two, but four large springs pumping thousands of gallons of water into the center of this pristine garden. After all these years with the encroachments of man, they were still there.

His valley was unique. The springs weren't a headwater (the start of a stream), but they did flow from an aquifer, an underground stream. In fact, they came from two different aquifers, which was what made the area so different.

The two western springs came from what scientists called the "Little Sandy Aquifer." This aquifer ran nearly due west and fed Little Sandy Creek. The two eastern springs came from the "Muddy Fork Aquifer." This aquifer ran east southeast and fed the Muddy Fork of Little Sandy. South of where Muddy Fork joined Little Sandy, the Still Fork came in and the stream became Big Sandy. Big Sandy flowed into the Tuscarawas River. The Tuscarawas flowed into the Muskingum. The Muskingum emptied into the Ohio and the Ohio into the Mississippi. As Ralph told it, these four springs were crucial to the economic development of the country.

He had a dream, or so he thought. Firmly ensconced on the family farm, his dream was unraveling. Every time he took one step down the path to fulfill his vision, he was knocked back two. Even his wife, Martha, seemed to be working against him. His life of contentment had turned to a life of chaos.

He met Martha in high school. Martha was a city girl. Her father moved the family to Minerva to take a job with the Cronin China. She met Ralph at a time when he was starting to spread his wings. She fell in love with Ralph's simplicity. He talked of grand things and the possibility of a great future. He even talked of college and a career. They were married as soon as they graduated from high school. But before Ralph could start college, his father died, and he was drawn back to the farm. He knew Martha always believed she could move him from the farm and on to bigger and better things. There was no question in his mind, Martha had never been happy as a farmer's wife. He felt she saw the loss of the farm as an opportunity to start a new life.

Ralph made $250,000 for the twenty acres he sold the state for the new highway. The sale would cut his farm in half. The barn would be on one side of the four-lane highway and his cows would be on the other. A quarter of a million dollars wouldn't be enough for him to start over. He couldn't blame the state. His valley was just perfect for anyone traveling east to west. Ralph tried to stop the road. He went to all the meetings. He participated in all the studies. He signed all the petitions. But in the end, it seemed as if nothing could stop the road. There was something not right about it. If he had a chance to stop it now, he would.

When they first mentioned the new road, Ralph did his homework about wetlands. All of the literature said that the existence of the springs constituted wetlands, and the road would have to go elsewhere. And that was what was so puzzling. The springs were important - important to the valley, to Muddy Fork and Little Sandy, and to all the people living along the two aquifers. He had proved that to the EPA. They told Ralph there was no way the highway could proceed through his valley. They would have to take Alternate C, which would move the road a mile south. Ralph was shown a draft of the report with this recommendation in it.

The next thing Ralph knew, he received a letter from the Department of Transportation offering to buy his land. When he asked about the EPA report, he was told there was no problem in building over the springs. A non-porous protective covering would be constructed so as not to disturb the springs. It would be like a small underground bridge to keep the road off the springs.

Ralph objected strenuously. He scoured engineering manuals and found nothing about "non-porous protective coverings." He scanned EPA regulations and again came up empty handed. Time and time again his complaints were rebutted. The only explanation was, "That was the way the bureaucracy worked."

Todd arrived at the house just after suppertime. Ralph had never had any dealings with him other than giving him a jar full of water from his spring, until last Friday when Martha judged his project. Ralph invited him into the living room while Martha finished the dishes in the kitchen.

Ralph's hobby was collecting historical artifacts. On the living room wall was a display honoring the early days of Minerva. Ralph's grandfather's muzzleloader hung as its centerpiece. Draped over one end was a hat made from the fur of a raccoon Ralph shot in his woods. It was complete with a twelve-inch tail. The bookshelf housed a replica of Remington's sculpture of a Plains Indian on horseback.

"Well, what brings you here, Todd? Since the science fair was over, I assumed you were through with water samples."

"I did, too," replied Todd, "but we messed up, so we decided to get more. I have to get ten new samples in an area from your farm to about a half mile East of here."

"Well, when you get this one done, I'll take you to the spring where you got your first sample. Then we'll go to my other three springs."

"You have three more?"

"Yep, they don't run as good as this one, but they're still here."

"That means there are four springs here."

"That's right."

"They don't form sort of a square, do they?"

Saling began to laugh. "They certainly do, and right smack in the center is the Tuscarawas Treasure."

"You know about the treasure?" quizzed Todd.

"Know about it? Son, I've lived it. The farm was supposedly the location of the skirmish where the French gold was lost," he explained. "For two and a half centuries, this place has been explored and dug up. But, to our knowledge, no one ever found it. I think the Indians got it," Ralph said.

"Indians?" Todd inquired.

"Yes, Indians," Ralph replied. "Iroquois, Mohawk, Cherokee, Chippewa, and Delaware all utilized our valley to travel from the Ohio River to Lake Erie. They called it the Great Trail. I have two big cigar boxes full of arrowheads I collected from the fields to prove it.

"This was a perfect place to camp," he continued. "The protection of the thick forests on either hill, the plush bed of grass in the bottom, and all the water you would ever need is at your fingertips. I can imagine seeing the smoke rise from a dozen campfires sprinkled among the magnificent teepees. I can see the Indian children running not too far into the woods because there were bear and mountain lion hiding in the brush. On a cool August morning, just at the break of day as the mist rose from the springs, the deer would venture out of the woods for a morning drink of nature's nectar," Ralph said, waxing poetic.

"When I was a boy, there were still plenty of trees on the hills - huge oak, maple and hickory. There was even a stand of birch in one corner of the valley. I always thought, if it were closer to Sandy Creek, the Indians would have used them to make canoes."

Todd puffed up his chest and said proudly, "I think we have found the treasure."

"How well I know," Ralph said. "But, you won't have to worry about any treasure when they finish putting the road through that field."

Kerr-boom! Another dump truck hit the chuckhole in front of the house. The windows rattled; the bookcase door flew open. A porcelain figurine fell off the shelf and bounced to the floor. The cows jumped back from the spring. The trustees had been told about the hole, but they weren't interested in fixing roads right now.

The truck was heading to Hopkins Hannum's farm with a load of debris from the new Route 30 construction. Hopkins was trying to fill in an old strip mine. It was mined before the companies had to reclaim the land, so Hopkins was doing it himself. Actually, the state decided to help after Hopkins threatened a lawsuit and dropped words like "a mining superfund" on legislators. In the old days, contractors were glad to get rid of the stuff, but these were the days of regulation.

From the living room window, Todd and Ralph could see the dust of the dump truck billowing down the road. The truck rounded the bend at Miller's and continued out the road toward Hannum's. The cows went back to grazing. Ralph said, leaning back in his recliner, "Todd, if you listen hard, you can probably hear the sounds of the approaching bulldozers."

"It's coming through here?" Todd asked.

"Just a hundred yards from this window will be the most beautiful stretch of four-lane highway this side of Kensington," said Martha who had finished the dishes and come in from the kitchen.

"How soon is it coming?" asked Todd.

"Before summer," she said. "They promised to give us a couple of weeks notice so we could move the cows. It won't be long. So if you're gonna find the gold, you'd better do it in a hurry."

Ralph looked at Todd staring off into space. He watched his countenance change. Todd's eyes began to sparkle in the way they did when he started on a new tangent. Suddenly, Todd was no longer simply a gold hunter. Based on Todd's performance at the science fair, Ralph could envision great clouds of dust swirling around him as Todd defiantly stood in front of the approaching monstrous earth movers. It would be like Todd to single-handedly stop the road and save the farm . . . or the gold . . . or something.

"Isn't there some way to stop the road?" he asked.

"For the longest time we thought the road would miss us," Martha said. "There were three possible routes. We went and testified against this one, but at the last moment, it was chosen. Our attorney finally said to give in. There was no use fighting the state."

She walked to the bookcase, picked up the fallen book and put it back in its place. Todd noticed only the top shelf was full of books. The other shelves were filled with boxes, which were meticulously labeled with their contents.

"It looks like you're ready to move," Todd said.

"All Ralph has to do is find us a place in town, and I could be ready for the moving van in two days," she replied.

"But you're going to leave this place," he protested, "and the gold will be lost forever. You can't stop fighting now."

"Todd," Martha was getting a little more than aggravated, "we've fought the fight, and now to finish the race we've got to move. The gold is going to have to stay lost."

Ralph jumped into the fray before it became too heated. "There comes a time when you have to accept the circumstances you've been given. The government says the road goes through the farm. We have to do what they think is best for the whole community, not just our own personal interests."

"But, Mr. Saling," Todd was almost in tears, "you've given us the first concrete information that the gold is real and that it might be here. If we just work together, I know we can find it and save the farm. Isn't that what you want?"

Martha had had enough. "Todd, grow up!" she snapped. "Some things are out of your control." She was heading for him with a granite bookend. He took one step closer to Ralph as she whisked past them and on to the fireplace on the other side of the living room.

She turned and waved the rock at Todd and Ralph. "My advice to you, young man, is to collect your samples, forget the road and forget the gold!" She spun around, placed the bookend against a line of books, then turned again and stood with both hands on her hips, staring at the two men.

Ralph nudged Todd toward the door as Martha watched them like a cat watching a fleeing mouse. Outside, they could still hear the repercussions of one very unhappy farmer's wife. Ralph was getting ready to explain to Todd the fine art of dealing with women when they were drawn to the sound of an approaching car.

A little green car with the broken grill came down the road. Calling the car green was kind. Ohio winters encouraged the

Henry Muselle's Treasure

growth of rust throughout the body of the late model car. Thanks to the weathering from the outside and the advancing rust from within, the car looked green, white, or brown depending on the way the sun hit it.

Ralph and Todd positioned themselves by the side of the road and prepared to wave at the driver as he passed. This was Minerva. It was customary to stop and visit with people who were coming from or going to some important chore. It could take more than an hour to travel a little over a mile on these roads because of the necessity to constantly stop and visit. The green car slowed and pulled off the road into the entrance of the drive. Ralph and Todd headed toward the car to greet the individual participating in the neighborly ritual.

"Hey, Mr. Muselle, what are you doing out in this neck of the woods?" Todd asked.

"I wanted to continue our discussion from lunch. I called your house and your mother said you were out collecting again. I went for a ride to see if I could find you."

"Mr. Muselle? . . . Ralph Saling," Ralph said, shoving his callused farm hand into the smooth hand of the teacher. He did not recognize Henry from the Science Fair. He was too preoccupied going in and too upset coming out to be sociable.

"I'm glad you stopped," said Todd. "The four springs are right here on Mr. Saling's farm. There's a road going to be built through the field. You have to help me convince Mr. Saling to fight the road so we can find the gold."

Ralph smiled and shook his head. "You have to forgive Todd. He has a very vivid imagination."

"I am all too well aware of Todd's imagination. I'm his history teacher. In fact, I have a personal interest in Todd's treasure. I'm curious to see his progress," Henry said.

"Well, we were just on our way to the field to look at the springs," said Ralph. "If you want to pull your car over there, you're more than welcome to traipse along with us."

As Henry moved the car, Todd and Ralph heard the kitchen window slam shut. This was followed by the sound of assorted drawers and cupboards being forcefully closed with an audible notice of disapproval.

Ralph looked like a farmer. He was not quite six feet tall with leathered sin than made him look a decade older than his fifty years. He was slightly built, but his wiry sinews turned into cords of steel when called upon. His hair was prematurely gray and getting uncomfortably thin. The ball cap he wore did necessarily go with the t-shirt and bibbed overall. He walked with a limp one of his disgruntled cows and given him.

The cowpath was the best route to the first spring, but April was not the time to be walking through the field. The cow presents dropped throughout remained moist for days thanks to the spring rains. As they matured, their color began to blend with the ground.

"Hi-ho little scientist," Ralph warned, "watch out for the . . ."

But Todd had already found it. His mother would kill him - again.

"Gotta watch where you're steppin'," Ralph reminded him.

"I know, I know," is all Todd said. He muttered other descriptions of his feelings, none of which would endear him to the adults in the area.

They arrived at the spring where Todd retrieved his first sample. Ralph bent over and cupped his hand. He swept the watercress away with the back of his hand and dipped his curved fingers beneath the surface of the water. He raised his hand to his mouth and sipped the sweet spring water.

I can never sell this place, he thought. The spring water was so good; his grandfather ran a tile culvert to a cistern next to the house. From there it was pumped up to the kitchen sink. Even after his father drilled the well and put in plumbing, the family still kept the cistern for the spring water. But there was the future to think about. How could he farm on two sides of a four-lane highway? The nearest exchange was three miles in one direction and seven miles in the other. He could find other work, but Martha would never stand living in a farmhouse so close to a highway.

Henry Muselle's Treasure

He took another drink. *This water sure has been good for our family,* he mused. It must have been good, Ralph's father lived to be ninety-six and his mother was still going strong at ninety. She was ambling about at Pleasant Rest Nursing Home with the use of a walker. Everyone was amazed at her recovery after she broke her hip falling off the ladder she erected to clean the leaves out of the gutter.

The next spring was about two hundred yards away beyond a little knoll. "You say you have a personal interest in this treasure?" Ralph asked.

"Yeah, his great-great grandpa or somebody was the only survivor of the battle," Todd chimed in.

"Really?" Ralph was beginning to get interested.

Henry corrected Todd, "He was *one* of the survivors. My ancestor was the quartermaster for the unit and was sent as a representative of the fort commander to account for the gold when it arrived at Fort Detroit. When he and the 10th Frenchman returned to Fort Duquesne without the gold, they were trapped between the triumph of the victory over Braddock and the failure of their mission. They decided their knowledge of the location of the gold would restore them to the good graces of the French generals. Instead of being honored as heroes of an English massacre, they were sent to Quebec where they were court-martialed and dishonorably discharged from the army.

"Since that time, one son in each generation of our family has been named Henry in hopes that someday the gold would be found and our name cleared."

"Very interesting," said Ralph. "I've heard many gold hunter's claims before, but yours is unique. Here's the second spring."

Todd quietly got his second sample. Ralph could tell he was impressed by Mr. Muselle's story. Ralph really didn't comment; he just led the entourage to the next spring. They walked down through the field away from the house and barn. They came upon a hole about four and a half feet in diameter and four feet deep. "This hole was from one of the prospectors. My father let him come out and dig. I've got four of these holes. They used to be eight feet deep, but I keep filling them in."

They walked a little farther and came upon the third spring. "They call this Cranberry Spring because of all the cranberry bushes around it," Ralph explained. Todd knelt down, got his sample and they headed through the pasture.

"See that pond over there?" Saling asked. There was a little pond about twenty feet in diameter in the middle of the field. To one side was a mound of dirt about five feet tall. "That's where they brought in the dragline. They went down about six feet and didn't hit anything."

"So, you don't think it's here?" asked Todd.

"I didn't say that," Ralph said with a grin.

They stopped at the fourth spring for Todd to get his sample. Ralph started back to the farmhouse.

"Are there any more springs around?" Henry asked.

"If you go in the half mile radius Todd wanted, I suspect you'd only find fifteen or twenty. I can tell you who owns which one and get you permission to get your samples."

"Great," said Todd, a little more than dejected. "Do any of them form a square?"

"Todd, when you get home, you plot all these springs on a map. I'll bet you could connect a hundred squares of four springs."

"Well, then why did so many people dig here? Why not someplace else?"

"The shovels, I suppose" Ralph replied, not really thinking.

"What shovels?" asked Todd, more encouraged.

"I remember my grandfather telling about digging up these shovels one year when he was plowing the field. Somebody said they were the ones used to bury the gold. He complained they created all kinds of ruckus around here."

"He dug them up? Where?" Henry was now extremely interested.

"I don't know. In one of these fields I guess," Ralph said.

"What ever happened to them?" Henry asked.

"There used to be one in the barn. I can remember playing with it as a child, but I don't know what grandpa ever did with the rest of them, if there were any more. Mom could tell us all about them. She knows the story better than I do."

"She does!" Todd's enthusiasm was back. "Can I talk to her? Is she here?"

"No, I'm afraid she lives now at Pleasant Rest Nursing Home," Ralph said.

"Can we go see her?" Henry asked. "This is the first live testimony I've ever run across. Maybe there was some fact she could recall that would irrefutably tie the shovels to the massacre."

"Sure," Ralph said. She loves company, and she loves telling about the treasure. I'll take you over Friday when I go to visit her." They were almost back to the farmhouse now.

"Come on, I think Martha will let us back inside. I'll get you permission to collect the rest of your samples."

"That'll be great," said Todd.

"Oh, and take your shoes off before you come into the house. It will be safer that way."

The bright spring Ohio sun was beginning to set. The orange globe was just low enough so its glow obliterated everything in the field. Ralph saw the reflection of the blazing sun on the springs. They looked like four gold markers. He gazed at the farmhouse. The sun made the white farmhouse glow orange. On the hill beyond, the sun cast shadows from the trees still in their winter starkness. He couldn't figure out why Martha disliked the country and all its wonders so much. Something could work. He wasn't sure what, but something could keep them on the farm.

"Moo!" called one of the cows. They were beginning to move down the valley, away from the springs, heading to the barn, food and milking. He followed the cows toward the barn. He stumbled on a flat rock at the side of the path, kicking it aside. When he looked back, he saw salamanders scurrying to find a new hiding place. *Wetlands habitat*, he instinctively thought. That was another thing he couldn't figure out. He couldn't figure out the sudden change in the EPA.

He watched the cows walk slowly down the path - some single file, others two abreast. Occasionally one would bellow at a slower cow and pass them.

"How funny," he thought, "just like people driving down a highway. This year it's cows; next year it will be cars and trucks. It hasn't been that long since it was railroads, canal boats, wagon trains, hunters and Indians. If this valley could talk, I wonder what stories it could tell?"

* * *

Corey was amazed at how gold fever was beginning to spread throughout Minerva. The Minerva Leader had run a sidebar story about the pollution experiment's modifications and the speculation it came from the lost French gold. Jason, the young local historian turned cub reporter, made the connection between the Henry Muselle in the story and Minerva's newest history teacher. He had begun badgering Henry for an interview. People began recalling family tales of gold searches. The old arguments about whether the legend was true now gained a new level of investigation - whether the students had actually discovered gold.

At the heart of the controversy, Corey and his team were redoubling their efforts to prove their conclusion. The "war room" was not a safe place to be, unless you were a scientist looking for pollution or a treasure hunter looking for gold. The room, which was normally immaculate, was strewn with jars filled with new samples. Another wall showcased the new hydrological map. Their drawing pad with the plan of attack was relegated to an obscure corner. The war was on and these little generals were immersed in the heat of battle.

Corey was at his usual station performing the tests on the samples. Michelle acted as his assistant, labeling tubes, preparing samples to be tested and recording results. Todd and Daniel transferred the location of the samples from one map to another. The drawing pad in the corner announced the progress of the battle:

Henry Muselle's Treasure

Task	Future Action
Original Experiment	*Complete Testing*

A new note written in red said, "In Progress."

Water Supply	*Needs More Research.*

On top of the second column in bold red letters and underlined was the word "Done."

French Gold.	*Collect More Samples.*

This was emblazoned with the word "Done."

There was a new list added to the pad. Corey had enumerated the clues to finding the lost gold.

Four Springs	*Found.*
Shovels	*Found.*

Corey was very optimistic.

Rock in Tree.
Deer Tree

The radio announced it was 8 PM, but no one made a move to put things away. There was an algebra test in the morning. The only "x's" and "y's" in Corey's mind was the "Why this sample has gold and that one doesn't?" Corey continued testing.

They were to have their parts memorized for the first act of "Romeo and Juliet." The Montagues must live on the west side of town, while the Capulets live on the east side, they imagined. Michelle, their Juliet, handed Corey the test tubes for sample 27 and logged the results for sample 26.

There was a geography quiz on U. S. rivers in the morning. Mississippi, Missouri, Rio Grande. There was only one body of water important to them. Dan placed a dot on the new map near Sandy Creek.

Todd had a report due on gold rushes in the U. S. It was apparent to Corey that the '49ers heading for California, the race to Cripple Creek in Colorado, and the discovery of gold in the Yukon had no significance for Todd because he had first hand knowledge about gold rushes, and he was about to start a new one.

Chapter Eight

Friday, April 21

There was an uneasiness in the black Suburban as in bounced along the country roads heading toward the nursing home. Maybe, it was because Ralph felt he was exposing his invalid mother to outside forces he did not understand. Or maybe, it was because this was a school day and two of its occupants were playing hooky. Whatever the reason, the tension in the vehicle was tactile, and all of Ralph's country music would not ease it.

"I wrote on my request for leave that today was a 'personal day to attend to family business'," Henry said as they went through the last traffic light in Minerva. "I've used very few school days in my search, and didn't want the multitude of secretaries through which my request had to pass to embellish upon my need for time off. The Science Fair project has the community in enough of a tizzy. I don't need my story to fan the flames any higher." Henry paused for a moment as Ralph guided the SUV under the underpass and through the step s-turn on Route 183.

Ralph noticed the nervous tension in Henry's voice. It had nothing to do with his driving. "The prospect of coming face to face with someone who has almost first hand knowledge about the treasure is unnerving. Today may be a journey through time I'm was not sure I am ready to make."

"Mr. Muselle, you will vouch for the fact I was 'sick' today, won't you?" Todd asked from the back seat.

"Did you call the attendance secretary in your best Mrs. Evans falsetto voice?" Henry asked. "If your mother ever really called you in sick, the school officials probably wouldn't believe her."

"I tried all week to tell her about the Science Fair. She rushed through and saw the First Place ribbon before she went to the restaurant. With her work and social schedule, our paths haven't crossed since."

"When I went downstairs this morning to get breakfast and leave, I went to her bedroom door. It was closed. I intended to tell her about today. When I stepped on the loose floorboard in front of the door, I heard a loud, long male snore from the room. As I turned to leave, I saw a dirty flannel shirt lying on top of the clothes hamper in the bathroom. I knew Mom had another 'friend' 'sleep over' last night. I wrote a note to school about my 'sickness' and stuck it in my book bag, so I won't forget it tomorrow." He paused for a moment. Ralph leaned forward to adjust the radio. He could see in the rear view mirror, Todd wipe his runny nose on his sleeve. "If I could find the gold, my mother would not have to live like this. We could have a real house, and a real income. I could provide for her like 'He' never would. I won't let the way my mom is stop me from finding the gold."

Ralph was beginning to realize how important this treasure was to other people. He'd never met anyone like Henry who was so passionate about finding it. And it was becoming the answer to all Todd's problems. He wasn't sure that was such a good idea, but then again kids had to have a dream.

Ralph's weekly visits to the nursing home were a bittersweet time of reflections, reminiscences and reminders. These were difficult visits. There was no joy in seeing his mother being able to ambulate only with assistance. She had worked so feverously on the farm to make sure her husband's and family's needs were met. Her mind was clear, at times, knowing the latest Congressional escapades; but, in the blink of an eye, she was fourteen again and remembering how she had met his father at the church social. Then would come the pain as she wiggled in her bed trying to find the next comfortable position. The visits were gut retching for Ralph. This one would be more difficult because he did not know how his mother would react to the strangers. It had been a long time since she had mentioned the shovels. Would she

Henry Muselle's Treasure

remember? Could she tell them precise enough directions so they could find them? And if these two gold hunters did find the shovels, what would that mean for the farm? Would it stop the road? Could it stop the road? The answers to these questions posed solutions Ralph had long since buried in the farthest corners of his subconscious. He was not sure he wanted them dug up today.

"You boys are awfully quiet for a couple of fellas in search of the 'Mother Lode'," Ralph playfully said to try and get a conversation started.

"It's not the 'Mother Lode'," Henry snapped. "I really resent when people talk about this treasure as if it were a naturally occurring gold treasure such as the 'Lost Dutchman Mine'. This was the financial depository of Fort Duquesne which was lost in transit to Fort Detroit." It was evident, Henry had the wording from the court martial memorized. "Unlike most prospectors, the men involved with this gold did not set out to find treasure. In fact, they never intended to lose it in the first place. They were lucky either of them got away. If the British had done their job, there would be no 'lost gold,' and a lot of people in my family would have been spared a great deal of suffering."

Ralph's plan hadn't worked. The uneasiness returned. On the radio, Johnny Cash groaned the last verse of "A Boy Named Sue."

"I hate that song," Henry said. "Any father who would lay a burden like that on a son should be shot."

"How about a mother?" The words were out of Todd's mouth before he could stop them. Ralph could tell the hurt and anger he felt were almost too much to bear. Today was supposed to be a happy day, but Todd's early morning discovery certainly was dampening his enthusiasm. Ralph supposed, finding a new man in his mother's bedroom Friday morning meant he would not see her now until Sunday afternoon. Ralph knew Todd had lost a father, he could see he was about to lose his mother.

"You know Ralph, you could have picked a different day to come here," Henry said.

"Why's that?"

"Well, this is the twenty-fifth anniversary of my father's death. Every year, I relive the anguish I felt as a teenager. Each memory rekindles the honor I felt when I first realized I had been named for a famous Frenchman, and the remorse that engulfed him when that legacy took my father's life."

Ralph couldn't respond. What could he say to either of these men? He didn't have any answers to their problems. His mother held the key - a key that would line up the four springs, a key that would authenticate the legend, a key that would turn today's events tolerable. It would not turn a mother's affections back toward her son. It would not take away the pain of a father's death. It might open a door and shed light on the mystery and eventually lead to its solving. Or, it might lead to a path so dark and sinister the treasure hunters would regret ever starting the journey.

* * *

Ralph felt walking into Pleasant Rest Nursing Home was like walking into another world. It was a Victorian house now used for geriatric patients. There were eight beds in the living room or main ward. The contrast of the modern hospital bed next to the ornate Victorian woodwork was perhaps fitting. For each of the beds was occupied by a person who was excited and well informed about current events yet trapped in a body ravaged by time. These women could talk about the current presidential election and compare it with Herbert Hoover's while, at the same time, needing help into the bathroom.

Ralph knew this was Edna Saling's problem. She had the mind of a seventy year old, trapped in a body of an antiquarian. Her thinning silver hair was always neatly done. She used her gnarled hands to wave and point as she spoke. Her scratchy voice gave a sense of urgency to everything she said.

Ralph came faithfully every Friday to visit. Edna's first order of business was to bring him up to date about the food and the care of the last week. Next came the report on patient expirations, departures and arrivals. It sounded more like a girl's dormitory than a nursing home.

Finally, it was Ralph's turn to tell his mother his happenings of the last week. Today would be different; Todd and Henry would take his turn instead. Henry would do the talking because Todd became too excited when he talked about the gold.

"Mom," Ralph started, "Henry and Todd want to ask you a couple of questions about the Tuscarawas Treasure. Do you? . . ."

"Lord, that treasure again," she started without hesitation. "You'd think after all these years we could just let it lay."

"Mrs. Saling," Henry asked gingerly, "Ralph told us you know where the shovels were found."

"Oh my yes," she said with a smile. Ralph could tell she had been asked the right question. "Ralph's grandfather found them under a large mound up on the hill. There were two of them - crossed like an 'X'. He always said that mound was an old tree stump. We used those shovels for years hauling ashes from the furnace."

"Do you remember where the mound was?" Henry asked again.

"Oh, you won't have any trouble finding it," she said. "One day a treasure hunter asked to take one of those shovels to examine it. He never came back. So, grandpa went up on the hill where he found the shovel, dug a hole, mixed up some wet cement and laid the shovel in the wet cement. He said anyone hunting for the treasure wouldn't have any trouble finding that clue."

"Then, according to the clues, all we have to do is hike 600 steps due South and we've found the treasure." Todd was unable to hold his enthusiasm.

Mrs. Saling began to laugh. "Honey child, if I had a dollar for every person who walked 600 steps from those shovels, I'd have more money than is in that treasure. Grandpa was a strapping big man. He hiked those steps a hundred times. He must have dug fifty times. He'd get down about three feet and the hole would fill up with water. The big flower bed down from the house is where he thought the treasure was." She paused and looked Todd straight in the eye.

"You're not planning on going after the gold are you?"

"Uh, no ma'am. We're just working on a project for school," he said.

"Good," she replied. "We don't need any more crazy people digging around Watertown."

"Watertown?" Henry was puzzled.

"That's what people called the area around the farm because of the twenty or so springs around. They used to call grandpa the Mayor of Watertown. When the canal came through, most folks moved out and grandpa ended up with most of the valley. Ralph did you fix the drain in the barn?"

Her question took them all by surprise. It was evident, to Ralph, she was back in the present and it was time to move on to other subjects. The weather, current events, crop reports, children and grandchildren stories all had their place in the discussion. Ralph tried to get back to the subject of the treasure, but each cue was deflected as if the subject never existed. At dinnertime, the men walk Edna to the dining room and said their good-byes.

The ride back from the nursing home was a quiet one. *'Up on the hill' wasn't a very precise location,* Ralph thought. It had been ten years since anyone had seriously looked for the gold. It would be difficult to find the crude grass level marker.

"Mr. Muselle, do you think we can find the gold?" asked Todd.

"I don't know. My family and a lot of other people have looked for a long time. I wouldn't get my hopes up."

"I think we should go back to the farm, step off those six hundred steps and start digging," Todd suggested.

"It's been done - hundreds of times - that's what Edna tried to tell you," Henry explained.

"Maybe this time we'll be in the right spot, or maybe it's deeper than anyone else has dug."

"It's been a long time since I saw that shovel," Ralph said. "But I'm willing to go up on the hill and see if I can find it.

Henry Muselle's Treasure

You have to realize that grandpa reburied it years after he found it. It might not even be close to its original location. Maybe you shouldn't count on it being the prime starting point for your search."

"Todd, have you kids tested your last batch of samples?" Henry asked.

"Not yet," Todd said.

"Why don't you go back and test them to see if they lead you any closer to the gold?"

Todd was quiet for a moment. Ralph figured he was imagining the map filling up with dots leading to the treasure. He watched out the window as they passed the many fields leading to Minerva. Ralph was daydreaming, too. Most were not filled with farm animals like his. They contained signs marking the future home of this church or that grocery store. So much had changed since the gold was buried, Ralph thought.

He worried about this pair of treasure hunters. He wondered if this partnership with Todd would ever really work. He was so young and impetuous. On the other hand if they were intent on finding the gold, Henry certainly was no dynamo. Unfortunately, Henry and Todd had some of the hardest evidence he could remember for finding the gold. Maybe he should . . . but he really needed to get into town and find an apartment until he and Martha could decide on a house.

Todd broke the silence. "Something's not right," he said. "Something in Watertown isn't as it appears to be. One plus one seems to equal three. Many people searched; no one found. There were too many clues and not enough evidence. In three hundred years, no one could put his finger on exactly what that 'something' is. Can we?"

"I agree, Todd, but do you think anything we've found thus far gives you the answer?" asked Ralph.

"I had one of your dreams, Mr. Muselle," Todd said weakly.

"What do you mean, Todd?" Henry asked.

"I had a dream about Indians."

"Go on," Henry said.

"In my dream were two Indians, one tall and one short. They were shooting arrows at two targets that appeared to be side by side. When they walked to the target to retrieve their arrows, the one the shorter Indian walked to be several yards closer than the taller Indian's target. I dreamed it several times. I don't understand what it means."

"Neither do I," said Henry. Ralph did not understand either, but he did realize that the bond between Todd and Henry was growing tighter. Who was this Guardian who was now infesting their dreams of gold hunting. Could the treasure be far away?

Chapter Nine

Henry Muselle's Journal
Saturday, 4:00 AM

He died twenty-five years ago. I held his hand until the last sign of life slipped out the tips of his fingers. As the pressure built within his head, he pulled me close to him and whispered with a sound slightly louder than the movement of his sheets. "Find the treasure, Henry. They weren't crooks. They didn't steal it. They didn't kill the patrol so they could run off with the money. The letter is true. It will be where the clues say it is. Follow the deer to Lisbon. Find the treasure." Those were his last words to me as he faded into unconsciousness.

My father, Henry, studied geology in hopes of using the knowledge to find the treasure. He was working for an oil company surveying the area for possible wells in the Minerva area. After a long day's work, he stopped in the Normandy Inn for dinner and a drink. The railroaders were there, too. They had been replacing the track between Minerva and Lisbon. They were large crude men who liked to unwind as the weekend grew near. This night, they were in an ugly mood. They had been informed that the money had run out for more track, and they were being laid off.

They lamented the fact that the job was easy going across the valley, and now should not be the time to stop them. Father began asking about the terrain, springs and old Indian trails. One very drunk Gandy dancer took exception to Father's comments, thinking he was making fun of them. Father found his shirt collar clenched in the Gandy dancer's fist. His attempt to explain his way out of the situation fell on deaf ears.

Holding my father high above the bar, the Gandy dancer proclaimed, "This here college professor thinks all his learning makes 'im better than us. He thinks instead of us building a railroad, we should look for some silly treasure. This is what we do to those whos sticks their noses where they shouldn't be."

With that he dropped my father toward the ground. As he was falling the Gandy dancer came around with a right hook and caught him squarely in the nose. Father went sprawling across two tables and into the wall. He picked himself up and staggered toward the door.

The Gandy dancer caught him. "And this is what we do to them that mouths off too much." He spun my father around, and as he fell toward him, the giant caught him in the mouth with an uppercut showering blood and teeth around the restaurant. Father fell dazed against the bar. Not to let well enough alone, the Gandy dancer approached one more time.

"And this is how we make our living, Mr. Professor . . . " He stood my father upright and raised both hands above his head. " . . . by pounding stakes into the rails." Clasping his hands together, he sent them smashing against my father's head. Father hit the floor and didn't move. Blood was streaming from his mouth, nose and ears. Jerry, the bartender, could not arouse him. The railroaders chased the rest of the patrons out of the bar. Sally called for the police and the ambulance.

My father made it to the hospital and had regained consciousness by the time my mother and I got there. The doctors said he had a severe depressed skull fracture and an intercranial bleed. They could not do surgery for fear of causing irreparable brain damage. The bleeding had to stop first.

It didn't.

Blindness came, followed by mini-seizures. He lost the ability to talk, and as they medicated him for the seizures, we could watch as he lost the use of each limb as the bleeding slowly suffocated the brain.

Henry Muselle's Treasure

After he spoke to me, I watched him struggle for each breath. They became deeper and less frequent. Finally, they stopped.

In twenty-five years, I have not been able to verbalize what happened that night. I have lived my life to this point trying to do what father challenged me to do on his deathbed. For the first time, I feel I am close enough to solving the mystery that our family may be freed from this terrible curse.

On the hillside north of the Saling farmhouse lays a clue - an honest to goodness clue. It is embedded in concrete, for Heaven's sake. I find nothing in my records of anyone knowing about this in the past. There are records of previous excavations, but none mention a permanent fixation of the shovels. Maybe it is a hoax. If these four springs are *the four springs* and these shovels are *the* shovels, then the treasure should have been discovered years ago.

I was awakened tonight by another dream about Guardian. I did not recognize the terrain where he was. He seemed afraid. He had taken shelter from a storm under an outcropping of rocks. He was not in this valley, as he had been in all my other dreams. It was as if he had fled. He looked terrified, and it was not from the rain, thunder and lightning. There was no story to this dream - no morals.

And now, shaken by the dream, I find myself working by candlelight because the power is out from our own storm. As the wind howls, the lightning outside illuminates the room. The search of my own papers reveals not verification of the cemented shovels, but tale after tale of thwarted explorations.

This one is most distressing, and I note it for posterity:

> *Clayton Robbins and a Mr. Pim, having dug feverishly past warning signs of a thunderstorm. They took refuge in a log cabin. They were both sitting on the same bench when a bolt of lightning struck Mr. Pim without fazing his partner. Clayton Robbins, practically assured that the man was dead, carried his limp body into the rain in an effort to revive him. He*

had little use of his arm the next day from the weight he mastered. The attempt was successful and Mr. Pim lived, although he lost the sight of one eye. Mr. Pim, being a devoutly religious man, took the shock as a form of God's warning that he was to forget about the gold, so this ended his conquest.

I am to meet Todd this morning to begin our search in earnest. I am frightened that events of this night are a terrible foreboding.

Chapter Ten

Saturday, April 22

Ralph was suddenly awake. The room was filled with light. It wasn't sunlight or moonlight, but it was the glow of an Ohio dawn preparing to burst forth over the rolling hills. He heard the noise again; not loud or frightening. It was just a noise - from the house.

The cobwebs cleared. And the noise - no noises, came again. Ralph slipped into his slippers. Then came the smell. It was not an odor, but more like a scent. He walked to the rocker and picked up his robe. There it was again - noises from downstairs and the smell of . . . bacon?

"Hey you people gonna sleep all day?"

Every Saturday, Howard Jackson visited his neighbor Ralph. He never came at the same time; and if he did, there was a joke involved with the visit. This Saturday, Howard chose to visit at 5:30 am and to cook his dear neighbor's breakfast.

"Good Heavens, man, do you know what time it is?" Ralph said, stumbling into the kitchen.

"Half past five by my watch," said Howard. He was a small man, for a farmer. His red hair was as short as his fuse. When he got riled up, folks called him a banty rooster. Ralph had seen that side of him a time or two.

As they made small talk in the kitchen, Ralph recalled their long friendship. Howard and Ralph had grown up together. In fact, their fathers and grandfathers had grown up together. Howard's family settled the valley first. They called it Watertown. As settlers began to frequent the Great Trail, they would pass through the valley and offer to settle. Hezekiah Jackson screened the potential neighbors. If they didn't appreciate the value of the resources of the valley, if they wanted to exploit the springs rather than coexist with them, he encouraged them to move on down the Trail to more fertile ground.

The Salings passed Jackson's muster and were sold ground next to his farm. Hezekiah lived to be 103 years old. He told stories of the Indians' respect for the land to a spellbound Howard Jackson. Hezekiah watched the canal reroute streams. He cringed as the railroad filled in swamps. Time after time he saw virginal pristine waters being used and abused. He said, "I wish we could give it back to the Indians. They knew what a real treasure was."

Ralph knew Howard cherished and respected the land. He was said to be "environmentally conscious." He greeted other "environmentally conscious" trespassers with a round of rock salt and BB's from his twelve-gauge shotgun. The Jackson's did not take kindly to people messing with the land.

The bacon crackled in the skillet. Howard tapped an egg on the edge of the pan, forced the shell open with his fingers and let the contents slide into the noisy grease.

"You like yours sunny side up?" Howard asked.

"Yes, I do," Ralph replied, "but not in the middle of the night."

"You have to get up to do the milking," Howard said. "Besides, if I can't sleep, you shouldn't sleep."

"Are you sick?" Ralph wanted to know of his friend.

"No, it's the construction," Howard said. "I didn't hear anything the first part of the week; then Wednesday they started night and day. Last night it was like Grand Central Station. They had dump trucks coming and going all night. I finally gave in and got up."

"Something is not right with this road," Ralph said, pulling up a chair to the kitchen table.

"No kidding," said Howard, flipping the egg. "Oops, you'll have to take this one over easy."

"I have the feeling somebody's not playing by the rules," Ralph continued.

"You've got that right," Howard slid the eggs on to a plate, added some bacon and home fries and set it in front of Ralph.

"Howard, I'm glad you came over this morning," Ralph said taking his first bite. "I've been having a tough time coming to grips with this road coming through here. I can't give up this place. I walk through the field and it's like I'm attacked by the ghosts of every Saling that ever lived here telling me not to give up. Every time I think I have something that might stop the road, one of those trucks goes by and reminds me it's too late. I don't think we could stop it now if we wanted to."

"I know, I know," Howard said, breaking another egg in the pan.

"Do you remember the report that Fernandez fellow wrote?" Ralph asked.

"Now that's another thing fishy about this whole deal," Howard said, placing more bacon in the pan.

"He came to my place a couple of years ago doing a survey for the EPA. He said he was doing a wetland survey for the road. He said he was looking for three things - wetland plants, evidence of water standing on top of the soil for significant periods, and soils that had a high content of decomposing material.

"I took him all over Watertown. I showed him the bottom that doesn't dry out until nearly June. We went past Catfish Pond, and he noted the watermark on the trees two hundred yards from the edge of the water. He'd stop every now and then to dig down just under the surface. He said he was looking for gray soil or muck. He found it more often than I thought he would. And plants! I never knew there were that many wetland plants. We found more cattails, bulrushes and willow trees than I ever knew were here."

"What did he tell you about the area being a wetland?" asked Ralph.

"I thought he said we were a Class One or First Class, I don't recall," Howard said.

"That's what I remember," Ralph exclaimed, mopping up the egg yolk with his bread. "He said they couldn't put the road through here. If only we could prove that's what he said."

"You know he came back?" Howard asked.

"He did! When?"

"This week. Monday or Tuesday. It was really weird. Everything was shut down like I said. This car pulls in with two guys from the EPA"

"Two guys?" Ralph almost jumped for joy.

"Enrico came with his boss. They didn't want me to show them around this time. His boss said he could find what he was looking for by himself."

"Do you think they're on to something? Would they have to stop if the EPA report was wrong?"

"I don't know how the government works. I just know there was a road heading Hell bent for election toward my back yard. The road stopped dead as a doornail for three days in the middle of the week. Two government officials come snooping around and the work starts like they have to have the road to East Liverpool by morning. It doesn't take a rocket scientist to figure out there's a snake in the woodpile." Howard answered in his down home Ohio wisdom.

"To answer your question, Ralph, I don't think there are enough brains between us to stop a project like this," Howard said, pulling up a chair to eat his own breakfast.

Martha slipped into the kitchen and sat down next to Ralph. Before Howard had a chance to say, "Good morning," she asked, "Do you think the gold is really buried out there?"

The question took them by surprise. They assumed they were having a man's chat. Martha's intrusion and question threatened to send them in an entirely different direction.

"I don't rightly know," Howard finally said. "One time I did mention to Edna that I thought it was just a tale. Lord, she'd like to have bitten my head off."

"What made you ask such a thing?" Ralph asked of Martha. "Yesterday, you were upset when you thought we were going to search for it."

Howard moved back to the stove to fix Martha some breakfast.

"I've been doing a lot of thinking," she began. "All I've ever wanted is for you to be happy. I thought the coming of the road would provide the opportunities we've always talked about. Now, I'm not so sure you wouldn't be happier if we stayed here. I tried to figure out a way. Now you two are talking about hanging your hopes on cattails and water lilies. It didn't seem like that much of a stretch to hope for lost French gold." Her eyes could hold the flood of tears no longer. They ran down her cheeks and dropped on the table like a spring rain.

"Now, Martha," Howard said, trying to lighten the atmosphere, "you'll have to stop or you'll get your toast soggy."

"That's right," Ralph said. "I agreed to go to town because I thought that would make you happy. If you want to stay, we'll have to figure out a way to stop that nasty old road."

"You'll have to hurry," Howard said placing Martha's breakfast before her. "As fast as they're moving now, they'll be here before you know it."

"Any suggestions?"

"Yeah, find that EPA report or dig up the gold," Howard said. "While you're doing that, I'm going to stick my cold little nose right between a contractor's eyes and see if I don't get some answers."

Howard took the time to finish breakfast with his friends. He even dried the dishes and put them away. Dump trucks rumbled past the house at an increasing pace. As the sun rose, it cast the shadow of a tree across an ancient shovel handle buried in concrete a little to the north of the farmhouse.

Chapter Eleven

This was Henry's first visit to a place, which was nearly a personal shrine for his family. Success would lay to rest the troubled souls of nine generations. Failure would mean passing on a box of weathered journals and cracking parchments to a new generation doomed to piece together a fleeting mystery.

He came to the field with his newfound protégé. More spitfire than scholar, he knew Todd would excavate the entire valley rather than conscientiously limit the search to an area where the probability of success was greatest. Todd had told him that he was certain they would leave the field in the next few hours with millions of dollars of French gold in hand.

The old green car sat abandoned in Saling's driveway. Two lone figures walked down the cow path into the field. Dressed in a hunting jacket and jeans, Henry Muselle was more reminiscent of the French fur trader who hunted the area three hundred years earlier than of today's French stereotype. His broad shoulders were crowned with a head of glorious brown curly locks. The hulk of a man sported a hat befitting a treasure hunter. It was a little outback explorer with a touch of Egyptian archeologist thrown in. To be sure, he looked nothing like his alter ego, the high school teacher.

His ancestors could never find all the clues. The goal today was for him and Todd to mark the landmarks they knew and then determine what needed to be done to bring the clues into alignment. He was sure of one thing - the accuracy of the original clues would be unswerving. The men who built the crude forts on the banks of wilderness rivers could just as easily have been in France building the Louvre or the Palace of Versailles. It was neither education, nor technology, which was lacking on the frontier. It was the availability of exotic materials.

Henry brought to the field the precision of his generation. He carried in his hand a gadget the size of a calculator. It was a GPS or Global Positioning System monitor. Henry could stand at a point and turn on the monitor. It searched the sky until it found at least three GPS satellites overhead. They were in geosynchronous orbits, which meant they circled the earth at the same speed the earth rotated, thus appearing to be stationary. The monitor's onboard computer calculated the latitude, longitude and altitude of the device and displayed it on the screen. This modern day compass could then remember the point, have other points added to it, calculate distances, give compass readings and a host of other hi-tech features.

They came to the first spring. Todd pushed the rod holding the orange banner into the soft ground with all the fanfare of a flag raising on the moon. Henry held the GPS monitor in his hand and pressed the start button. The message "Please wait" faded onto the screen. "Acquiring satellites," it proclaimed. One . . . two . . . then three icons appeared indicating it found its prey. The screen faded and then the coordinates for the location of the spring appeared. With the dexterity of a classical pianist, Henry picked one button after another until the information was saved.

Henry was unusually quiet as they proceeded on their mission. He stopped for a moment along the path and surveyed the area, looking for clues, traveling back in time, imagining the valley as it might have been, listening for the voices of three centuries ago. The farmhouses and barns seemed to disappear. Trees grew again on the hillside. The meadow was waist deep with Queen Anne's lace, knotweed and Christmas ferns. Only a single, well-worn path dissected the scene.

Through the valley from the East came the sound of men and horses. The rhythmic plodding of the horses and creaking of the leather straps struggling to contain the King's treasure punctuated idle conversation.

From the West the orderly sound of British soldiers resonated through the woods. They spoke not a word, the whoosh of wooden gunstocks chafing against their bright red uniforms. The staccato of brass cufflinks ricocheting off canteens and bayonets broke the calm.

Between the two mighty forces, a "native savage", as the aristocratic European intruders called him, slipped silently on doeskin slippers not on the well-worn path, but effortlessly through the virginal vegetation. He was not acting out of a sense of loyalty to one side or another, but as a protector of his land and lifestyle.

Two squirrels played in the trees above, content to ignore their unarmed friend in the woods. The unnatural sound of metal on metal and flashes of scarlet through the leaves alerted the warrior to impending trouble. He scampered through the woods toward the column of blue and brown.

"I wish there was something I could do to make them go away," the reluctant messenger thought. "I wish they'd leave us and our land alone."

Todd was already at the second spring and planted the second flag. Henry caught up with him and took another reading. He felt the spirits of departed soldiers surrounded them. How many times through the centuries had they reenacted the skirmish? How many times had the gold been buried? Age after age had passed and not one spirit had come forth to reveal the location of the treasure.

"Here's Cranberry Spring," said Todd, planting the third flag. Henry wasn't listening. He was concentrating on his measurement.

Todd went to a nearby bush. Hanging from its branches were clusters of buds ready to burst forth in marvelous color. In a few short weeks they would bear beautiful purple berries suitable for Martha's pies and jams.

"Are these cranberries?" Todd asked.

Henry finished playing his "save the location" symphony on the GPS unit and looked at the bush.

"No," he said, "these are elderberries."

"Are there any cranberries around?" Todd asked.

Henry makes a quick survey of the area. "Not that I see," he said.

"Then why don't they call this 'Elderberry Spring'?" the youngster quizzed.

"Well, Ralph didn't say when they named the spring, so it's possible the cranberries died off and were replaced by elderberries," Henry explained.

He could tell that was good enough for Todd. They resumed their reverie. It was too bad they were treasure hunters and not botanists, or they might have noticed the plethora of cranberry bushes on either side of the path twenty yards from the spring.

They reached the fourth spring, planted the flag and recorded the coordinates. Henry let Todd watch as he made the GPS computer perform its magic. First, he plotted a course around the springs. *Yes. It formed 'sort of a square.'* Todd was excited. Next, Henry asked it to plot a course from spring one to spring three and spring two to spring four. *It formed an "x" on the screen.* Todd was ecstatic. Finally, Henry asked for the coordinates for the center of the "x" and the direction and distance from where they were standing.

"Do you want me to get the shovels?" Todd asked.

"No," Henry replied, "we agreed that we were just going to mark the places today. The digging will come when we're absolutely certain we're in the right spot."

"But, we know it's the right spot," Todd said, fidgeting around like a young pup waiting for a bone.

Henry was determined not to jump the gun. Too many times his ancestors' search had ended in ridicule because they failed to wait until they had all the answers.

"Have you ever heard of triangulation?" Henry asked his student friend.

"I don't think so," Todd said.

"Triangulation is a process by which you locate an object by referencing three other points. It's the way the GPS computer works. It calculates how far we are from the three satellites. When we have the shovels, the rock and the deer head we can triangulate to the center of the springs which should be the point to which we are now heading."

"Oh," was the only reply Todd could muster.

Henry stopped abruptly. He took another reading and then plotted a corrected course to bring him to his desired goal.

Todd followed impatiently, but obediently. Finally, Henry declared, "Here it is!"

Todd pushed a blue flag into the ground. He was sure the clunk he heard when the rod stopped was the top of the boxes of treasure. Henry heard the sound, too. Was it the same sound that had echoed through the valley centuries before? He could sense the spirits around him.

In the elysian fields of times gone by, the Indian guide watched from the protection of the woods as the Frenchmen threw the last shovel of dirt over the treasure. The report of muskets to the West announced the arrival of the British forces.

Young Henry heard the gunfire. He and his partner hurried to bury the shovels. The rest of the French patrol formed a defensive perimeter. The young men knew with the skill and cunning of the French warrior, the battle would be over in a short time. The Indian also knew what the outcome would be. He had seen the French fight before.

A thunderous volley of rifle fire echoed through the valley. Screams of dying men followed.

Henry and his comrade picked up their guns to join the battle. They started through the valley. They took only a few steps when off to the right they could see a wall of red coats raise their weapons.

The crack of the weapons sent a cloud of smoke through the woods obliterating the first line of men kneeling to reload. The popping of three or four return shots told them it was futile to continue. A large rock provided cover for them to watch the final slaughter of friends and comrades. They watched as the British took time to gather spoils, which amounted to personal effects and military trinkets.

The soldiers captured most of the horses and were overjoyed with the additional provisions. They took no time to evaluate why this small group was so far from Fort Duquesne.

They assumed the British were more concerned with getting back to Fort Necessity and General Braddock. It was later that a lowly supply sergeant at the fort checking in the spoils questioned why such a small band of French soldiers had so many empty packhorses.

In less than twenty minutes it was finished and the last red coat disappeared into the woods. As the Frenchmen sat stunned by the course of events, a lone buckskin warrior appeared. He walked among the dead, kneeling occasionally to close open eyes. He was careful not to leave a trace of his presence. It was evident he did not want his kind be blamed for the massacre.

They watched as he moved to the area where the treasure was buried. He picked up a handful of loose dirt and sifted it through his fingers. He walked around the treasure at a distance of about thirty yards scrutinizing the landscape, making a mental map of every rock and tree.

The Frenchmen knew they were in foreign territory. They knew the native knew the land far better than they. He had not been there when they buried the treasure. He had been watching for the British. He made them uneasy because he always seemed to know what was happening. It was as if he could read their minds. Had he seen it all? Did he know about the treasure? Suddenly, when they looked, he was gone.

Henry took the old compass from his pocket. A casual observer would have mistaken it for a pocket watch. The ornate gold etching had been worn smooth near the edges.

It was Henry's grandfather's compass. He had used it to walk the Great Trail. He traveled east and west over what he could find of the trail. He searched north and south of areas that seemed to resemble the description laid out in the letter. He never had the precise landmarks Henry now thought he had. He opened the case and let the needle settle on zero degrees – north. He and Todd began to walk . . . one pace . . . two paces . . . three paces toward what might be their first tangible confirmation.

At one hundred paces they left the pasture. Two hundred paces they were near the farmhouse and stopped at Henry's car to pick up his metal detector. Three hundred paces was the far side of the road starting up the hill through an old field of oats. Four hundred paces put Todd and Henry at the edge of the oat field. The hill became so steep it would have been dangerous to drive a tractor across the front of it. The terrain responded by producing a wall of thorny blackberry bushes, thistles, and hawthorns to keep intruders out of the woods above.

It seemed like it took hours for Henry to blaze a trail through the thicket to the edge of the woods. As near as he could calculate, the edge of the woods was approximately five hundred paces from the center of the springs. He stepped through the tree line into a new world. Golden leaves lay undisturbed on the ground like a newly laid carpet. Throughout the forest were fallen trees in various stages of decay, presenting obstacles for Todd and him, but slides and mazes for squirrels, raccoons, possum and rabbits. It was evident no one had been in these woods for a long time. Henry supposed Ralph's children explored every nook and cranny of their wilderness pretending to be Daniel Boone or Davey Crockett. But, perhaps a generation raised on video games and television did not have the gumption to tackle a world guarded by gnats, mosquitoes, and spiders. Possibly the last explorers of this primal forest were Ralph and his grandfather.

From the size of the trees, Henry could tell that the areas near the edge of the woods had only been forested about fifty years. The trees to the west were much, much older. Although the slope of the hill would discourage a modern traveler, a skilled farmer with a team of horses and a plow could have tamed the land with no problem. About fifty paces into the woods, the treasure hunters paused to get their bearings.

"We should had brought water," Todd said.

"I didn't realize it would be such a difficult climb," Henry said, struggling for each breath.

"Now what are we going to do?"

"It's pretty obvious that this part of the woods is relatively new. My suggestion is that we start at the east edge of the woods and walk up the hill another hundred paces or so, sweeping with the metal detector. Then we will move over a little and sweep back down the hill. We'll do that until we find the shovels or wear ourselves out." For the next couple of hours they hiked up and down the hill stopping to uncover empty beer cans, crumpled up cigarette packages, an old plow blade, and other broken and discarded implements.

They were nearly to the old stand of trees when the buzzer on the metal detector sounded. Henry moved the sensor until he got the strongest signal. Todd took the metal rod they had uncovered an hour ago and probed the dry leaves of the forest floor. He hit something, but instead of the clang of metal, there was a dull thud. He moved six inches on either side of his initial contact point – same sound. Could it be?

Henry knelt down and brushed away the loose leaves. There was nothing there but more leaves. He dug down through the leaves and dry topsoil until his fingers hit something hard and rough. He cleaned a spot ten inches in diameter – concrete.

Now Todd was beside him leaves and dirt flying as they raced to find the edges of the cement. When they had outlined an area nearly four feet square, they moved the debris from the center. There on the side of the hill at the edge of an old field, lying in a kind of an "x", buried in concrete were two old shovels.

Henry knelt down and touched them. Nine generations ago it was in his forefather's hands. Henry began to cry, banging his fist on his forehead. Then he fell to his knees and he wept, his tears cleansing the concrete. Finally, he collapsed on the ground sobbing uncontrollably. He had done what no one in his family had been able to accomplish. He found the first tangible evidence of the treasure.

When Henry regained his composure, he saw Todd sitting silently on the ground next to the marker. He had been crying, too. "C'mon," said Henry, "let's see if this all means anything."

Todd placed an orange flag at the marker. Henry set the GPS computer for 180°, due south, and stepped off six hundred paces. It soon became painfully evident they were not heading toward the blue flag in the center of the springs. The farther they walked, the more Todd insisted they veer from the appointed course. "It's not logical that we could possibly be this far off course. We can't be wrong - we just can't."

Finally, Henry came to a stop and told Todd to place a blue flag in the ground. They were nearly a hundred yards short of the center of the springs and nearly thirty yards west. Henry was not pleased. He pushed button after button on his new fangled GPS contraption. He looked back at the pockmarked earth they have just traversed. The debris from prior searches was scattered over a two thousand square foot area. *Hopeless, he thought.*

Todd looked toward the marker on the hill. Henry could tell he was beginning to appreciate the enormity of the problem. "Are you sure we went the in right direction?" Todd asked. "Maybe South didn't mean the same thing back then."

"That's it!" Henry exclaimed. "We took our bearing from magnetic north. If they were in a hurry, they might have taken their heading from the sun - true north."

He punched a couple of buttons and shouted, "Ah ha, the angle of declination at this latitude is four degrees. We did head in the wrong direction."

He started off at a dead run for the marker on the hill. His long strides made it difficult for Todd to catch up.

"What was all that compass talk back there?" Todd inquired between breaths.

"True north points to the North Pole at the top of the earth. Compasses point to magnetic north, which lies a distance away from the pole. Some places on earth they are in line with one another. Other places, they are not. The difference between the two points is the angle of declination."

They arrived at the shovel and took only enough time to correct their reading before Henry was off again. The closer they got to the field, the more obvious it became; they were not heading for the previous flag. It was also soon clear that they were not on course for the flag in the center of the springs.

When they reached the appointed spot, Todd placed a third blue flag. Henry saved the data in the hand-held computer. Henry dropped to the ground and surveyed the flags waving defiantly in the breeze. He tried to envision what his ancestors had done.

The two Frenchmen, their plan for survival well entrenched in their heads, ascended the hill. They hurried to provide a common shallow grave for their comrades. They decided to mark the spot so next of kin could find it later.

They wanted to be able to retrieve the treasure and be heroes to their superiors. The first clue was the four springs surrounding the treasure. The second marker was the shovels buried six hundred paces to the North. Louis LeSeur headed west to make a sign only he would know. Henry went east to do the same. Each man knew three signs, neither knew all four. The coming summer months would quickly hide all trace of the day's events. Only those who knew what to look for could ever find the treasure. They were partners forever - the 10th Frenchman, Henry and . . .

"Nine generations we've searched," said a twenty-first century Henry. "Nine generation have been this far off. Maybe it really isn't here."

"Don't give up, Mr. Muselle," Todd consoled his friend. "Remember, we have another clue. There's gold in the water."

"I'm still not convinced," said Henry, "but I'm willing to stay in the game a little longer."

He reviewed the information in the GPS computer before turning it off. He and Todd walked slowly back to the car. His dream of saving the family reputation was badly tarnished, but he would continue if only to help Todd.

Todd grabbed Henry's belt to help himself up the gentle slope. Henry offered a friendly hand to his diminutive partner. As they walked west toward their green steed parked in the driveway, two ancient silhouettes were reunited with their frightened horses. Separated by a third of a millennium, heading in opposite directions, one pair was creating the destiny the other hoped to fulfill.

Chapter Twelve

Johnson stood in the bay window of his trailer office surveying the valley. From the hilltop perch, he believed he could see the tree line falling away to the Ohio River. Actually, he could see into the next county, which was good enough for now.

In front and below him laid the resolution of the first major entanglement of this undertaking. There was always something to throw a monkey wrench into a project. At Johnson Center, it was an ancient fault line that had to be ignored. Here there were springs . . . lots and lots of springs.

Things were going well. A tree fell in the distance as his men worked like little beavers clearing a path for the approaching bulldozers. Each tree meant more money for Johnson. The state got the money from the timber, but Johnson tacked on a significant "handling fee" for each tree cut and taken to the mill.

On the other side of the stand of trees was the next complication. The four springs at Salings almost stopped the project once. He couldn't remember who came up with the bright idea to build a platform over them, but that ingenious solution saved the state hundreds of millions of dollars. His bonus money was coming from those savings. The next trick would be to give the appearance of building the platform while racing through to complete the road by the August 1 deadline.

As he envisioned the progress, he noticed Huntsinger talking with someone at the bottom of the hill. Even from this distance, Johnson could tell Huntsinger was doing more listening than talking. The more Johnson watched, the more he could tell the problem was not going to go away easily. The verbal assailant was not getting any satisfaction. Johnson would have to handle this one himself. The discussion outside was about to get physical.

* * *

"It's evident you finagled until you got the road to go through my farm. You're pushing so hard, it's obvious you're trying to hide something," Howard Jackson said to Huntsinger, his face giving new meaning to the term 'beet red'. "What's the hurry?"
"It's business, Mr. Jackson, simply business," Johnson said. The field office was more than five hundred yards from where Jackson and Huntsinger were arguing. And yet, Johnson was able to transport himself almost effortlessly and inject himself into the conversation without appearing mussed, fussed or out of breath. His unannounced appearance even startled Huntsinger.
"Howard Jackson, this is Fred Johnson, owner of Johnson Construction," the ever-efficient hired man said.
"You don't need to introduce me. I've heard about his shenanigans," Howard snapped.
"And I am well aware of Mr. Jackson's reputation," Johnson replied cordially. "I apologize for the inconvenience a road makes, but as a farmer, you are well aware of the need to stick to a schedule. All I am trying to do is bring the road in on time and under budget."
"Then, what was all the starting and stopping last week? How are you gonna finish a road, if you don't work?" Jackson demanded.
"You should know, Mr. Jackson, you can't plant corn if the plow's broken," Johnson began his well-rehearsed answer. "Our lead bulldozer threw a track. We have found that it is more productive to shut down the entire operation than to either wait upon or catch up to a portion of the crew experiencing down time. Once all the equipment is operational, we can very quickly get back on schedule."
"That's what I've been trying to explain to Mr. Jackson for the last half hour," Huntsinger interjected. "Now, if you'll

excuse us, Mr. Johnson and I have some important business to discuss."

Johnson extended his arm as a peace offering. He was confident that he had dissuaded any fears.

"I will not excuse you. There is no excuse for you," Jackson was apparently going to take this opportunity to meet the devil in his den. "Some of us around here think you're building this road in the wrong place."

Johnson pulled back his hand. This was not going to be as easy as he had hoped. "Mr. Jackson, I am building the road where the government says to build the road."

"Well, Ralph Saling and I think you'd build the road through my kitchen if the government told you."

Johnson was getting irritated. "Tell Mr. Saling, he's correct. My job is to build this road. The way it goes is not important. I am as concerned about the ground as the cow patties that lay upon it." He turned to walk away.

"I knew it. You don't give a damn about the people whose lives you're destroying. You're just looking for that paycheck at the end of the yellow brick road."

Johnson whirled around, "Mr. Jackson, I will not stand here and have you impugn my integrity. I am simply doing my job in my usually efficient manner." Johnson put his arm around Huntsinger to lead him from the confrontation.

"You no good so-and-so." Jackson continued, following after them, his red hair nearly on fire in the midday sun. "You buried my spring. It wasn't just a puddle of water that never goes away. It was a spring - a pool of crystal clear water filtered through God's good earth. It provided sustenance for my ancestors. They could live without food, but they couldn't live without water. They built their homes near the spring and brought the roads to meet them.

"That spring had a name. It was important to the farm and me. We called it 'Sweet Spring' because of the taste of the water. The Indians used to camp here just to get a taste of the water. They felt it had healing qualities. Three hundred years that spring was here. The Indians knew it. I knew it. The EPA knew it, and by God, you knew it.

"You city-slickin', gotta-get-the-job-done son-of-a-freckled frog buried it. You sneaked in here in the middle of the night on a weekend and buried it."

Johnson and Huntsinger walked up the hill away from the salvo of accusations. They were used to this, but the fury of Jackson's wrath was disconcerting.

"I watched you. You no account coward. How come you're getting dirt from a cement company? I don't see any cement." There was no response from the men walking up the hill.

"Don't answer me. I have pictures before and after. I'm taking them to Johnson Center to the EPA. If they won't listen, I'm going to the prosecutor. Hell, I'll go to the President if I have to. You don't scare me."

Fred was beginning to realize, ignoring Howard Jackson might not have been the smartest thing he had ever done. He and Huntsinger stood by the door of the trailer. They could hear Howard yelling. They could see his arms flailing in the air. They got inside to get out of the cold April air and plan the strategy to overcome their newest entanglement.

"Sit down, George," Johnson said, moving toward the refrigerator. "You want a soda?"

"Sure, root beer," Huntsinger replied.

"I just witnessed a very poor job of public relations," Johnson said, handing him the can. "I am very disappointed in you."

"Fred, how was I supposed to know that spring had such sentimental value to the old codger?"

"It's your job," Johnson said, sitting on the loveseat across from Huntsinger. "Now we have a problem. It's a small problem, but it could get out of control. It could jeopardize the project. My future is beginning to look a little uncertain. If I were you, George, I'd be a little concerned."

"Oh, I am concerned, Fred," Huntsinger said, "but, I think I have a solution. Jackson has a small pond, which won't stay filled. I could take some of the men and we could dredge, drain and landscape that pond into a respectable little lake. You could donate the materials for a swimming platform, dock and picnic gazebo. It could be a real showplace. I think it would take his mind off things."

"What if it didn't, George," Johnson said, leaning back in his seat and running his fingers through his salt and pepper hair. "What if in spite of the nicety you propose, Mr. Jackson goes to the EPA and tells them about 'Sweet Spring'? Do you think they'll appreciate our landscaping efforts?"

Johnson got up from the loveseat located in the decision area of his office. He walked around his desk and sat down in his chair. He looked across the expanse between him and George and issued his decree.

"I want you to take Mr. Jackson's mind off "Sweet Spring'. I want you to make Mr. Jackson forget the inconvenience Johnson Construction is causing him. I want Mr. Jackson to be concerned with personal matters. I want him to be very concerned about his future . . . I want you to burn down his house."

Huntsinger jumped to his feet. "Fred, you know I can't do that. I'll go to jail."

"Then why did you suggest it?" Johnson pushed a memo across the desk. It was from George to Fred suggesting the arson.

"There are other persons in my employ," Johnson explained, "some who type memos on your word processor, others who watch over potential problems, still others who solve those problems in other ways.

"It is all set. The timer is set. It will burn. It's only a matter of time."

The look on Huntsinger's face showed he knew he had been had - again. "When?" was all he could ask.

"Soon," Johnson answered. "You really don't want to know, do you? Just go about your routine. It'll be over before you know it."

That's what George was afraid of.

* * *

George got up and stumbled to the door, sweating so profusely he could hardly turn the doorknob. He slipped into the antechamber and leaned against the wall. It was hard for him to breathe. It felt like a vise was tightening around his chest. He was sick to his stomach.

If I could just have heart attack and die, he thought. He slid down the wall to the floor. His eyes rolled back in his head. The room was spinning. He lifted his hand to ward off the darkness closing in on him.

He knew Johnson was once again in control of the situation. The fire would so consume Howard Jackson that he would not have time to bother with the road project. If anything should go wrong, George knew the paper trail leading to him would be hard to refute.

Paper trail! The darkness started to subside. His mind began to clear. Behind any white collar crime was a paper trail. Just as Superman recovers after kryptonite is taken away, or Popeye breaks loose after eating spinach, George could feel his symptoms subside.

"There is a paper trail," he thought, struggling to his feet. "But it doesn't lead to me. I have to see Fernandez." He staggered out of the trailer like an old drunk. He got to his little red car and unlocked the door. As he stepped back to open the door, he could see Johnson standing in the bay window surveying the workers. He was smiling that big "I've got you now" smile.

Huntsinger mustered a smile. "If he only knew . . . "

* * *

Corey had a great sense of timing. He arrived at Howard Jackson's farm after nearly being run over three times by monstrous dump trucks. As he crested the hill before the farm, he noticed there was a new road to the right. It led to the construction area. He was peering down the road when a red Escort came barreling out of nowhere. In a cloud of dust, throwing dirt and rocks, the car careened onto the main road without stopping.

The driver looked crazed. He was either high on drugs, or about to have a heart attack. Corey watched as the car headed toward Minerva. It never stopped as it approached the stop sign at the "y." Fortunately, the intersection was out in the country and no one was coming the other way.

He righted his bike, pushed off and headed over the hill toward Jackson's. *At least the new road will give the crazies a place to go,* he thought.

Corey arrived at Howard's and rang the doorbell. Through the screen door, he could see Howard was searching drawers, hunting piles of papers and looking through stacks of old mail. He could tell Howard was in no mood for visitors. Howard stopped his searching.

"Mr. Jackson?" said the semi-adult voice through the screen door. "I'm Corey Wagner."

"I don't like candy. I don't need any magazines. I don't want to go to church. Please leave me alone," came the terse answer from the usually pleasant Jackson.

"Please, Mr. Jackson," Corey pleaded, "I'm not selling anything. I'm here about our science experiment. Did Todd Evans get some water samples from you?"

"Yes, he did, but I don't have time to get you any more."

"But Mr. Jackson, we think we've found pollution in your water. May I please talk to you about it?"

He saw Howard plop a stack of papers on the coffee table and head for the door. "Come on in, Corey," he said. "Polluted water would just make my day."

They walked into the living room. The furnishings were comfortable, but old. Family antiques were supplemented with a thirty-year-old couch and recliner. Throws hid the worn cushions and tattered arms.

"Let me show you what we've found," said Corey, taking a seat on the couch. He unfolded a county road map on which he had marked the location of the polluted samples.

"As you know, we collected samples to test for pollution. Todd added something to the samples and in these we got a precipitate. We're trying to figure out what it is and where it came from."

"What do you think it is?" Howard asked.

"Some of our group thinks it's gold . . . "

Howard began to laugh. "Gold! Now I remember you. You were at the science fair."

"Yes, we were," Corey replied.

Howard said, still chuckling, "Where in the world do you think the gold would come from?"

"Since then, we've come up with new information that makes us think it might be the Tuscarawas Treasure," Corey said seriously.

Howard nearly fell on the floor laughing. "Everyone thinks they've found the Treasure, but . . . this is the most ingenious technique I've heard of yet."

"But Mr. Jackson," Corey continued. "All the samples that had a precipitate lie along one aquifer."

Howard brought himself under control. "So what do you want from me?" Howard asked.

"I want to verify the location of the water source for the two samples Todd got from you," Corey explained.

Corey was glad Howard finally took him seriously. He wanted to get the gold question resolved one way or another. He needed to summarize the results so they could get the project ready for Mrs. Talkington.

"How do you know it's gold?" Howard asked.

"Well, we don't for sure," Corey replied.

"I suggest you find out," Jackson retorted. "You might be barking up the wrong tree."

"I guess we should," Corey said, a little embarrassed.

"Is there the same amount of precipitate in each sample," Howard asked. He was slowly picking this theory apart. "You know if the concentration is greater in these samples on the right than there on the left, and your aquifer flows from right to left, it would prove your source was here on the right," he said, pointing to the map.

Corey tried to visualize the test tubes in the war room. He knew there were different amounts in different tubes, but he couldn't, off the top of his head, correlate them to the map. Being the teenage pragmatist, he simply believed it was his fate to discover the gold, if there was any. Now he realized, he had overlooked a couple of key points.

"Who could help us?" Corey asked.

"Oh, any chemist could probably tell you if it is gold and what the concentration is," said Howard.

"Maybe Dan's dad could help," Corey said. "He's a chemist."

"Could be," replied Howard.

Suddenly, Howard concentrated on the map. "Corey," he asked, "how accurate is this map?"

"Not very," he said, "that's the reason I'm here. I want to verify where each sample was collected. This map just shows how many samples were collected and their approximate location."

"The map shows Todd collected two samples at my place. Is that right?" he asked.

Corey flipped through his notes. "That's right - one at the spring house and one in the field southwest of the house."

"Sweet Spring! He got one from 'Sweet Spring'!" Howard shouted.

"I don't know. Is one of these 'Sweet Spring'?"

"It has to be!" Howard said. "How well did you document its location?"

"We counted paces from fixed objects and took compass readings. If it was out in a field like that one, we took measurements from two different directions."

Howard pressed him further. "You young scientists might have the independent documentation of "Sweet Spring" I need to show the EPA. Do you have these directions?"

"Back home. I don't have them with me," Corey said.

"Son, if you get me those directions, I'll help you find the gold," Howard promised.

"Yes sir," Corey shouted, folding the map. He thanked Howard a hundred times between the living room and his bike. He'd hurry home, find and copy the data sheets for Howard, and try to convince Dan's dad to analyze the samples for them. A dump truck rumbled past the house. He had to hurry. Time was running out.

Chapter Thirteen

It was nearly dark and Corey was still testing the new samples. Saturday night was not a night usually set aside for homework, but tonight the "war room" at Corey's house was a flurry of activity, as the young scientists tried to bring the gold portion of the experiment to a conclusion.

Michelle quietly shut the door, so she didn't disturb the rest of the house. "If only we would find the key to the treasure," she said.

"The answer is here," Corey replied. "We just have to find it."

Corey had assigned each team member with a specific job. Michelle filled the test tube with water. Corey added the cyanide and the zinc. Daniel marked the sample location on the map. Todd paced like an expectant father.

"Can't you hurry up?" Todd fussed at Corey.

"Todd, you're worse than my baby sister," Corey said. "I've told you a million times; we have to do this right."

"We know it's on Saling's farm. I've seen the prospecting holes," he complained.

"That's right, and if we don't pinpoint exactly where the treasure is, we could dig up the whole field and not find it," said Corey.

"I know," said Todd. "I have the picture of three very nonaligned, blue flags vividly emblazoned in my mind."

They didn't talk much more. There was too much work to be done. As the music on the radio talked of lost loves and lives gone awry, the pieces of the puzzle slowly came together on the map.

Finally, Corey announced the results of the final sample. "There's gold in it," he said.

There was gold in all the new samples. They had been right to collecting more. The map now showed a larger area running east to west south of Minerva.

"Now what?" asked Todd. "There's gold all over the place."

"Maybe it's from a vein and not from the treasure."

"Aren't we assuming the gold is traveling along the water table?" asked Dan.

"Yes, I guess we are," said Corey.

"There's one other problem," Michelle piped in. "We really don't know if this is gold."

A gloom started to fall on the room when Corey jumped in with the solution. "Mr. Jackson pointed that out to me this afternoon. Dan, your dad is a chemist, isn't he?"

"He sure is."

"Give him a call. See if he can tell us if this is gold and what concentration is in each of the samples."

Dan was gone in a second. The best part of the experiment was that after two hundred and fifty years of treasure hunting, most people in Minerva jumped at the possibility of finding the gold. Dan was back in a few minutes with the expected news. "My dad wants three or four of the last samples. If they test positive for gold, he will replicate our experiment to find the concentrations."

Suddenly Corey's heart sank. Were they now off course? Had they crossed the terrible line Mrs. Talkington had drawn? Precipitate equals pollution, Corey thought. This was the only way he could rationalize this part of the experiment.

Todd was rummaging around in the corner.

"What are you looking for?" Corey asked.

"I want the hydrological map Dan brought. Your silly map doesn't show where the springs are."

"What are you trying to do?"

"I want to mark the springs and the shovels Mr. Muselle and I found this afternoon."

They stretched the map out on the floor. Using the measurements from the computer, they were able to figure fairly precisely where each flag has been placed.

"Now if we could superimpose this map over the one on the wall, we could see if our water samples were close to the gold," said Michelle.

"And who made you Miss Scientific-Know-It-All," Todd interjected.

"It was just a suggestion, Todd. You don't have to bite my head off," Michelle said, defending herself.

"What, your *Daddy* suggest it to you?"

"Todd, just because I have a Dad to ask is no reason to talk to me that way." Corey sensed trouble brewing. He knew it had been nearly two years since Michelle had told her mother she met "the most obnoxious boy in the entire school." He had watched as she tried to avoid him, but Todd seemed to appear out of nowhere at the most inopportune moments. Corey was there the day Benny Kizler cornered her outside the band room, insisting she go out with him and engage in extraordinary sexual activity, Todd materialized from the locker room across the hall.

"Leave her alone, slime ball. She doesn't do things like that," he heard him say.

"Yeah, and how do you know? She turn you down?" Benny taunted.

He saw Todd take her by the elbow. "Come on, Michelle. You don't have to take this." The argument was drawing a crowd of kids anxious to see the school bully take on the school whipping boy.

"Enjoy her Todd. If she's half as good as your mother, it'll be a night in heaven."

Michelle was between Todd and Benny. Todd spun her into the crowd. He used his left hand to propel her out of the way and build momentum for his right hand to shatter Benny's unsuspecting jaw. The crack of the punch sounded like a pistol shot in the nearly empty hallway. A dazed Benny flew face first into the wall. A red smudge marked the impact point of his nose. He rolled down the wall and into a bloody blob on the floor.

"My mother says *all* women deserve respect," Todd said, retrieving Michelle and leading away from the battlefield.

Michelle had told Corey that the altercation cost both boys a three-day suspension, but it won Michelle's heart. She found Todd not only had a chivalrous side, but a romantic one, too.

The best Todd and Michelle story he had heard was about one brisk fall day when Todd took Michelle to a park for a picnic dinner. Instead of using a table, he found a secluded spot in the woods and laid a blanket on the forest floor.

After dinner of tuna salad sandwiches and potato chips, Todd pulled two plastic champagne glasses and a bottle of sparkling cider out of the basket. They toasted to their friendship and then went for a walk.

A little ways down the path, they found an elm tree, its bark rutted and falling off. "It'll be dead soon, from the blight," Todd said.

"Let's hug it," said Michelle.

"Hug a tree?"

"Sure, my mother says if you hug a tree it will live longer."

"OK, if you say so."

The young couple surrounded the ancient tree with their arms. Their hands entwined, Todd felt Michelle pull him into the tree. Not to be outdone, he pulled her toward him until she complained, "Stop, the tree might live, but I can't breath." He let go and as Michelle slipped around the tree to join him, she tripped on a root and stumbled into his arms. Todd helped her gain her balance. Their eyes met, and then their lips.

Michelle had told Corey, she was hooked. From that moment on she was Todd's chief defender. But lately Corey noticed his violent outbreaks were becoming more frequent and more severe.

"I'll talk to you any way I want - woman," Todd snapped, bring Corey back to reality. "That's the trouble with you broads, just because a guy's nice to you, you think you own 'em."

In his whiniest voice, Todd said, "Girls are smarter than boys. Find a good man with lots of money so you can sit on your butts watching soap operas and getting fat, their mommies tell them. Well, your mommy hooked the right sucker and she ain't doin' too bad in the fat department!"

Calm, quiet Michelle's face turned crimson red. "Of all the nerve. You're the son of a cradle robbing adulterer and a drunken whore, and you have the gall to criticize my parents?"

"Whoa bitch," Todd said trying to gain control.

Michelle's open palm struck Todd's cheek with a ferocity he had not felt in years. "Don't you ever . . . ever call me that again," she said adamantly. "Now get out. We have work to do and we don't need your childish antics interrupting us."

"But, Michelle . . . "

"Get out . . . and grow up," she repeated her finger pointing toward the door.

Todd gathered his things and followed her finger to the door. Corey had never heard her talk to anyone like that before – let alone Todd. She had banished him from his dream. Todd slowly closed the door. Through the silence, his slow plodding footsteps could be heard leaving the building. Finally, Corey broke the uneasy stillness.

"I don't know," Corey complained. "This is getting too complicated. People have searched for this gold for a long time and haven't found it. Why should we kids think we could achieve what adults a lot smarter than we are haven't been able to accomplish?"

"I think I know how we can combine the maps," said Dan.

"How?" asked Michelle. "The maps aren't drawn to the same scale."

"Then maybe what we need is GIS," he said.

"GIS?" Michelle asked, "What's that?"

"When I took Conservation merit badge, I spent the day with a guy at the Department of Natural Resources. He showed me a Geographic Information System. It's a computer system, which assembles, stores, manipulates and displays geographic information. He said if you can mark it on a map, he can use it.

"Is that the system Mr. Muselle said they used to find the Roman cities?" Corey asked.

"Yeah, the fellow said this program is like a large cake. He puts census information in one layer, road maps in another, hydrology maps in another and bingo, out comes a nifty report."

"Reports like what?" Michelle wanted to know.

"Well, he was telling me about this report they did for the county hazardous materials team. They wanted to know where the chemicals would go if the chemical plant had a spill. He said they were able to simulate the spill and track it through the ground water and down the creek."

"So how does that help us?" Michelle asked.

"When I looked at our map, I wondered why we couldn't put our gold findings in and reverse the process to find out where our 'spill' came from."

"That's brilliant," said Corey.

"Do you think he'd help us?" Michelle asked.

"He might," Dan said smiling, "for a portion of the thirteen million dollars."

"Well, don't just stand there," Michelle snapped. "Call him, ask him. Let's get moving."

The Tuscarawas Treasure just leaped into the twenty-first century. But even if the answers lie in the future, the rest of the clues lay in the past.

* * *

The grandfather clock in the hallway was just striking nine o'clock when Corey left the house with Michelle to walk her home. Her parents would be home late tonight and Corey did not want her to go into the empty house alone.

After a thorough search of the house to make sure there were no bad guys lurking about, Michelle said to Corey, "Come upstairs. I want to show you what my mother found this morning." Michelle led him to the corner of the attic where an old humpback trunk sat open. A stack of old clothes, lace and linen were piled precariously on the floor next to a stool.

"Mom said, we kids have this town in a tizzy asking about the gold. She said she remembered hearing my grandmother talk about it, so she came up to look through her trunk."

Corey knew one of the things that had excited Michelle about this new angle to the project was its history. Coming from Coshocton, she had grown up and played in the Roscoe Village section of the town. She was there when it was restored to its nineteenth century elegance as a canal town. She became a docent at the museum explaining the community's history to anyone who would listen.

Michelle had told Corey about her father, a Civil War buff. She had complained that she had vacationed on more battlefields than she could count. Corey knew she appreciated the value of history.

"Let me show you a treasure," Michelle said as she reached in the trunk and pulled out a bundle wrapped in cloth. She gingerly unwrapped the parcel to reveal a hand-painted porcelain figurine.

"This was made by my great uncle. He worked at the pottery. He made them from his own mold and hand painted each one."

"It's beautiful," said Corey.

"Turn it over," she coaxed.

On the bottom in fine gold hand-written letters was the name of the delicate creature - Michelle.

"Each doll was different. He said each piece had its own personality, so it deserved to be painted in its own way. This was the last one he did, two months before he died. He said it was his favorite."

A girl with sparkling blue eyes, a mischievous smile and long blond hair wore the long, flowing Victorian gown with the slightly revealing bodice.

"I was born a year after he died. Mom said they couldn't name me anything else," Michelle said wiping a tear from her cheek. "I wish boys would see me like this," she complained.

"I'm tired of being 'one of the guys.' I want them to see 'me'."

"They will," Corey said, trying to console her.

"That Todd is so rude. I wish he'd grow up. He screwed around with the samples and now there's this stuff in the water. I know Mrs. Talkington will flunk us - all because of Todd. Dan's tired of it, too. We had a good project until Todd blew it all out of proportion. If it weren't for you, Corey, we wouldn't have gotten as far as we did."

"Michelle, Todd has a lot of problems," Corey replied, as he rewrapped the fragile doll. "He's just acting out his frustrations."

"Dan says I should break up with him."

"I can't disagree. I know how his mother is and I know how Todd reacts to her escapades. I'm worried he'll take his frustrations out on you some day. Now that the science fair is over, you don't have to be around him anymore. I think he got your message tonight."

"But Corey, I think I love him," Michelle said, pulling a strand of her golden hair over her shoulder and coquettishly stroking it.

Corey didn't want to hear this. They had worked together so many years; he could have fallen for her. And now here they were alone in her attic, her parents not expected to return for hours. But Corey resisted the temptation and responded in the counseling role he had learned to adopt. "Michelle, at our age, love is like a river. Some parts of it are smooth and calm, other parts are nearly torn apart by the rocks and debris on the bottom and the narrowness of the gorge the river is forced to flow through.

"Our Senior year is like one of those rapids. Every place we look, there are rocks and boulders forcing us this way and that. Who knows, we might even find a waterfall or two before we come out the other end. Todd's been through a lot of rapids. He's given up without a father. His mother is turning into a drunken whore. He rebels at every inkling of authority and deliberately tried to destroy our project. Unless somebody or something gets a hold of him, he'll not make it through these rapids. Do you want the responsibility of rescuing him? Are you willing to brave the currents and go after him when he's drowning even if it means you'll drown, too?" Corey waited for a response, hoping it would be in his favor, but it never came.

Michelle reached into the trunk and pulled out a yellow picture in an ornate antique frame. A very handsome, very bearded man dressed in a swallow-tailed mourning coat stood next to a very dainty extremely feminine woman dressed in a lacy white Victorian dress complete with parasol. "These are my grandparents," she said proudly. "The picture was taken in the 1930's during the celebration of Minerva's centennial. My grandparents dressed as they might have in the late 1800's when the Efflemeyer's, my mother's family, first came to town." Michelle started to put the picture in the trunk, and then realizing there was no place for it, handed it to Corey.

"What's that package there in the corner," Corey asked.

"I don't know, Corey. That picture was the last thing Mom and I looked at this morning. We were interrupted when the phone rang and we never came back."

In the bottom corner of the trunk was an odd-shaped package wrapped in heavy brown paper and tied with thick green string. It was dusty and dirty - evidence it had not been moved during the many nostalgic cleanings the trunk endured through the years.

Tonight, the spring moonlight streaming through the attic windows created an almost magical atmosphere. The package seemed lonely and begged to be part of the party. Michelle picked it up, laid it in her lap and gently wiped the years of neglect from its surface.

"What is it?" Corey inquired.

"I don't know," Michelle replied. "I've never seen it before."

It was triangular in shape. It weighed a ton. In the dim light, she could see writing on the paper. It was ancient writing done with a wide lead pencil. It read "gold tree stone."

"What does that mean?" Corey asked, the mystery growing. "You don't suppose . . . "

Michelle carefully untied the string and unfolded the paper. On her lap laid a triangular piece of limestone approximately eight inches on a side and three inches thick. It looked like any rock one might find lying by the road. Lying on top of the stone was a newspaper clipping from the Minerva Gazette dated August 4, 1897. The headline announced "Storm Uncovers Lost Gold Rock." Corey and Michelle were holding their breaths.

"The terrible storm which passed through Minerva last Monday night left much destruction from high winds and lightening.

"For John Efflemeyer, lightning may lead to a fortune. Tuesday, while inspecting the damage to his farm, John found a tree in his east pasture had fallen due to being struck by lightening. The tree, estimated to be over a hundred years old, split from the top through its main fork nearly to the ground. While cutting the tree, John noticed a triangular shaped rock that must have been wedged into the tree many years ago.

"This tree, nearly due west of the four springs located on the Saling property fueled speculation that it might be the lost rock of Tuscarawas Treasure fame.

"Joshua Saling reported chasing off several treasure hunters since news of the rock's discovery became known."

For an eternity, neither person made a sound. "I remember my mother telling me about her grandfather taking her to a gate in the fence row bordering Howard Jackson's," Michelle finally began. "She said the stump the gate hooked to was the remnants of that tree. I never understood what she was talking about."

Corey speculated in his mind on the importance of the discovery. Limestone doesn't glisten, but to Corey, this rock did. It reflected the thousands of gold coins whose location it helped pinpoint.

"You know, Corey, I've been skeptical that this gold really existed."

"I am well aware of that," Corey acknowledged.

"Treasure hunting is a heart thing. In my head, I know the rock is not enough to find the gold. In my heart, I know I have to try." She held the rock in her lap. She caressed it. She outlined every ridge and every valley with her finger. "This is my gold flake."

"What?"

"This is my poof that the gold exists, just like the gold flakes are Todd's. If he can believe, so can I." Corey reluctantly realized she and Todd now had a bond that went beyond popcorn and a movie. "I've got to find a way to apologize for what I said tonight. We've got to help him find this treasure."

It was long after midnight when Corey and Michelle put everything back in the trunk, except the stone and the letter. Michelle walked him to the door. "I think I'm going to put the rock under my pillow."

"Why do you want the 'rock fairy' will take it and leave you a treasure?"

"No, I'm hoping it will whisper to me in my dreams the secret of the lost French gold. Some of us believe in things other than science."

She leaned up and kissed Corey on the cheek. Michelle opened the door and nudged him to the doorstep. She gave him a girlish wave and shut the door.

This was not the way Corey had hoped the evening would end, but then, scientists never get the girl.

Chapter Fourteen

Henry Muselle's Journal
Late Saturday Night

After the events of this afternoon, I had resolved not to write in my journal tonight. I am so exasperated. I cannot stand it. How I ever let myself be led around by these juveniles is beyond me. Five hours in the middle of a cow pasture produced nothing. The shovels don't line up with the center of the springs. We have no earthly idea where the rock and the deer tree are. How did I ever hope to find this treasure? I should have followed my original hunch, which was to use primary account material to locate it.

After I left Todd, I went back to the nursing home to visit Edna. When I told her my name, she became like a little girl reciting the words of her grandfather. He knew Henry Muselle. Henry Muselle was a frequent deer hunter on the Saling farm. But Henry Muselle never shot any deer. Henry Muselle came at the wrong time of day to hunt deer. Henry Muselle could be seen walking in the fields away from the deer trail. Her grandfather caught Henry Muselle looking through the storage sheds and the barn.

It was Henry Muselle who saw Edna's grandfather shoveling manure with the ancient shovel. Henry Muselle took the shovel and when Hezekiah Judson asked for it back, Henry said he couldn't find it. That's when Hezekiah buried the shovels and banished Muselle from Watertown.

God plays mischievous games by clouding the present in an old woman's brain and opening a portal to the past of which time travelers would be jealous. I witnessed the failure of my grandfather, which led to his bestowing the mantle of discovery upon my father. That coronation led to his death and my misery.

The pace of coincidence quickens. Ghosts haunt me at every turn. To make matters worse, that damned Indian won't leave me alone! Not only did I feel his presence in the field all afternoon, but also when I lay down after I got home, he appeared again in one of my dreams.

He walked into Saling's barn and lifted two bales out of the haymow. In the hole was one of the springs. He laid two crossed sticks in the spring. Next he placed an odd-shaped rock in the hole. A tiny deer went in next. He pulled a piece of parchment from his leather vest and opened it. It appeared to be an ancient map. He laid it on top of the rest of the material in the spring.

In my dream I wanted to ask what it all meant. He turned and addressed me as if I were in my own dream watching him.

"When nothing seems to be going right, don't worry," he said. "Answers come from places we least expect."

Chapter Fifteen

Sunday, April 23

Banished, Todd had taken refuge in the bushes at Hennigers and waited as moonstruck lovers passed him, petting and pawing their way down Chestnut Street. The Wolfs walked their Highland terriers who obediently announced the presence of the unseen spy and were chastised for trying to devour a chipmunk. The sound of plastic on denim awakened Todd as Mrs. Sloan struggled with her bag of milk and cigarettes. The spent butt of the Winston hit him in the head as she disposed of her cigarette and headed for home.

He did not know why he had said those things to Michelle. She had done nothing to hurt him. Maybe he had been so close to accomplishing his dream that he lashed out at the person he cared about the most to soften any defeat he might incur. The feeling in the room at the time was almost like a championship baseball game, and thanks to his father, he hated baseball.

All he ever dreamed of was being a pitcher. As Todd relentlessly practiced throwing the ball at the hand drawn target on the wall and catching it on the rebound, his father would sneak up and snag it then refuse to give it back. Practice was important. He could have been the starting pitcher if he could have improved his accuracy and velocity.

His father, who saw no use for sports, considered Todd's efforts a waste of time. As his relationship with Todd's teacher intensified, his ridicule of Todd increased. It would be easier to abandon his family if they didn't like him.

The more his father tormented Todd, the harder he tried – until that day when the tryouts to decide who would be the starting pitcher in the playoffs. That day, practicing with his father, he threw thirty-one strikes in a row. His father told him anyone could throw that many strikes, standing ten feet from the plate. Todd threw number thirty-two. His dad caught the ball on the rebound and walked into the house. Todd didn't go after him. Todd quit the team and vowed to never again let an adult take advantage of him. Michelle was no adult. Michelle was his friend.

Todd finally mustered enough courage to return to the war room and see how much damage he had really caused. It was nearly one AM and the lights were still on. Todd found the garage door unlocked. He made his way through the house and into the room. It had not changed much except for a few more dots on the map. Corey was engrossed in his work when Todd tapped lightly on the door.

"Mind if I come in," he said.

"Oh no, of course," Corey said, never looking up.

"How badly did I screw things up tonight?"

Corey paused, put his pencil down and turned to his friend. "Todd, we're tired of catching the flack for your tough life. If you want to wallow in it, be our guest. But we have our lives to live, our futures to plan, and we're tired of being dragged down into your cesspool."

Todd did not expect this - first Michelle and now Corey.

"Don't you understand what you've done?" Corey continued.

"Yeah, I screwed up the experiment."

"No, you've opened up an opportunity to go beyond the experiment. You've got this whole town in a dither. *I* think we're on to something. *Dan's dad* thinks we're on the right track. And all *you* do is sit around and whine about your lousy parents.

"Do you understand that before this year is out, you could drop out of school, join the Army, vote, get married, own your own car or do anything else your parents can do?"

"I guess I do."

"I'm sorry you're parents are such losers. You have a choice. You can follow in their footsteps or you can take control of your life and set a different course. I can't be your father. I can't fix your mother. And neither can you. But you can make something of yourself."

"I can have a dream?"

"You've got a dream, dum-dum. Look around. I'd say finding $13 million in lost gold is a pretty good dream. Are you too dumb or too scared to latch on to it?"

Todd didn't acknowledge his friend's words. As Corey went back to writing, Todd slipped out of the house. A light breeze with a hint of summer greeted him as he walked outside. The rumblings of distant thunder warned of the approach of another round of spring rains. He was not anxious to go home and be met with an empty house or, worse yet, the raucous giggles and carrying on of another sleep over. Somewhere he had to find a new resolve.

He wandered the streets of Minerva searching for it. The old Victorian houses lay silent and dark, an occasional flickering television revealing an insomniac, a dim nightlight illuminating the way to the bathroom for the elderly or the young. He passed Mr. Muselle's house and saw one light in the study and a shape stooped over the desk. He shouldn't be grading papers this late on a Saturday night. He wondered what he was writing. Maybe he was writing in one of his journals. What would be so important to write at this time of night?

A flash of lightening followed by an immediate clap of thunder darkened Henry's house as well as all of the streetlights on Line Street. There was a storm brewing. Todd ran for his house and whatever shelter it provided.

* * *

The warm rain blowing through the slightly opened window awakened Ralph. He had not been sleeping well, anyway. He dreamed about Fred Johnson and trying to stop him building the road. Fred waved the EPA report at him and laughed hideously as he rode past Ralph bulldozing one cow after another. Even though he felt helpless, Ralph had a feeling everything would work out all right.

The flash of lightening sent a long, low, rumbling wave of thunder down the valley. Its sound and the numerous slashes of lightning announced a good nurturing, soaking spring rain. The fields would be happy. Tomorrow, as the sun wakened the ground with its warming rays, the newly planted seeds would burst forth above the ground. Rabbits and groundhogs would feast on the young sprouts in the cool of the afternoon.

Ralph really didn't know what he would do after he left the farm. He would probably become a handyman for some business in town. Andrew Muth, the undertaker, said Ralph could work for him part time. He couldn't imagine spending his time doing electrical work around dead bodies. He was too much of an outdoorsman to be cooped up in a funeral home.

He had not given up on stopping the road, but he didn't see how they were going to pull it off. Finding the gold was an interesting diversion, but he wasn't sure it was an option based in reality.

Since he was awake, he decided to look for more answers. He laid his hand on the bed to get up and realized Martha was not there. This had become a routine over the last several months. They would start out the night sleeping together, but for one reason or another, one or the other of them would end up on the couch before morning. Ralph assumed the storm made Martha move tonight.

He went to his desk in the corner of the bedroom and turned on the desk lamp. After several clicks and an attempt at the floor lamp nearby, Ralph realized electricity was not an option this morning. He fumbled his way back to the bed and found his flashlight on the floor under the bed. He returned to the desk and began searching through the file drawer. It was not hard to find the right file even in the dark. The Route 30 file was nearly four inches thick. The trick was pulling all of the papers out of the drawer at the same time.

His mission accomplished, he began looking through the correspondence. Martha's filing system which put each correspondence in the file in chronological order, made the task easier. He read about the public meetings for the proposed road. He was informed about the estimated purchase price for his land if the road should go that direction. Next was the correspondence with the EPA about the status of his property. He found the letter from Enrico Fernandez, which stated the farm, was wetlands and would probably be bypassed. The very next piece of paper was a letter from Washington informing him of the eminent domain purchase of his property in order to construct a four-lane highway. It still didn't make sense.

The rain pounded on the roof in tense agreement with his findings. It was almost as if the rain gods were applauding him to encourage his quest. He went to the closet, like a prospector in search of gold, and retrieved an old metal box from the top shelf. He laid it on the bed and opened it. Inside were all of his and Martha's important papers. There were life insurance policies, certificates of deposit, car titles, wills and most importantly deeds. He had the deeds and abstracts for the property dating back to Hezekiah Saling. Maybe in one of the abstracts would be the ammunition he would need. He knew that the EPA had reviewed them, but look at what they had decided from the information.

As the rain came and went outside, Ralph scoured the records for over an hour. He found a lot of curios information, but nothing that he believed could be used against the EPA. Nearly exhausted, he rearranged the items in the box so all would fit in it again. He picked their wills up and moved them against the back wall of the box. In the bottom was a small circular object wrapped in tissue and bound with black fishing line. On a scrap of paper was scrawled, "Lost Gold Coin."

How could it be lost if it's in here, Ralph wondered. He carefully untied the string and unfolded the paper. Inside was a dirty old coin. It was nearly black. Ralph licked the edge of the coin and then massaged it with his fingers. The edge turned gold. *What in the . . .*

He laid the coin flat and held his light close. He could not make out the inscription. He took it to the desk, put a piece of paper over it and rubbed over the coin with a pencil. When he was finished, he examined his work with the light.

In the center of the coin was the head of a royal figure, Ralph decided from the crown. Underneath he could make out the inscription Louis XV, and the date 1753.

* * *

    Todd groped his way into the house. He was soaked from head to foot. The rain was coming down in sheets. He stripped down to his underwear and wrung his clothes out in the sink. He tiptoed passed his mother's room and sneaked upstairs. He took his emergency candle from his bottom dresser drawer and lit it. Emergencies were thunderstorms when the lights were out and late nights when he did not want his mother to know when he was up.
    He sat the candle on his desk and took a new notebook from the drawer. He did not know which class this was supposed to be for, but it didn't make any difference. The rain beat on his window. The lightening was almost strobe-like and illuminated the flooding streets. He was not frightened. He lived a storm worse than the one raging outside.
    If Mr. Muselle can keep a journal where he recorded his most intimate thoughts, then so can I, he thought. *I have a dream,* he wrote. *I have a dream. I have a dream. I have a dream. I have a **dream**.* The tears streamed down his face quicker than the rain outside. The page in his notebook became spotted and stained.
    *Tonight I set my sights on something larger than I am. I nearly lost my only friends in the entire world. To hell with my mother, my father and all of the demons who surround them. I have a dream. I **have** a dream. I have a dream. I have a **dream**.*
    My dream is to find the lost French gold. When I do, I will prove to Corey that I am a true friend, willing to put aside my problems to help him. I will prove to Michelle that I am worthy of her love, not just her sympathy. I will help Mr. Muselle end his family's torment. I will prove to me that I can accomplish something important on my own.

I have a dream. I have a dream. I have a dream. I have a dream.

The rain, wind, lightening and thunder hid his weeping. He cried himself to sleep like he had the day he watched his father drive away with his new girlfriend and shatter Todd's every dream. The spring rains were certainly bringing a new beginning.

* * *

Sunday mornings were special in Minerva. It took the town until after lunch to get up to twenty-first century speed. The spring morning was announced before sunrise by the tunes of songbirds returned from their winter hiatus. Miniature bunnies and tiny squirrels ventured from well-hidden nests to feast on fresh shoots of grass and newly fallen seeds.

At eight o'clock, the carillon of the Christian Church serenaded the village with hymns, reminding everyone it was time to get up. The Catholic Church bells were the first to sound a call to worship at nine. Father Mike's homily would deal with the need for parishioners to reach out to one another in time of crisis. In the Church of God, Pastor Fred would blast the malls for violating the sanctity of the Sabbath. Rev. Susan at the Methodist Church would try to convince the congregation that God was in control of all the events affecting their lives.

* * *

High on top of the hill outside Minerva, Fred Johnson was taking full advantage of the interlude to plan his next move. Trophies attesting his total control of projects surrounded his desk. On the office love seat sat newly hired, highly paid engineer Joe Davis. He was easy pickings for the shrewd operator.

"Now Mr. Davis, I cannot impress upon you enough the importance of finishing on schedule. Not only is this taxpayer money, we have been given the honor of safeguarding; it is the very reputation of Johnson Construction that is at stake.

"As many of my employees will tell you, some of whom have been with me since I purchased my first backhoe, when Fred Johnson prospers, everybody prospers. There have been occasions, however, when certain employees felt they knew better how to run the company than I did. They certainly never received a gold watch, and many times unexpectedly fell upon hard times, if you catch my meaning."

Davis gulped. "Well, Mr. Johnson, I do have the plans for the 'environmental cover' we are supposed to build. We will pour a series of pilings and then connect them with steel girders. We will then lay a flooring, and finally apply the roadbed over top. The sides will be graded so when it is finished, no one will be able to tell it is there."

"Very nice, very nice," Fred said. "But *this* is the way we're going to do it."

"I want the pilings poured, but then construct the sides and make them solid. After dark, we will fill it with a mixture of concrete and dirt. This will take care of any moisture in the ground and provide a solid base.

"During the day, the cross members and other building material will enter the site from the west. Anything we don't need haul out the east end of the project at night and take it to our building site in Cadiz." He didn't mention that he rebilled the state for materials he used at that site.

"But Mr. Johnson," Davis began.

"Mr. Davis, life is a series of choices. You chose this job. I chose to hire you. I always choose what's best for the company. I have my way to do things and you have your way. Now which way do you think is right?"

* * *

Davis heard the siren first. There were certain sounds that were always welcome on a Sunday morning in Minerva. Church bells, choirs, cars quietly moving to family gatherings were all appropriate Sunday morning sounds. Sirens were

Henry Muselle's Treasure

never welcome. Sirens meant sickness or accident or . . . fire. High atop city hall, the junior high school and the water tower were old air raid sirens. First utilized to alert citizens to impending Russian missile attacks, they now warned of approaching tornadoes and called volunteer firemen to their trucks.

"Mr. Johnson, do you want me to go to my truck and call my buddies on the CB to find out where the fire is?" The timing of the siren was usually an indication of the crisis it announced. Weekdays were industrial fires and auto accidents. Nighttime was accident and accidental house fires. Saturdays were careless fires. But Sunday mornings were unattended house fires observed by passersby. Sunday morning fires were not good. Johnson simply looked at his watch. He had a puzzled look - like the siren was blowing at the wrong time.

Davis became more uncomfortable when the fire trucks went by on the road next to the trailer. Johnson finished his briefing without interruption, then said, "C'mon, let's go see what the ruckus is all about."

Outside the bay window, huge plumes of black smoke soared into the sky. Johnson did not act surprised. He walked Davis to the car as casually as if they were going out to lunch.

* * *

Churchgoers knew that all they had to do was walk into church with an inkling of a problem and something in the sermon would reach out and grab them. On any given Sunday, the sermons presented to the community provided solutions to most of its problems. At the Pentecostal church downtown, Pastor Livingston was trying to explain the various ways God spoke to people. He used Moses as his example.

"And the angel of the Lord appeared to him in a blazing fire from the midst of a bush; and he looked and behold the bush was burning with fire and yet the bush was not consumed."

As he paused for effect and moved to the far side of the platform, the fire siren started. The congregation chuckled. Several firemen got up to leave.

"Beware of burning bushes," Livingston quipped. "They may be harder to put out than you expect." The congregation roared with approval.

* * *

Todd rode to Howard Jackson's house to give him the location of "Sweet Spring" that Corey had found. As he crested the hill, he saw a small plume of gray smoke coming from the direction of Howard's house. Grass fires were not that uncommon this time of year. Debris from the fall dried out. Careless smokers and children testing their fire building skills started most fires. The wind quickly spread them.

When he got to the house, he found a fire in the ditch across the road. It was moving through the debris in the ditch and was starting to climb into the bushes at the edge of the woods. It was already too big for him to handle. He dropped his bike and ran into the house.

"Mr. Jackson, Mr. Jackson, there's a fire across the road. He ran through the house, but found no sign of Howard. As he reached for the phone to call for help, he heard siren approaching. Someone must have called from a cell phone. He went back to the road. A couple of cars had stopped. One man was directing traffic through Howard's yard to keep the cars away from the fire that had grown to almost fifty feet in length and had flames leaping ten to fifteen feet into the air and engulfing many of the bushes.

No sooner did the firemen reach the scene and begin their work than Todd heard the squeal of tires and watched a car bounce off the road, into the ditch and up against a power pole.

"Hey, one of you EMT's, go down and check out the driver," called Chief Everett.

"He's bleeding pretty badly, somebody call an ambulance," yelled a bystander near the car.

Henry Muselle's Treasure

"And get the sheriff out here to control traffic before somebody ends up in Howard's front porch," cried the Chief.

More sirens. Todd watched in amazement as the crisis grew.

"More water. I need more water," screamed one fireman.

"I'm giving you everything I've got. The pump's not working."

"What do you mean the pump's not working? That truck's not thirty days old. Call Robertsville. Have them send us theirs."

The roadside bushes were now fully involved and the fire was quickly spreading through the pine needles and licking at the low dead branches of the trees.

"Get some men into those pines and start a fire line"

More sirens pierced the air. The ambulance arrived. "Hey, can you guys radio base for another squad? This guy's wife is having chest pain, and we don't have any service on our cell phone where we're parked."

Todd watched in astonishment as Robertsville Fire Department arrived and set up a portable reservoir next to Howard's house. The additional manpower and water started to bring the fire under control.

"Where's my pressure. I need pressure."

"The reservoir's leaking. I thought you patched that!"

"Call Augusta," yelled the chief. "Maybe they've got something that works."

A call went out for assistance. Police sirens screamed through the quiet village.

* * *

People sitting in church were becoming extremely uncomfortable. Scanner listeners who could stand it no longer began to get into their cars and go to the fire.

When Todd saw Johnson pull in next to Howard's house, there were three fire departments, two ambulances, two sheriff's cruisers, two Minerva Police cars and forty cars and trucks parked in the fields around Howard Jackson's house.

All these are necessary to extinguish a half-acre blaze? Todd noticed how extremely agitated Johnson was about a fire which really didn't concern him.

Elsewhere, there was a party atmosphere with neighbors visiting each other and commenting on the fire fighting techniques. The party stopped abruptly with the sound of breaking glass and the sight of flames and smoke shooting from Howard's basement window.

"Somebody give me a hose," yelled a fireman and he quickly sent a blast of water through the window. Another fireman jerked open the basement door and went charging downstairs with a two-inch line. There was no more smoke coming from the house when the fire chief stuck his head out the basement door and called for the sheriff.

* * *

The excitement of a Sunday morning fire gave way to curiosity surrounding a structure fire of suspicious origin. Johnson had imagined a passing car finding the burning house. Instead, two hundred people had witnessed the ignition of the blaze.

As the crowd moved closer to the house to catch tidbits from the investigators, Johnson hustled Davis back to the car. They now had no time to lose in implementing phase two. Johnson was amazed at the makeup of the membership of the congregation that gathered at Howard Jackson's farm on Sunday morning to worship the fire god.

He bet Huntsinger had heard the location of the fire on the scanner because he nearly beat the fire trucks to the scene. Johnson watched as he stayed far enough back in the crowd to catch the rumors on the first bounce. Johnson knew there was no doubt from the time the firemen entered the basement that they suspected the fire was arson. He could see George listening intently to the conversations. He was almost certainly planning his excuses.

He saw Ralph there, too. He probably came to make sure his farm was not in the path of the flames. Johnson was afraid this turn of events would lend credence to Howard's dirty trick theory.

He also spotted a Hispanic face in the crowd. Some inexplicable force must have drawn Fernandez to the valley where his troubles began. Johnson didn't know if Fernandez suspected he was involved in this, but he certainly had a feeling.

There was an unfamiliar face in the crowd. Johnson had only seen pictures of Joe Gunther. He couldn't imagine why he had come to Minerva. Johnson never anticipated investigators finding a treasure-trove like this fire.

* * *

Todd finally found Howard. He was in the barn talking to the sheriff. "I kept the cows in so they wouldn't be hurt in the confusion," he explained. "As a volunteer fireman myself, and member of the County Arson Task Force, I knew what I'd found in my basement. I didn't disturb it, but I did shut off the gas to the other gas appliances in the house. I couldn't be sure if or when it would go off, but I knew who ever set it would show up and watch his handiwork. So, I lit a greasy paper towel and threw it in the dry leaves across the road for a little insurance. Your arsonist should have been in the crowd, and my video camera sitting in the front window should have his picture," he smirked.

* * *

"Vengeance is mine, saith the Lord," the pastor of the Presbyterian Church shouted. It was Sunday morning in Minerva.

Chapter Sixteen

Monday, April 24

George had left Joe Gunther a frantic message about the road and requested a meeting. This was the reason Joe had been in Minerva over the weekend and by chance witnessed the fire. In addition to George, Joe had invited Howard Jackson and Enrico Fernandez to attend to a ten o'clock meeting. Howard brought Ralph and Martha Saling for moral support.

Joe Gunther's office was not a typical E. P. A. District Manager's office. Johnson made sure that the people in Johnson Center, whose help he needed the most, had all the comforts of home while at work.

The raised gold letters proclaiming the domicile of the Environmental Protection Agency were mounted on a marble fascia above the receptionist's mahogany desk. The matching wainscoting and molding complemented the floral wallpaper. The atmosphere of well-spent tax dollars radiated a sense of protection alluded to in the agency's name.

Gunther's office carried through with the elegant atmosphere. His massive mahogany desk overlooked plush couches and formal overstuffed chairs. Clients were overcome with their comfort as they sank into luxury while awaiting Gunther's bureaucratic decisions.

"Thank you all for coming," Gunther began. "I understand you have some concerns with the manner in which the Route 30 project is progressing. So do I. I am hoping your input today will help resolve them. Anyone care to begin?"

"I will," George said. "I'm George Huntsinger; and I've worked for Fred Johnson for several years. I've noticed that he has an obsession for completing this project on time. I'm afraid he might be breaking some rules."

"Ha," cried Howard, "come look at my basement. I'll show you what he's broken. Do you want to know what I think is going on?"

"Yes I would," said Gunther popping a breath mint into his mouth, coming around the desk to sit on its corner.

"I think Johnson tried to burn my house as a diversion so he could hurry up and get the road past Ralph's."

"Why would he want to do that?" Gunther prodded.

"You see," Howard continued. "Ralph's and my fields are full of springs. Johnson's already buried one of mine. But Ralph here has too many. Your EPA plan calls for some sort of 'environmental cover' over Ralph's. I think it's too expensive to build and Johnson wants everybody's attention some place else while he flimflams the state one more time. Besides, he wouldn't be where he is today if old Jose over there hadn't done a new report for him."

Gunther never flinched. George couldn't tell from his body language whether Jackson was right or wrong.

"George? Enrico? Would either of you care to respond?" he asked calmly.

Huntsinger spoke first. "As I said, I've worked for Fred Johnson for a number of years. Recently, I have become uneasy with the manner in which he conducts his business, but I really have no idea what Mr. Jackson is talking about."

"You lying so and so," Howard snapped. "You buried my spring." He held up a crumpled piece of notebook paper. "This kid doing a science experiment got water from my 'Sweet Spring' four weeks before the road got to my place. He took pretty accurate bearings and I followed them. According to my calculations, that spring is twelve feet from the edge of your road under about two feet of fill. If it was there four weeks ago, it was there a year ago when this Spanish speaking wetback did his report. I think Johnson paid him to doctor it up."

"Please, Mr. Jackson," Enrico finally said, "you may question the quality of my work, but do not question my loyalty to my country. My family is proud to live in Puerto Rico. It has been a territory of the United States for a long time. We pay taxes just like you. I am proud to work for my federal government. Please stick to the issues."

"Mr. Jackson," Gunther said, reaching for another mint. "This is a fact-finding mission and not a witch hunt. I'll deal with my employees if that is necessary."

He moved from his desk pulling a black chair with his college's logo painted on the back closer to the group. Gunther sat down. George liked the fact that he would talk with people eyeball to eyeball.

"As you may know, Mr. Jackson," Gunther began, "I did my own survey of the area. I do not agree with Mr. Fernandez's findings. I also find Mr. Johnson's actions unusual for a contractor. I do have some solutions, but first I'd like to hear Mr. and Mrs. Saling's view of the situation.

"Well," Ralph started, "I'm generally a peacemaker. I don't like to make waves. I ask a lot of questions before I make up my mind. If I lose an argument, I'll submit to the winner. This Johnson fellow, though, doesn't seem to play by any rules. I didn't believe it at first, but I agree with Howard - I think Johnson set that fire. It didn't get enough of a start to destroy the fuse. It was lucky for Howard that he left his muzzleloader's black powder on the windowsill. If it hadn't exploded and blown out the window, we might not have found the fire for a long time.

"Mr. Johnson paid me a visit last week. He wanted permission to bring heavy equipment past my house and through the field to where the road was going. I told him they'd damage the other springs in the field. He said he didn't care. He said they'd be ruined anyway after the road went through. I told him there was nothing in the purchase agreement that said I had to give him access. I told him to get a letter from the Department of Transportation and I'd let him do it. He said he didn't have time for any letter and offered me ten thousand dollars - cash.

"Mr. Gunther, ten thousand dollars is a lot of money. I've lost my livelihood. I've lost my heritage. When I leave my farm, it doesn't matter if there's one spring there because it will never be a farm again. But I got one thing left, and every Saling that ever lived on that farm gave that to me. I've got my convictions. If I have to live by the rules, then why doesn't he? I'm not for sale for ten thousand dollars or any price."

George sat with his head down. He didn't dare look up. He couldn't speak. He had only imagined what his actions were doing to the local people. Now he was in the same room with them and he was afraid it was too late to rectify what he had done.

Martha laid her head on Ralph's shoulder and sobbed. Gunther got out of his chair and went to the window. He stood with his back to the group, not saying a word. Fernandez excused himself and went to the restroom. Howard had wanted to say more, but the lump in his throat caused by the events of the last several days prevented him from speaking. The silence was deafening, broken only by Martha's occasional sniffles. When Fernandez returned, Gunther assumed his post behind the desk.

"I want to assure you all that I am aware of everything that has transpired. I am the lowest level of a high level group of government officials who realize a very large mistake was made in the granting of the Route 30 project. They understand there is a major problem with Johnson Construction. Their goal is to stop the road, correct the problems and build it the way it should have been built in the first place."

Howard jumped right on Gunther's statement. "Are you saying . . .?"

"I've said all I am going to say on that issue. On the issues you have raised, I have two choices. I can reveal that in a routine follow-up environmental study, I found glaring conflicts with the final report. I could file for a restraining order to stop construction until the discrepancies can be resolved."

"That's great news," said Ralph.

"No, that's the good news," Gunther continued. "The bad news is because the report was originally accepted at the highest levels, the argument is moot."

"OK. What's the second choice?" Howard asked.

"The second choice would be to admit fraud in this office," he said. "The restraining order would not be granted. Johnson would claim he was not involved and finish the road. Heads would roll in this office, but the likelihood of Johnson being named in a criminal action would be slim."

"Great," said Howard. "The bad guys win again."

"However, if someone came forward with evidence of Johnson's crimes, I've been told to offer them immunity from prosecution." Huntsinger perked up a little. He didn't want to appear too obvious.

"Our task is to find some loophole which would stop Johnson's progress until the legal process can catch up with him. I sent Johnson a letter, which he should receive today, requiring him to send us core samples from Saling's farm. I told him we want to make sure the ground is stable enough to support the 'environmental cover'. It's all bureaucratic babble that will buy us some time.

"Also, as we speak, law enforcement has a suspect under surveillance in the attempted arson of Howard's house. But we still don't have any way to stop Johnson."

Fernandez finally spoke up. "He did bury a spring which is destruction of a wetland. Can't we stop him on that?"

"I'm afraid that points a finger back at us," Gunther replied. "But before I rule that out, let me run it by the others."

The struggle going on inside Huntsinger was intense. He didn't want to betray his boss and friend, but Johnson had placed him in a tenuous position. Immunity might be a way out. He whispered to Enrico. They excused themselves and left the room.

Still searching for answers, Gunther asked, "How did you say you determined the location of that spring, Howard?"

"Some kids doing a science project gave me their bearings," he said.

"Are they the ones who think they found gold?" Gunther asked. "I heard a teacher or somebody talking about it in the grocery store."

"Actually, I think they were looking for pollution, but have decided they've found the gold buried on our farm," Ralph added.

"Is that the lost Indian gold?" Howard asked. Then he added, chuckling, "You know, if you spend enough time buying groceries and getting your hair cut in this town, you don't need CNN for your news." They all laughed. It was the first light moment of the morning.

"It was lost French gold which is supposed to be buried on our farm," Martha gently corrected him.

"Is this fact or legend?" Gunther asked.

"Fact," said Ralph.

"Legend," said Howard.

"Maybe a little of both," Martha said sheepishly.

Gunther reached in his desk file and pulled out a form. He ran his finger down the checklist. "Uh huh, just what I thought," he said. He walked to the bookcase, selected one of the many black binders, brought it back to his desk and searched its pages.

"Here it is," he finally said. "If we can show that this gold is a historical site, the road has to stop. Johnson cannot proceed until the government has determined it has collected all artifacts. It might even stop the road entirely."

"That's great," shouted Ralph.

"Hot digity, Hallelujah," Howard said jumping up from the couch.

"I don't believe it," Martha said breaking into tears again.

"What do we have to do to prove it?" Ralph asked.

"I'm not a historical expert," Gunther said, "but I imagine proving the story through documents of the period would be a start."

"One of the men helping the students is a direct descendent of the man who buried the gold," Martha said. "Perhaps he has some documents."

"It's worth a try," Gunther said.

"What if we find the gold?" asked Ralph. Martha and Howard were stunned. What a question from old Mr. Never-

Take-A-Side. Maybe he was getting excited about something other than cows and corn.

Gunther didn't realize the significance of the question. "Any physical finds would certainly immediately stop construction."

"Is this physical enough?" Ralph said pulling the gold coin from his pocket. Gunther examined it carefully.

"Where did you get that?" Martha asked.

"I found it in the lock box at home. It was among grandpa's papers. I don't ever remember seeing it before."

"If we could prove this came from your treasure, I'm sure the road would be in jeopardy," Gunther admitted.

"Well, we'd better be getting home," said Martha. "I promised Todd I'd find some things for him."

Howard and the Salings got up to leave. Gunther thanked them for their help and promised to keep them informed. Huntsinger and Fernandez came back into the room.

"Mr. Gunther," Huntsinger said, "Enrico and I are tired of having Fred Johnson control our lives. We need to talk to you. But first, may we use your phone? We'd like to call our attorneys."

* * *

Fred was thrilled when he read the newspaper. The article about the fire in the Minerva Leader had an unexpected twist. There was no mention of Howard Jackson's house and the ongoing investigation. The description of the grass fire focused on the proximity to Johnson Construction equipment. Kim, the reporter, made a big to do of the damage that could have occurred and how much it would have set the project back. There were flowery references about the benefits Minerva was going to derive from the new road and altruistic references to Fred Johnson and his contributions to the community. Praises were also heaped upon the various fire departments and EMS units, which responded to the blaze and contained it to such a small area. It was evident, to Fred, who had gotten to whom about the article.

Fred had originally given the job of spinning of the local news to George Huntsinger. Now that Huntsinger had mysteriously vanished, that job fell to Davis. It was vital to control the news because even though the road was well under way, there was still a very vocal group of citizens opposed to it. The northern route would have benefited more small communities. This route would encourage more national franchises to locate in Minerva, but would spoil some of its small town atmosphere. As the debate continued to rage, Fred made sure that any press was slanted in his favor. Davis had done well on his first assignment.

Delighted, Johnson turned the page and noticed tucked in the lower right corner of page two was a story only the most conscientious newspaper reader would find.

High School Students Search for Lost French Gold

Four Minerva High School students have taken their award winning Science Fair project and put it to practical use. Their pollution experiment, designed by Senior Corey Wagner produced results none of the students expected when they began.

"The kids found a precipitate in their samples," explained General Color Chemist and father of one of the students, John Jones. "I tested it at our lab and determined it was a low grade refined gold."

Chief student investigator, Todd Evans believes he knows the source of the gold. "It's coming from the lost French gold."

Skeptics abound about the discovery. "People have been searching for that treasure since it was lost in 1755," says science teacher Mrs. Talkington. "The children have a nice theory, but I don't believe they will ever prove it."

Team member Dan Jones says they have enlisted the help of Dr. James Dorman of the Department of Natural Resources to analyze their data. Dr. Dorman was unavailable for comment.

Michelle Bobinger, the only female in the group, says their initial investigation leads them to believe the treasure is buried on the Ralph Saling property. Mr. Saling would not return phone calls to this newspaper.

Unfortunately for the young treasure hunters, the area in question lies in the path of the new Route 30.

The longer he read, the more crimson his face became. This article gave the young scientists the legitimacy they were searching for. When he saw the last line, he screamed, "Davis. Get in here. You've got a problem."

* * *

Todd walked up the rickety front porch steps and rang Henry Muselle's doorbell. From deep within the bowls of the house, he could hear the Westminster chimes announce a visitor at the door. Even though the storm had been over for hours, electricity had not yet been restored to this block. As Henry opened the door with candle in hand, Todd though he was reminiscent of Ebenezer Scrooge in the many adaptations of *A Christmas Carol* he had seen as a child.

Mr. Muselle's home was plain and under spoken, just as he was. Much of the furnishings he had inherited from his parents. The living room furniture had been reupholstered several times and lay hidden from view under ancient throws. "I brought my journal to show you," Todd began.

"Good, I want to read it sometime."

"Read it now."

"Some other time, Todd. I want to get your opinion on this."

"Read it now," Todd insisted. Finally Henry acquiesced. Tears began to form in Henry's eyes as he read the entry about the dream. Henry cleared his throat and gained his composure. "That's very nice," was all he could muster.

"I wrote it because of you."

"Thank you, I appreciate that," Henry said trying to get on with the business at hand and away from Todd's gratitude which was hitting entirely too close to home. "I want to show you what I have here," he finally said directing Todd to the table.

Henry escorted Todd to the dining room where he had a topographical map pasted to a mounting board, and was using stick pins to recreate their findings in the field. It took Todd a minute to decipher the map. Finally he recognized the road in front of the farmhouse. Closely spaced lines represented the hill in front of the house and a gold pin marked the GPS location of the shovels.

The map clearly showed the outbuildings of the farm and the pasture behind the house. It was recent enough to show the blemishes where prior diggings disturbed the neat contours of the map. Four gold pins marked their four springs and a gold pin with a top painted red with marker indicated their center. A gold pin with a blue top marked their second attempt at finding the center, and a third pin with a blue top marked the calculated center of the square.

Nearly an inch away to the west of each gold pin was a clear pin. A clear pin with a blue top was stuck in the apparent center of that square. The colored top pins formed a mosaic nearly four inches long by three inches wide.

"There's our problem, Todd," Henry explained. The centers of those four springs, based on our various ways to look at it cover nearly half an acre.

"What are the clear pins? I don't remember taking a second set of readings on the springs."

"Those are the location of the springs as my father recorded them in 1935." Henry handed Todd a tattered notebook with the words "Henry Muselle's Journal 1934-1936" inscribed on the cover in the finest of penmanship. There was a bookmark stuck about three quarters of the way toward the back of the notebook. Todd opened to the spot. The notation read:

> *June 25, 1935 I have identified what I believe to be the four springs mentioned in the correspondence.*

The center of them lays approximately six hundred paces from where Mr. Saling says he found the shovel. The University at Leone, France examined the shovel I borrowed from Mr. Saling and has verified it is the type that would have been used by French troops on the frontier at the time in question. I anxiously await its return be Parcel Post. Mrs. Saling is becoming increasingly agitated by its absence.

While the Saling's were in church today, I surveyed the locations of the four springs, the rock tree and the shovel. I have indicated their positions here.

In typical Muselle precision, the six locations were precisely recorded.

"What do you think it means?" Todd asked.

"I don't know. That's why I asked you to come over. Maybe between the two of us, we can put together the missing pieces."

"And what is this 'stone tree'? I don't see it mentioned here."

"I forgot about that one." Henry took the notebook and reviewed the tree's location. Using two straight edges, he carefully followed the grid on the map until they crossed at the appropriate point. He stuck a clear pin at the point and then removed the guides.

"Isn't this curious," he said motioning to Todd.

The pinhead had punctured the letter "a" in the word "Trail" which was part of a notation centered in a dotted path meandering through the pasture and up the hill behind the Saling farm. It was marked "The Great Trail."

"I wonder if that might be the tree where the rock was lodged?" Henry pondered. "It's impossible to know, and how could we possibly find that tree today?"

"Your dad kept really good notes."

"Yes, he did."

"Was he a good father?"

The question took Henry by surprise. He had never considered it before.

"Todd, you have to realize that when I was growing up, we had just come out of The Great Depression. Work was scarce. Many husbands abandoned their families because they could not support him. Men who had work, worked long hours just to be able to buy food. My father had an education and worked for the university. We were not wealthy, but we had enough. His position placed us in an upper class society. I was fortunate. My father was around a lot. He made sure we had what we needed - food, clothes, a good education, respect for family and heritage. Yes, Todd, he was a good father."

"How did he do all this surveying and stuff?"

"He used his position at the university to research the legend and put it together much like when we tried to find the gold."

"How did he die?"

Henry was absolutely not prepared for this question. He sat for a moment not saying anything, then rose and left the room. It was obvious; Todd didn't know what to do next. He was just curious. It was an innocent question. Todd got up to leave when Henry reentered the room carrying his journal.

"Todd, I have never told a soul about my father's death. I'm not sure I can tell you. But, for the first time, I was able to write about it. Here, read this. Then if you have more questions, I'll see if I'm able to answer them."

Todd sat down on the couch and read the journal entry. As he read, tears began to form in his eyes. Henry watched as one then another dropped into Todd's lap. As they began to flow freely and Todd wiped his nose on his sleeve, Henry felt the lump in his throat begin to climb. Tears began to well up in his eyes. He sat down next to Todd on the couch.

Todd finished the entry and wiped his nose again. He looked up at his teacher whose lip was quivering, tears overflowing from both eyes.

"Oh, Mr. Muselle, you do understand," Todd said lunging forward into Henry's open arms, the journal sliding to the floor.

"More than you'll ever know, Todd," Henry said as he began to sob.

"It isn't fair," Todd wailed, the tears flowing freely now.

"No it isn't, Todd. No, it isn't." Henry moaned. That was the last word said for nearly twenty minutes as student and teacher bawled, wailed, grieved and mourned a childhood cut short by the loss of a father. The treasure they sought in finding the lost gold just became priceless.

Chapter Seventeen

Ralph sat at his bedroom desk slowly tumbling the coin in his fingers. Downstairs he could hear Martha preparing Edna's birthday dinner. Howard left early this morning to pick her up at the nursing home.

He had handled the coin so much that the tarnish was falling on the EPA report on the desk. Its corners turned down to mark important passages and handwritten notes scribbled in the margins, the recent report looked defiled lying next to the original deed for the farm.

He was not looking forward to his mother's last visit to the home where she raised her family. He did not know how she would take the news. In her current state of dementia, she might revert to her childhood or race forward to her dying days banished to the nursing home. No one, not even her doctors, could predict how she might react. But Ralph knew she needed to be here today despite the consequences.

As he flipped the coin and it landed on the desk, a pan serendipitously hit the table downstairs. Martha seemed to be taking the move in stride, but he was not sure with the revelations of the last several days whether her heart was really in it.

Howard had volunteered to pick up "his old sparring partner." He had agreed not to tell her, but Ralph knew that Howard was forlorn over the loss of the farm, his own near miss not withstanding.

King Louis's crown was beginning to shine again from the wear as Ralph pondered the future of his new friend Todd. The farm meant nothing to him, but the possibility of losing the treasure was becoming an escalating dilemma.

The coin slipped out of Ralph's fingers and lit on top of the report. "The Environmental Impact of the Proposed US

Route 30 on the Counties of Stark, Carroll and Columbiana" was the title. The coin landed heads up and covered the word "environmental." It seemed to Ralph as if King Louis was smiling. "The ___ Impact of the Proposed US Route 30 on the Counties of Stark, Carroll and Columbiana," the paper read. Ralph smiled. Impact indeed. The EPA certainly was not concerned with the personal impact of a new road. The closer the road got, the less he liked it. Under the title, during one of his fits of rage, he had scribbled, "How do we stop this thing?"

He was not sure if Fernandez's and Huntsinger's change of heart would be enough. Howard said the police weren't saying a word about any investigation into his fire; so as much as they felt it pointed to Johnson, the Police were mum on the issue. That left King Louis, his gold, a seventeen year old and a crazy history teacher to stop, in a very short period of time, more bureaucracies than Ralph could count.

"Surprise!" yelled Martha and Howard.

Ralph knew his pensive time was over. He abdicated his role of chief investigator to King Louis and scurried down the back steps into the kitchen to wish his mother a Happy Birthday.

* * *

Edna was standing in the doorway of the living room, tears of joy welling up in her eyes. Howard had stopped at the nursing home and used the excuse of taking her for one of their many spring rides to get her to come. Her home was decorated with balloons and banners celebrating ninety-one years since her birth. For about an hour they visited, joked and reminisced. When it came time to party, Edna insisted on being the hostess. She scurried to the kitchen as sprightly as her antique legs would carry her. She returned almost as quickly sans coffee cup and with a look of consternation, which concerned everyone.

"Martha," she said, "I went to get a cup from the cupboard, and it was full of boxes."

"That's right, Mother Saling," Martha replied. "Ralph and I are getting ready to move."

"Move? Whatever for?" Edna asked, her lips quivering.

"We've told you, Mother," Ralph said, the moment he had feared now upon them. He steered her to her favorite chair. "There's a new road being built through the farm. As soon as Martha and I find a place, we're going to sell the farm and move to town."

"So that's why you brought this old lady home," Edna wailed. "You don't want to celebrate my birthday. You want to kill me." She clutched her chest. "Oh, my heart. Howard, get my pills." Then mustering her last ounce of strength, she pointed her finger at her little boy. "If your father were alive, he wouldn't sell the farm. It meant something to him. He had respect for what was given to him. He didn't squander it on some old road. We didn't have much, but we worked hard for what we had."

She paused long enough to take the nitroglycerin tablet from Howard. She made a face as it melted under her tongue. She took a deep breath and beseechingly looked at Howard. "Your grandfather would be so disappointed. He worked so hard to find the gold, and now it will be buried under this road."

Howard knelt down and took Edna's hand. "Now, Edna, you silly old thing, you know there's no gold." With all the vivaciousness left in her ninety-one year old body, she rose from her chair, knocking Howard backward.

"Howard Jackson," she shouted, "you know darn well there's a treasure. John Efflemeyer found that triangular rock wedged in your tree at the property line. He made the tree into a gatepost so everyone would always know where the tree was."

Ralph watched his mother in amazement. Howard tried to crawl away from her wrath.

"And you, Ralph Saling, remember when the man surveying the valley said he found a deer carved in a tree over at Snode's? But not one of you want to believe a senile old woman!" Edna said, sobbing her way to the kitchen.

Ralph, befuddled and bewildered at this new revelation, didn't know whether to console his mother or confront her antagonist.

"Did you hear that?" Howard said, pulling himself to his feet.

Ralph chose the latter. "You crusty old fart," Ralph began. "You know mentioning the treasure upsets her. You did it on purpose."

"I was hoping she had some historical information that I could use to save my farm," Howard said, dusting off his behind. "It didn't take Johnson trying to burn my house down to get me moving," he said, starting toward the kitchen. "Hell, if it was you, a case of dynamite wouldn't get your attention."

Ralph cut Howard off at the couch. "I love my farm as much as you love yours."

Howard belly-butted Ralph. "I'd lie down in front of one of those bulldozers to stop it. You'd go out, give the driver cookies and milk and ask him to stop."

"I would not!" Ralph started to belly-butt back, but his belly being considerably higher than Howard's settled for a shoulder shove. "You can't bully Johnson around the way he does us. You have to present him with facts and legal obstructions."

"Facts," Howard shouted, "like what?"

Howard grabbed the replica of Remington's sculpture of a Plains Indian on horseback from the bookshelf and waved it at Ralph.

"Facts. Like there used to be an Indian trail where he wants to put his road?"

"Maybe," said Ralph, moving closer to rescue his prize.

Howard maneuvered just ahead of Ralph until he could snatch the raccoon hat. Waving it high above his head, he said, "Facts. Like there were these French guys carrying gold through your back yard?" He dropped the coonskin hat on his head.

"Could be," Ralph said, jockeying for position.

In an instant, Howard jerked Ralph's grandfather's muzzleloader off the wall, stuck the butt under his arm and feigned aiming it. "Facts. Like the British gentlemen shot 'em after the French buried the gold?"

"Of course," Ralph said. Howard backed around the living room fending off Ralph's attacks with the barrel of the gun.

"Are you crazy?" Ralph yelled at his friend. "Are you out of your mind? Nobody's found that gold in two hundred and fifty years. What makes you think you can find it in four days?" The pace of the race around the living room picked up.

"Gunther said all we need is some evidence and we can stop them," Ralph yelled.

"Gunther doesn't know his rear from a row of trees," Howard said, thrusting occasionally on the offensive. "The only thing Johnson understands is force. We've got to blow up a dozer, shoot one of his men or something."

Ralph stopped dead in his tracks and roared at his friend, "Stop being irrational!"

Waving an eighteenth century rifle in one hand, the statue of a native American in the other and shaking his head until the tail nearly fell off his coonskin cap, Howard shrieked at the top of his lungs, "Who's being irrational!!!"

And that's when the cow patties went through the manure spreader.

"Now boys, settle down," said Edna, reentering the room with a tray full of cookies in hand. "Sit down on the couch together and have some cookies and milk."

Ralph was well aware that in Minerva, universal Truths are still recognized. People in Chicago may live under a revised Law of the Jungle, but in Minerva respect for elders and submission to authority are qualities instilled in every young person. The times may chip away at these qualities, but when really challenged, folks tended to revert to their upbringing.

Howard went around the couch one way and put his toys back in their proper place. Ralph went the other way, sat down and grabbed the first cookie from the tray.

Edna sat in her chair and smiled approvingly. Martha who was escorted by Todd followed her into the living room.

Ralph wiped off his milk mustache and asked the parental question, "Why aren't you in school?"

Todd, frustrated by his day's work, snapped, "We're on spring break."

"What brings you back to the farm when you could be doing things with your friends?" Martha asked.

"You all know we're trying to find the gold," he began. "I followed Mr. Muselle all over the farm last week trying to mark the location of the gold based on the springs and the shovels.

"He's a nice man and great history teacher. I'm not sure he knows diddlysquat about science and navigation. I rechecked the location of the springs, and their center point. That was OK. But when I measured south from the shovels, I wasn't even close to where he finished. He was way past the springs, and I am way short. I don't know what we're doing wrong," he said, taking another cookie.

Forgetting the law, which said to not talk with food in his mouth, Todd continued dropping crumbs as he went. "We've got to find it by Friday. Corey said if we don't, we'll have to work all weekend redoing our results from the Science Fair. It's due Monday."

Martha sat on the love seat next to Todd. "I told you in the beginning this was an impossible task." She looked at Ralph and Howard. "There are two little boys who wouldn't listen either." They hung their heads, grabbed the same cookie, which broke in two, giggled like kindergarten kids caught robbing the cookie jar and continued eating. "They have pinned their entire future on finding the gold and stopping a multi-million dollar highway."

"All you have to do is find the surveyor who found the deer carved in the tree and you have all the clues mentioned in the letter," Edna said, refilling everyone's glass.

"Now, Martha," Ralph said, defending his maleness. "We're not trying to find the gold, simply some historical facts that verify its existence. It's these kids chasing gold flakes in the water who are on a wild goose chase."

"Actually, Dr. Dorman doesn't think so," said Todd.

"Dorman?" asked Howard. "Isn't he that crazy professor who works at the Conservation Department?"

"He is," said Todd. "He's taken our data and is running it through his GIS program."

"What in the world is a GIS program?" Howard asked.

"Here, let me explain it the way Dr. Dorman explained it to us," Todd said scooting up to the coffee table. "Suppose the newspaper is the hydrological map Mrs. Yant gave us. Dr. Dorman enters it into the computer. Next he takes Corey's data, this magazine and enters it." He laid the magazine on top of the newspaper. "We add the clues from the letter and any other information we have, represented by this book and it pulls all the information together and spits it out on this plate." He ceremoniously placed it on top of his wobbly pile.

"He's adding a couple of embellishments of his own to the program. He says when he's done, he'll serve us the treasure on a silver platter," Todd said raising the plate in the air.

"You really think it will work," Asked Ralph.

"Sure," replied Todd.

"You kids really rely too much on computers," snorted Howard.

"Ralph," asked Edna as she straightened the Remington sculpture on the bookcase, "did I ever show you the plat map of Watertown your grandfather made?"

"No, Mother," Ralph replied.

"It's upstairs in the bottom drawer of my dresser," she said. "He platted the town. He envisioned a resort community like Harlem Springs where people would come from miles around to get our spring water. Minerva and Oneida filed their plats first, so he never bothered."

"Howard," she said adjusting the coonskin cap, "your grandfather was so upset thinking my grandfather might make money from your springs, he drew a detailed map of all the water in Watertown."

"When was that, Mother Saling?" Martha asked.

"Oh, about 1829, 1830, around in there," she said.

"And you're sure the maps are still around?" asked Ralph.

"Oh my, yes," she said. "The Jacksons and the Salings used to argue worse than the Hatfields and McCoys. Those maps were the only things that kept blood from being shed."

Ralph noticed Howard and Todd were ready to pounce upon Edna for more details.

Martha saved her mother-in-law from their attack. "We'll look for maps later," Martha said. "We have a birthday to celebrate." She went to the kitchen and returned with a cake ablaze with ninety-one candles.

"Oh my," Edna exclaimed, "I can't blow all those out."

"We'll help," said Howard.

The five of them gathered around the coffee table where the cake blazed. Ralph watched as they took their collective deep breath, the gold flames reflected off their faces and danced in their eyes. They blew and blew and blew until the last candle went out. No one asked Edna's birthday wish. She'd already told them.

Chapter Eighteen

Tuesday, April 25

There was no smoke coming from the trailer, but he was certainly on fire. "What do you mean the EPA wants us to submit core samples before we can begin to build at Saling's?" Johnson blared into the telephone. "Fernandez, I paid you big bucks so this project would go smoothly. Don't you screw things up now."

Johnson's neck was red. His face was red. He held the phone first in one hand and then the other. He pranced wildly around the room. He slammed the phone with such force that he knocked the picture of him and the governor off the wall.

"I do care if Gunther wants inspectors there when you get the samples. You work for Gunther; you get the inspectors. This is not my problem, Enrico. And Enrico, we'll do this by Friday, right? I don't want held up past Friday."

He walked to the refrigerator and poured himself one of his favorite drinks. He strolled back to the map on his wall.

Taking his fist, he hit the map. "I *will* finish this road."

He hit it again harder. "I will *finish* this road."

He hit it harder still. "I will finish *this* road."

Then, almost putting his fist through the wall, he smashed his Styrofoam cup on top of Saling's farm. "I will finish this *road.*"

"Mr. Johnson?" came a voice from the other side of the desk.

"My God, Mary Lou, are you trying to scare me to death?" he snapped.

"No sir, it's just that you've been on the phone and Mr. Davis is here to see you."

"Send him in," he said. Then realizing who was coming shouted, "Where is Huntsinger?"

* * *

In a conference room in Fred Johnson's greatest achievement, Johnson Center, George Huntsinger, his attorney and Joe Gunther sat down to have a discussion.

"Mr. Martin," Gunther began, "I have a letter here from the Secretary of Commerce stating that we are granting your client, George Huntsinger, immunity from prosecution in exchange for his testimony in this matter. Have you explained to your client the ramifications of his cooperation?"

"Yes, I have," Martin said. "He understands and wants to cooperate fully."

"Good," said Gunther. "This is an informational meeting which I would like to tape. We'll do a sworn deposition after we file charges against Johnson."

"You know," Huntsinger began, "I'd hoped it would never come to this. I've tried for months to get him to change. But every time I mention moving one step toward the right way of doing things, he takes two diabolical steps the other way."

* * *

"Davis," Johnson said, still pacing and chewing on the end of an imported cigar – and Johnson didn't smoke. "We have a problem. We're running out of time. We have to have this road to the Ohio River by August first or I lose a great deal of money. It could force me into bankruptcy. This environmental cover that I brought you in to build is critical. Understand? It is critical to us being able to finish on time."

"Now Huntsinger has been doing a good job . . . " He paused. "Mary Lou . . . find me Huntsinger!"

* * *

"I really liked my job," Huntsinger told Gunther. "I liked working with the men. I enjoyed working with the subcontractors. I liked getting the job done on time. But Fred?. . . Now I understand about being a businessman and all, but he was obsessed with money. He just couldn't make it quick enough."

* * *

"Now Davis," Johnson continued. "I don't like to sit around and wait for things to happen. I go out and make them happen. Everyone who works for me makes things happen." He knelt down, placed his hands on Davis's knees, looked him in the eyes and said, "And I want <u>you</u> to make things happen."

He jumped up and shouted at the office door. "Mary Lou, find Huntsinger. If he's not in my office in thirty minutes, tell him to find another job."

* * *

Gunther handed Huntsinger a cup of coffee. "Mr. Gunther," Huntsinger said, "I just couldn't go on working like that. I know how it was. I know how I wanted it to be. Your offer is going to make everything all right."

* * *

"I don't know why I tolerate peons like Huntsinger," Johnson said, supplicating at the top of his lungs. "I can have the best of anything I need. I hired you, didn't I?"

Davis shrank into the couch, agreeing out of self-defense.

"Huntsinger thinks he is so great - so self-righteous. But I'll show him who's boss."

* * *

Huntsinger walked around the room, coffee cup in hand. "It was a real struggle. It got to the point that everything he asked me to do was a moral decision. Everything to save a buck. I was trapped. I couldn't stand the total control. He acted like he was your friend, but he knew your every move."

* * *

"Will you help me?" Johnson was on his knees again to Davis. "Will you help me finish my road?"

"Certainly sir," Davis replied, "That's why I asked for the job in the first place."

"Good boy, good boy," Johnson said, rising to his feet. "Now, the other day I explained your job with the environmental cover. Now let me explain the big picture." Johnson was nearly back to normal. He retreated to his seat behind the desk and peered at his map.

Davis mustered his courage and approached the desk. "Mr. Johnson, I really appreciate everything you confided in me today . . . "

Johnson turned his chair around. He knew he didn't like what was coming. "But? . . . "

"We got a letter from the EPA insisting we send them core samples before we proceed."

"Is that all?" Johnson said, relieved. "I took care of that. We'll know tomorrow what we have to do."

"Thank heavens," said a conciliated Davis.

* * *

Huntsinger was beginning to relate the events leading to the second EPA report when he stopped and looked deep into Gunther's eyes. "Mr. Gunther, you are aware that if Fred Johnson finds out I'm here, he'll have me killed?"

"Don't worry, Mr. Huntsinger, "You'll have plenty of protection. Besides, how will he find out?"

* * *

Henry Muselle's Treasure

"Welcome to the Department of Natural Resources' Geographical Information System Laboratory," said Dr. Dorman, straightening his tie under his lab coat. He led his newfound pupils into the twelve foot by twenty-foot climate controlled room. They clanked across the raised floor as each of the tile slid into its metal frame.

Corey was awestruck with the potential he saw in the room. It was a simple lab. Makeshift bookshelves held hundreds of manuals. Movable racks stored reams of printouts. In one corner, a plotter slowly spit out a full color map. Dot matrix, laser and ink jet printers were strategically positioned around the room to produce reports and analyze data as required. On the desktop, flatbed scanners provided input to the two computer towers on the floor. The focal point of the room was a twenty-four inch monitor sitting in front of an ergonomically correct keyboard.

"So this is GIS," Corey said.

"Wow," was all Daniel could muster.

"Yes, Dan, we've added a couple of things since you were here," said Dr. Dorman. He was always adding things. When Dan suggested they could find the lost gold using GIS, he paused only a moment before accepting the assignment. Corey hoped Dr. Dorman would let him input some of the data. He was certain this computer held the answer to their quest.

"Let me show you what I've done," said Dr. Dorman sitting in front of his giant screen. "We are looking for one spot in which to dig," he began. "Corey, you kids think you found it through your experiment. Using your data and the related maps, we'll come up with a point we'll call the reverse pollution site. This will be one layer in the GIS program.

"Todd, you and Mr. Muselle have been following the clues to the lost gold. This will make a second layer. The intersection of the center of the springs should correspond to the intersection of lines drawn between the shovels, the rock tree and the deer tree.

"In the meantime, I have ordered a Landsat picture of the search area. If the NASA satellite photo shows what I think it will show, we should have a third layer."

"What are you talking about?" Corey asked.

"Since the 1980's NASA has been mapping the earth using different remote sensing technologies. The Landsat program identifies mineral deposits beneath the surface. None of the scientists who initially examined the photos would be looking for gold in a farm field in Ohio - especially not an area as isolated as two hundred square feet. My friends are going to do some enhancing for me. They are looking for a mineralogical anomaly on the Saling farm.

"If we then stack the three points on top of one another, we should be able to drive an imaginary stake through them straight to the gold. Let me show what we have thus far."

Dr. Dorman began his tour of the information stored in the GIS computer. "We have a topographical map of the area already loaded into the computer. We'll use it to reference the terrain." A map very similar to the one on the wall of the war room appeared on the screen.

"Next, I took our hydrological map. It was more up-to-date than yours. Through satellite remote sensing and radar imaging, we have an accurate map of surface and ground water."

"Finally, I took your data from the water samples . . . " Corey was elated. Now was when he would prove what a great scientist he was.

"Your measurements were very good, but a little too imprecise for GIS." Corey's ego deflated a bit.

"I used a census map and, from your descriptions of the collection points, assigned each of them a GPS location. I'm allowing a margin of error of plus or minus three percent.

"As Dan's dad told you, the highest concentration of precipitate was near the Saling farm. I factored those numbers into your data and did the reverse spill calculations Dan asked about." Corey nodded in agreement, although he was not quite sure he understood.

"I have great news. I have narrowed the point of pollution to an eight acre site on the Saling farm."

Eight acres, Corey thought. *That's not good enough.*

"That's about half the size of the Love Canal. It's a

bit large, but it's our first reference point," Dr. Dorman continued.

"I added the data from Mr. Muselle. As you know, the center of the springs and the triangulation of the other markers do not match. They do, however, fall within my eight acre site."

"So what are you saying," asked Corey.

"I'm saying what you already know," Dr. Dorman said. "The gold is there, but we need more precise data to find it."

"How do we do that?" Dan asked.

"Your job is to accurately pinpoint the location of the last two clues mentioned in the letter. While you do that, I'll be running a probability program.

"What in the world is a probability program?" asked Corey.

"I'm telling the computer to take each data point and vary it until they all point to a single location - i.e. the gold. It will then give me the land area necessary for that probability to occur. Watch."

He typed frantically as screen after screen popped on and off the monitor. Finally, he arrived at the proper program and hit the enter key. In a moment the computer had the answer.

Latitude: 40° 44' 28"
Longitude: 82° 28' 14"

"There's your gold," Dr. Dorman said, chuckling.

"Really?" asked Dan.

"The latitude and longitude give the exact map location in degrees, minutes and seconds," Dorman replied. "However, a square second covers quite a little piece of ground. I have asked the computer to be more precise." A few keystrokes later, the screen changed.

Correlation: 100%
Coverage Area: 30 acres

"Does this mean we start to dig?" asked Michelle.

"Only if you want to dig up thirty acres. This is the smallest area where we can get all our points to overlap."

"I don't understand what it's doing," said Corey.

"The computer takes the estimated location of the gold in one of the layers, let's say Corey's pollution layer, and draws a circle around it. The program moves to the possible gold location in the next layer - we'll make that the center of the springs at Saling's - and makes another circle. The computer then lays one circle over the other. If my two circles overlap, the computer assumes the original points are identical and it says there is a 100% correlation. It draws a square around the overlapping circles, and describes it as being the land area necessary for that to happen. If I shrink the coverage area, the computer will tell me how much of the overlapping circles lie within the area. After work, I will ask it to use every variation possible to find a point within our eight acres. The more points we can give it, the more accurate and quicker it will be."

"How close are we now?" Dan wanted to know.

"Well, let's see," said Dr. Dorman.

A couple of keystrokes later, the computer began thinking. It took much longer. Finally, the screen displayed:

Correlation: **5%**
Coverage Area: **8 acres**

"There is only a five percent correlation. Only five percent of two layers overlap. We have much work to do," Dr. Dorman said.

The young scientists, now turned treasure hunters, agreed.

* * *

"Well Mr. Johnson, I am happy to report that everything is going fine," Davis said. "The collection of core samples went just as planned.'

"That's good. That's good," Johnson replied.

"Fernandez will have inspectors at the job site right on schedule."

"Fine job. Fine job," Johnson remarked not really paying attention.

"I'm going to oversee the work. I've been told that Mr. Huntsinger is in isolation in the Mercy Hospital with hepatitis."

"Well, I guess he'll have to be excused. He could have had someone call," Johnson complained.

"I can't see any reason why we can't be to the river by August first." The phone rang. Johnson answered it.

"Uh huh . . . Oh, he is . . . You don't say. Imagine that . . . That's very interesting. Don't worry. I'll take care of it. Thanks very much for calling. Good-bye."

He looked at Davis with a menacing glare. "That was my good friend and employee, the maintenance man at Johnson Center. It seems Mr. Huntsinger is not in the hospital. He and his attorney have been having long talks with Mr. Gunther." He leafed through his personal phone book, and then dialed a number. "Listen to this."

"Hey Guido, Johnson here. How you doing? Listen, I have a favor to ask. Do you remember my good friend George Huntsinger? No, I don't want you should break his legs," Johnson said chuckling. He then became dead serious. "I want you to go to Mercy Hospital, room 312. I want you should smash his head. Then take his body and chop it into little pieces. Then put them in little baggies and do the compassionate thing. Sell them to the missionaries who preach to the cannibals. Have them give it to their converts as instant people - just add water."

Davis could hear the laughter on the other end of the phone.

"Guido, by the weekend. I'm in kind of a hurry. Thanks, bye,"

"You weren't serious, were you?" asked Davis, half afraid to hear the answer.

"No, it was all a joke," said Johnson, smiling. "But when you read about it in the papers Monday, remember you heard it here first." He swung around in his chair and then swung back. "Which, by the way, makes you an accessory to murder. Have a nice day."

* * *

Henry traipsed along with the menagerie through Howard Jackson's woods. Corey had invited him to come along with the young scientists to find the tree where the stone had been lodged. Tired of being assaulted in the teacher's lounge for encouraging "such foolishness in the minds of promising young scientists," Henry invited Mrs. Talkington to join them. She brought up the rear as Todd, Corey, Dan and Michelle marched behind Howard.

Howard led the group at a pretty good pace. Corey was trying to carry on a conversation while dodging tree limbs.

Henry's mind wandered. He thought about the significance of a trail in the woods for a hiker. He wondered how his ancestors might determine if they were on a right trail. The first plan might be to follow the well-worn areas made by the many people who traveled that way before. As the terrain becomes rougher, they might look for trail markers left for their benefit. If the trail was well traveled, prior travelers may have left a milepost. These mileposts would not only indicate how far it was to their destination, but also how far they'd come. Fellow travelers on the same trail probably used different techniques to keep them on the trail, but at a milepost, they would stop and contemplate the difficulties between the techniques and their individual goals.

Henry imagined that many times several travelers probably converged at a milepost, providing different options for reaching the same goal. Similarly, it was important to recognize mileposts along the trail of life. Perhaps this tree was one of them as he set out to find more clues to his ancestor's treasure.

"But Mr. Jackson," Henry heard Corey say to Howard, "I know our probability of correlation is only five percent. That's why finding this tree is so important. It will give us another marker to narrow our search field."

Henry Muselle's Treasure   181

"I don't give a hoot about GPS, GIS or gee whiz," Howard commented. "My only concern is finding that tree and some sort of marking to prove this is a historical site. Did you bring the rock, Michelle?"

"Yes, sir," she replied, hurrying along the well-worn trail.

"Michelle, do you really think this is the rock out of the tree?" Todd asked.

"Personally, I thought you were all crazy until Corey and I came across the package with the rock in it," she said, tolerating his presence. "It was really bizarre. I asked my Mom about it and she said she doesn't remember anyone in the family ever mentioning it. It had to be in the trunk a long time."

Henry smiled as he listened to Todd. "It looks like everyone has a stake in finding the gold," Todd remarked, apparently trying to get back in Michelle's good graces. "For your sake, I hope we find it."

"Todd, I didn't know you cared," Michelle said, with a coquettish smile and a flirting flip of her hair.

He blushed. "I'd better wait for Mr. Muselle," he said, letting her go on ahead. They came out of the woods into a clearing, which joined the backside of Ralph Saling's field. About twenty feet from the edge of the woods was a dilapidated fencerow. A combination of spit rails and stone pillars, the fence had long ago been replaced by a single strand of electrified wire. It was so remote; it didn't even warrant repairs for ornamental reasons. Just the same, it was recognizable as a fence. The old gate lay as a pile of rubble next to the tree stump. Its supportive bolts and nails had turned to rust decades ago.

The tree stump was nearly six feet tall. It was cut cleanly at the top. A notch on one side, the uneven taper of the trunk and a split, which ran nearly to the ground, indicated the tree met its demise in a violent manner. The split on Saling's side of the tree was nearly perfect. It was as if someone had driven a wedge in the top of the tree. On the Jackson side, however, the split began with an indentation. It looked like something had been stuck in the tree but removed.

"OK, this is it. My old stump is now a historic landmark. Who's going to try the stone?" Howard asked.

"I think Mr. Muselle should. It's his treasure," Mrs. Talkington said rather facetiously.

"It's not my treasure, Mrs. Talkington. I just have a very large interest in it," Henry said. The group all laughed.

"I would be honored to see if this fits. Michelle, the stone please." The group tittered as the stone passed from hand to hand until Henry held it above the hole in the stump. He examined the stone, and then laid it gently in the tree.

"Well, it doesn't fit that way," he said downheartedly.

"No, look at that bump," said Todd. "Turn it this way and it will go." It still sat precariously on its perch.

"No, no," Howard said. "Look at the groove. Turn it a quarter turn to the right and it will go.

Henry picked up the stone, turned it slightly and sat it in the hole. Although the top of the stone extended beyond the top of the tree, the bottom fit like the piece of a puzzle.

As he placed it there, flashbacks of times past raced through his head. The 10th Frenchman had placed the rock in the tree. It was his sign to future hunters of the burial site of the gold. Placed away from the treasure, it pointed to unthinkable wealth. Henry wondered how his grandfather found the location of the stone. What made the Frenchman tell him?

"Well, I'll be," said Howard. "I always thought squirrels or a coon made that hole."

"Well, that proves it, Mrs. Talkington," said Todd. "We've found the gold."

"No," she said. "This is very intriguing. I've heard so much about this lost gold, but this is the first time I've seen proof it really might exist."

"Would you say this is historical evidence?" Howard asked hopefully.

"It at least supports the claims in the letter," she replied. "But it doesn't validate the existence of the gold." Howard took a picture of the rock in the tree anyway.

"Now back to your question, Todd," she said, being the teacher again. "Remember, yours is a pollution experiment. I understand you've identified your pollution as gold. If you include that in your results, you must be able to identify the source for your gold. The legend of the lost gold is not an identifiable source."

The group discussed for a while what they had and had not found. This was truly a milepost. As Henry examined the tree and the rock, his hopes were encouraged. Each person counted the costs of continuing or not continuing to the goal. New strategies were planned and new commitments were made.

Michelle put the rock back in her daypack and set off with Howard, Dan, Corey and Mrs. T. through the woods to Howard's house.

After they left, and Henry and Todd were alone, Henry pulled out his trusty GPS computer and took a reading at the tree. "Let's follow this due east and see where it takes us."

"Sounds good to me," Todd quipped.

Henry could tell Todd still wanted to dig now. He explained to Todd that with Corey's revelation of the GIS results and Howard's need for documentation he'd have to be more patient than he had ever been.

The tree was closer to the Saling farm than Henry realized. They went just a short distance when they could begin seeing the flags marking the springs blowing in the breeze. Henry was wearing a new gadget, a counter to measure mileage as he walked. They were not concerned when they ended north of the center of the springs. It didn't bother them that the location a half-mile from the tree was a little short of where they thought it should be.

Henry took another reading. Dr. Dorman would now have two more trail markers to add to his computer program. Back in the lab, the computer was thinking. The display read:

Correlation: 100%
Coverage Area: 28 acres

Chapter Nineteen

Henry Muselle's Journal
Tuesday, April 25

We located another clue today, however, I fear there will be no happy ending to this story. Our faith lies in a computer. Ten of us are frantically racing the clock to solve an unsolvable mystery. One madman threatens to quash us all. We are all acting in a Pollyanna world where nothing can harm us, and yet I feel bad things may be right around the corner.

I want to believe in Guardian's guiding, but his tribe's fate was worse than mine. The people he worked so hard to help enslaved him. They took his treasure, his land, his lifestyle and his culture and denigrated him and his nation to a lower than second-class status.

We have traded faith in a Creator for faith in the Creation. Worse than that, we look for solutions not in people, but in things. These things - this technology - become the focal point of our search. Now the Creation has become the Creator and our search for answers is found in our reverence for bytes. Truth, justice and love are simply virtues studied in fairy tales.

Why can't we learn from our past mistakes? Can't these treasure hunters see that there is more to lose or gain here than $13 million?

The search must go on. We cannot stop now. Too many people have too much to lose.

Chapter Twenty

Thursday, April 24

Correlation: 5%
Coverage Area: 8 acres

Corey and Todd had finally convinced Mrs. Talkington to come with them to the Department of Natural Resources to see how their experiment was progressing. For her, even eight-thirty in the morning was not too early to get started on science.

"As you can see, Mrs. Talkington," Dr. Dorman said showing her the computer, "the information the children have given us is providing some very interesting outcomes."

"Just what does all this mean?" she asked.

"Has Corey explained the theory of GIS to you?" Dr. Dorman inquired.

"Yes, he has."

"My contribution to the GIS system has been to enable us to determine the correlation between points in multiple layers," Dorman explained. "We are having difficulty, however, finding a common point in the gold layer. Here, let me show you."

He took a piece of paper and drew four "X's" and a circle in the middle. "Here are the four springs on the hydrological map with the center marked with a circle." He drew a large square encompassing all the marks. "This is the target area our program identified as the source of the pollution the kids found. As you can see, the center of the springs is included in that area and so there is a 100% correlation."

"So you haven't proved anything," she said curtly.

"No, not yet," Dr. Dorman said disconcertingly. "But the kids gave us other clues which are in a different layer. Here is where our problem begins. The first clue is the shovels, which are supposed to be six hundred paces north of the approximate center of the four springs. However, we have four points, two, which Mr. Muselle determined, and two, which Todd discovered. None of these are within twenty yards of the center of the springs."

Mrs. Talkington was unimpressed.

"We also have the location of the stone tree one half mile to the west. However, an easterly line drawn through any of the four shovel points does not intersect the center of the springs. According to the computer, the probability of these points leading to a single point requires a land area of 30 acres. That's why we need more points to compare."

"My assistant has been loading the map of Watertown and the water rights map into the system. We have been very fortunate thus far, because all the maps have used the benchmarks from the original survey of the territory done in 1797. That insures us of the proper alignment of each map."

Mrs. T. listened intently.

Corey was elated. He was nearly to his goal. It didn't dawn on him the number of people with whom he had talked. He didn't realize how aggressive he had been to get to this point. He just knew he'd gone from his basement workroom to a state of the art laboratory and he could not contain himself.

"Now let me see if I understand," Mrs. T. finally said. "The results of the pollution experiment are represented by this square."

"That's right," Dr. Dorman said.

"And because you can't precisely say there is gold buried here, you cannot pinpoint any more accurately than this box, the source of the pollution," she continued.

"That's also correct," Dr. Dorman agreed.

"Then it is safe to say that your calculations neither support nor reject the students' hypothesis since the clues you refer to are based on folklore and not historical fact?" the old biddy continued in self-righteous indignation.

"I'm afraid," Dr. Dorman admitted, scratching his head, "as a scientist, I have to agree."

"Well then children," she gloated, "forget the gold. Concentrate on pollution and turn your project in by Monday." She thanked Dr. Dorman for his enlightening discussion, then turned and walked out of the lab.

The young scientists were crushed. Dr. Dorman tried to console them. He congratulated them on their initiative and resourcefulness. He noted most great scientists did not find what they were hunting for on the first attempt. It didn't matter. Corey was content to finish the report, as he had wanted to do all along. They left the lab, climbed on their bikes and headed home.

"Dr. Dorman?" the secretary's voice came over the speakerphone. "NASA's on line one. They have your satellite photograph. Dr. Murdoch wants you to come to Cleveland right away. He says you won't believe what he's found."

* * *

Ralph tapped his spoon on the side of the coffee cup and asked everyone to take their seats. He was hosting an unusual meeting at the farmhouse. The rumbling of the dump trucks going by and the cloud of dust on the hill reminded every one of the urgency of the task.

"I've asked you all to come here this morning," Ralph began. "You are the people I believe have the knowledge and ability to stop the road."

The four young scientists were there as well as Henry. Howard wouldn't be kept away, and of course Martha was there to help her husband.

"You all have been running all over my farm for nearly two weeks bothering me about this lost gold," Ralph continued. "Martha and I have talked it over. We've decided all the lawyers and politicians in the world can't stop this road. But if we find the gold, we can."

"All right," Todd shouted. The others whispered approval among themselves.

"There are two ways we can approach this," Ralph said, pacing back and forth like Patton addressing the troops. "The first is to find some historical documentation which we can get to Gunther in Canton. I spoke to him this morning. He says he has all the paperwork ready. All he has to do is fill in the name of the historical document and then present it to the judge who will issue the injunction."

"What's the second way?" Corey inquired.

"We physically dig up the gold," he replied. A hush fell over the room.

"It's really not going to be all that difficult," Ralph continued.

"The kids discovered the GIS program. According to Dr. Dorman, on both the water map and the plat of Watertown, in 1829 there are four springs north and west of where we find them today. Since both those maps were made before the canal was built, he assumed that construction might have disturbed a great deal of the water table in the area. Our 100% correlation area is now only 12 acres."

The group gasped. "The area is cut in half by finding just one point," Howard exclaimed.

"Now, he's still working to get Michelle's stone tree in the picture. The Department of Natural Resources feels there's enough merit to the project, they have given him the go ahead to work on this full time."

"I wonder if Gunther's group had anything to do with that?" added Howard.

Corey spoke up. "Dr. Dorman's lab left a message on our answering machine. He is going to Cleveland to pick up the satellite photograph from NASA. He seems to think it was an important discovery."

"As Corey and Dr. Dorman work on the scientific aspects, we must concentrate on finding historical documentation," Ralph said. "And, we must hurry."

"What's the big rush?" asked Howard. "Aside from those bulldozers bearing down on your field?"

"Gunther says he can't stall Johnson beyond Monday. The results of the core samples will be in tomorrow, and he'll have to give the go ahead," Ralph explained.

"I've taken the liberty to assign you to search in different locations. As near as I can figure, we want to look for material, which came from the years 1750-1755.

"Dan, Michelle and Corey, I want you to go to the historical society and the library. They both have good collections, but I don't know if they go back that far.

"Henry and Todd. There's an old museum near Hanoverton. They specialize in Indian history of the area. Maybe there's something there."

"Martha and I will go to Lisbon and search the court records. I'm interested in the survey of 1797. They might have some early information on the area."

"And what do I do?" asked Howard.

"You go home and keep an eye on Johnson. If anybody finds anything, they'll call you, and you can call Gunther."

"Any questions?" Ralph asked. No one raised a hand. "Good. We'll meet back here at five and see what we need to do tomorrow."

They finished eating Martha's breakfast snacks then climbed on bicycles and into cars to begin the final hunt.

* * *

Corey, Dan and Michelle reached the library and split up. Michelle went to the genealogy room and began searching. Corey browsed through the computerized card catalog. Dan went downstairs and rifled through the Ohio History collection.

Once each hour, they met in the reading room. They finally agreed there was a void from 1750-1755. They moved on to the historical society. It was housed in an old bank building on the square downtown. The bank lobby was where the main collection was housed. Pictures adorned the walls. Display cases were filled with memorabilia from defunct industries. After looking at the collection and perusing the archives, they got permission to look through uncataloged items. They went down the narrow staircase into the dimly lit basement. The room was lined with boxes stacked waist deep on both sides of the room. On each box was a piece of masking tape with the donor's name and a general description of the contents. There was an empty space at the end of the row. They scrutinized each box and then moved it into the empty space. They worked their way down the wall searching and moving.

About half way down the room, they found a box donated by Cecil Wright. Cecil spent his life collecting artifacts of Ohio Indians. He had a collection of more than three thousand arrowheads, tomahawks, pieces of Indian pottery and other relics. These were neatly framed and packaged for display. One box contained books, magazines and journals from the nineteenth century. Many of these were from the original settlers of Minerva. They emptied the box on top of the other boxes and began sorting through its contents.

"I've never seen this much old stuff before," said Dan.

"You should see our attic," Michelle said. "I don't think anyone in our family ever threw anything away."

Corey was absorbed in the wealth of information at their fingertips.

"Do you really think we'll find something?" Dan asked.

"Before I found the rock, I'd have said no," Michelle commented. "Now I think anything is possible."

Dan pulled out a roll of paper about eighteen inches long. "What's this?" he asked.

Corey was intrigued. "I don't know. Let's see."

They unrolled a map printed in 1806, which had the title, *The Great Indian Trail in The Seven Ranges*. There, in great detail, were the communities from the state line into Tuscarawas County. The map was drawn to scale and the benchmarks from the 1797 survey were highlighted. Also rolled with the map was a sheet of onionskin paper with a section of map traced on it.

Corey compared it to the original map. "These are Minerva landmarks around 1800. Look, here's Minerva, Oneida, Malvern and Watertown."

"What good does this do us?" Michelle asked.

"Yeah, we already have a map of Watertown," said Dan.

"But this one shows where the Great Trail went through town," Corey said.

"So?" Michelle was not impressed.

"What if east wasn't east and west wasn't west?" Corey asked, contemplating the two maps.

"Now what are you talking about?" Dan asked.

"If someone asks you where Minerva is in relation to Canton, you tell them we are eighteen miles southeast, right?" Corey replied.

"I guess so," Dan said.

"But the road doesn't travel due Southeast," Corey explained. "It goes south, then east, then north, then back south. When you're finished, you've traveled eighteen miles and you're southeast of Canton."

"Speak English, man," Michelle said.

"The stone tree is supposed to be a half mile west of the gold and the deer tree is supposed to be a mile east. Maybe it's west along the Great Trail, not due west. This map shows where the Great Trail was. It's another clue!"

"This might be the last clue we need for the GIS puzzle," said Michelle.

"No, we have to find the deer in the tree," Corey reminded them.

"Well, we can't worry about that now. Don't just stand there," Dan said beginning to put things back. "Let's get this to Dr. Dorman."

* * *

It was a long ride from Minerva to Lisbon. It gave Ralph and Martha the opportunity to talk about the many possible outcomes now at hand.

"I don't believe we're doing this," said Ralph. "Last week everything seemed so simple. The road was going to wreck our lives."

"I know, I could never have imagined that scuffle at the science fair would lead to this," Martha agreed. "Do you really think that Henry Muselle is who he says he is?"

"I didn't," said Ralph, "but I don't know why anyone would be this dedicated to a story this old if he didn't have something to gain from it. And that Todd sure is a terror isn't he?" Ralph said smiling.

"I couldn't believe him at the science fair," Martha said. In all my years of being a judge, no one has ever put on a performance like he did."

Ralph turned serious. "If he hadn't pushed the issue, you and I wouldn't be on our way to Lisbon."

"I know, he certainly made me appreciate what we have," Martha replied.

"If we lose this, do you think we ought to stay and make a go of it somehow?" Ralph asked with a quiver in his voice.

"I sure would be willing to try," Martha said. "Isn't that the courthouse up there on the right?"

They walked into the courthouse and started their search. It didn't take long to figure out the people in the county government were more interested in preserving their jobs than in preserving history. Ralph and Martha went first to the Recorder's Office to see if he had a record of the survey. He told them it was done ten years before the county was established. He had no reason to have it.

They went to the Probate Court to find estate records of the period and documents of land transfers. The clerk had the same problem as the recorder. The county was not in existence during the period they were searching. In addition, Ralph and Martha needed to know the name of the deceased who owned the land in order to find his estate.

Finally, in desperation, they ended up in the Engineer's office. He certainly would be the keeper of the county maps. George Weir was the third member of his family to serve as County Engineer. He was protective of his professional privacy and had trained the office staff to shield him from routine public inquiries. However, the staff had come into his office so many times to find old maps, he had to make an appearance to find out who was so inquisitive about early county history.

Ralph and Martha explained the problem at hand. George invited them into his office where the older maps were kept. George's office had been a judge's chamber before the courthouse was remodeled. He had an abundance of shelves, which were filled with antique plat books and ancient maps. The old oak desk and filing cabinets were reminiscent of another century. On top of one of the cabinets was the cross-section of a tree nearly a foot high. The bark had fallen off long ago. The grain was weathered and faded. At first glance it looked like a circular file on top of the cabinet. As Ralph walked past to look at a map hanging on the wall, he glanced at the carving on the stump, but paid no attention.

It was Martha who stopped and studied the likeness of a deer carved in the tree. "What is this, Mr. Weir?" she asked.

"Oh, that's part of a tree my grandfather found when he was surveying near Minerva," George replied.

"Why did he keep it?" Ralph asked.

"I don't really know. It was supposed to be a part of some local legend. He always collected interesting artifacts he stumbled upon."

"Do you have any idea exactly where he found it?" Martha asked.

George walked to the cabinet and turned the piece on end. "I remember there was something painted on the bottom. I never paid much attention. We have so much junk like this around the house. We're afraid to throw any of it away for fear it might be important. It's all going to go to the Historical Society some day"

"Oh, it's important all right," Martha said.

On the bottom of the stump, the surveyor had painted the latitude and longitude of the stump with the notation "lost gold deer tree 7/8/04."

Ralph and Martha gazed in amazement at this unexpected treasure. The final clue. Stuck on top of a filing cabinet twenty miles and ninety years from where it was supposed to be.

Ralph asked George, "Do you have a piece of paper? I know someone who is very interested in these numbers."

* * *

Hanoverton was known as a canal town. Located on the banks of Sandy Creek, it was at the crossroads of two major thoroughfares and the Sandy Beaver Canal. It didn't reach its prime as a stopping place for stagecoach lines until long after the French and Indian War. But its history as a resting spot along The Great Trail and a gathering place for local tribes was remembered at Fort Hanover. Although fictitious, the Fort attempted to recreate the pre-Revolutionary atmosphere of the area. The stockade fence bordered by two blockhouses welcomed visitors to a bygone era.

The sight took Henry's breath away. The log buildings with their dirt floors gave him a sense of deja vu. Mannequins dressed in French uniforms and Indian war dress were an eerie sight to Todd and Henry. He could see Todd was ready to overturn rocks and dig up the weapons magazine to find the clue for which they were searching. Henry, in his usual tactful manner, explained to the owner his history and their quest.

They were escorted through the trading post and into the barracks. In the back of the barracks on a bed with ropes woven back and forth for springs laid an old leather suitcase.

"Henry," the owner said, "I was given this by a French family from Pittsburgh. They said their ancestor was a supply sergeant at Fort Duquesne. They said the historical society in Pittsburgh wasn't interested in its contents because this fellow wasn't important enough. They heard about my museum and brought it here."

Henry slowly opened the suitcase. It was filled to overflowing with manuscripts written with quill pen and India ink. One by one, Todd and Henry unfolded each piece.

They found supply lists, pay vouchers, rosters and equipment requisitions all dated 1754 and 1755. There were several documents where the name Henry Muselle appeared. Henry laid those aside. They were important, but he didn't feel any of these were the key to their search. After about an hour, they had several stacks of manuscripts. They were separated in piles according to their content.

"This is all very interesting, but I think we're just wasting our time."

"I think the answer's here. We can't quit now," Todd said. He reached into the suitcase and pulled out another slip. He gently unfolded it. His eyes grew twice their size. "Mr. Muselle," he gasped. "Look at this."

Henry took the piece of paper. It was a requisition for sixteen pack horses, shovels, rifles and provisions for an expedition to Fort Detroit. The purpose of the expedition was to transport the "financial resources" of the fort to Fort Detroit for safekeeping. It listed the ten men assigned to the expedition. Henry Muselle was one of them!

"This is it. This proves it. Come on, let's thank Mr. Weir and get this to Gunther." They put the requisition in a small brown pouch for safekeeping, jumped in the little green car and headed for Minerva.

It was only eight miles from the fort to Minerva, but in the green car a little jaunt could turn into a great adventure. The headliner had long ago been ripped out because it sagged so much it hindered the driver's view. The vinyl seats were split in so many places it was almost uncomfortable to sit on the thin cloth seat covers.

Todd had ridden in the car before, and he had sworn he would never ride in it again. He wasn't sure if it was because the floor mat only partially covered the hole in the floor or because the front seat didn't lock on the passenger's side, but it seemed the only thing holding him into the car when it came to a stop was the seatbelt.

They went only a couple of miles when, for no apparent reason, the car stopped running. Henry let it coast to the side of the highway. "I'll bet the battery cable has come loose again."

"Why don't you buy a new car?" Todd asked.

"On my salary? Why do you think I'm hunting for this treasure?"

Henry popped the hood and inspected the battery. Everything seemed fine. He wiggled each spark plug wire. Every one was tight. He touched the distributor cap to make sure it was tight. As he gave it a slight turn, it exploded into a thousand pieces. "Well, so much for a quick fix." He looked at his watch. "It's three o'clock. We have to have the document to Gunther by four-thirty so he can make it to the court before five."

He handed the pouch to Todd. "Take this and start walking toward Minerva. The first house you come to, call Howard. Tell him to alert Gunther and then come and pick you up. Then keep walking. Every minute counts."

Todd took the pouch, stuck it inside his shirt and began walking toward Minerva.

"By the way, tell Howard to send me a tow truck."

* * *

Todd walked the quarter mile to the next house and called Howard. Howard said he'd call Gunther and come get Todd. It would take about ten minutes. He said he would be in his red pickup.

Todd left the house and started for Minerva at a dead run. It only lasted a hundred yards. Feet became yards and seconds turned into minutes as he contemplated his mission. He could visualize the GIS computer narrowing the search area. He imagined bells and sirens sounding as it spit out the location of the gold.

He stumbled over a chuckhole. The pouch bounced underneath his shirt. He could see the rage in Johnson's face as Gunther handed him the injunction. Imagine, he thought, a multimillion dollar road project and I'm carrying the document which can stop it.

Todd never noticed the red pickup cross the centerline and pull in behind him. The sound of the horn nearly scared him to death. When he saw the color of the truck, he ran back, opened the door and jumped in the front seat.

"Need a ride to Minerva?" the driver asked.

"You're not Howard," Todd said, realizing his mistake.

"Howard?" the man inquired.

"Howard Jackson. He's on his way to pick me up," Todd said.

"It's not safe for a boy like you to walk along a busy highway," the man continued. "I know Howard. Why don't I take you to his place? We'll watch for his truck along the way."

Todd figured it was a good way to make up some time, so he agreed. Besides, this was Minerva, and neighbors always helped neighbors. There was nothing to worry about accepting a ride from a stranger.

"Thanks a lot," said Todd. "You're a real lifesaver." He held out his hand to shake the man's hand. "I'm Todd Evans."

The man took his hand and shook it vigorously. "Nice to meet you Todd . . . I'm Fred Johnson."

Chapter Twenty-One

If there was one problem Todd had, it was knowing when to keep his mouth shut. He had no reason to know the Fred Johnson who was kind enough to give him a ride was the same Fred Johnson he had vowed to stop.

"Aren't you the man from the science fair?" Todd asked.

"Sure am, best judge at the show," Johnson remarked. "That was some experiment of yours."

"Yeah, we think we found the lost French gold."

"Oh really, is that what you're doing way out here - hunting for it?"

"No, we think it's on Mr. Saling's farm."

"Really, on Mr. Saling's farm. Have you told him?"

"Oh, yes. In fact, *he's* the reason I'm out here."

"He is?"

"Yeah, he had this big meeting with Mr. Gunther of the EPA and he told us if we found this document that could prove that the treasure was real, they'd have to stop building the road."

Now he had Johnson's attention. "But it's just a legend, right?"

"No, Dr. Dorman over at the Department of Natural Resources thinks with our data, and his stuff, he can tell us where to dig."

"And where might that be?"

"Right in the middle of the four springs at Mr. Saling's." Todd bounced in his seat as the right front tire of the truck dropped off the pavement.

"Sorry," Johnson said, "but you don't have any real proof that the gold existed."

"Oh yeah, Mr. Muselle and I just found this old paper which told all the details of the expedition. He thinks it's just what Mr. Gunther wanted."

Todd glowed when he talked about his friendships with Ralph Saling and Henry Muselle. He paid no attention to the myriad of turns Fred was making, and that the roads were becoming less and less familiar.

Fred's demeanor was changing. "So, did Henry give you the memo to deliver to Howard?" he asked. Todd started to answer, but realizing he was in unfamiliar territory he hesitated.

"Well, did Henry give you the paper?" Fred insisted. The trees were flying passed at an increasing pace. The truck fishtailed as it slid through a particularly sharp turn. Fred was breathing harder. The veins on his neck were bulging.

"Did he?" Fred's eyes were wild with rage. Todd moved closer to the door of the truck.

"Yeah . . . uh, no . . . I mean," Todd stammered and clutched his chest where the pouch was hidden.

"You've got it, you little gutter snipe," Fred yelled. He reached for Todd and dragged him across the seat by the front of his shirt. The truck slid to the side of the road. Fred threw Todd into the door, grabbed the steering wheel and pulled the truck back onto the road.

Todd grasped his head where it hit the door leaving his chest exposed. In an instant, Fred ripped open Todd's shirt and grabbed the pouch.

"I've got it now!" Fred screamed.

"Oh, no you don't," Todd yelled. Suddenly it was not an ancient memo he was fighting for. It was his prize possession – a baseball. He was not looking at Fred Johnson, but his father - taunting him, teasing him, ridiculing his every pitch. Todd lunged at Fred, caught the pouch in one hand and pulled down on the steering wheel with the other.

The truck skidded sideways down the road. Fred, still in command of the pouch, stretched Todd's arm until it almost came out of its socket. At the same time his huge left hand let go of the steering wheel and came crashing into Todd's face.

Youthful blood splattered the inside of the truck as Todd's limp body crashed again into the passenger's door leaving Fred holding the contested pouch. In one movement, Fred stuffed the pouch under his leg and gained control of the runaway vehicle. "No one stops Fred Johnson!" he proclaimed. "No one!"

The truck picked up speed. He maneuvered closer and closer to the edge of the road. The hillside dropped away precipitously. Todd's bloody body lay dazed and bruised on the seat next to him. Johnson reached over and unlatched the door. Holding the truck on a steady course, he picked up Todd's limp body and threw it toward the loosened door. "Here's where you get out kid!" he yelled. Todd's body flew out of the truck and disappeared in the underbrush.

The door of the truck smashed into an oncoming tree. The impact hurled the door back toward the truck. The door slammed shut and thousands of pieces of glass from the shattered window filled the cab. "Damn tree!!" Fred exclaimed, "I got too close." The truck careened down the road at its breakneck pace.

Todd's body flew through the air like a bullet shot from a gun. The underbrush grabbed at his clothing, ripping and tearing his new outfit, but barely slowing him down. The laws of physics finally took control and he descended into the underbrush. He collided with small trees, medium size bushes and large rocks before finally coming to rest.

The dust settled in the road. The trees regained their composure after their battle with the man-made tornado. Once again, all was quiet on the country road. On the side of the hill laid the crumpled remains of a boy whose only crime was that he wanted to do something important.

* * *

It didn't take long to get from the Historical Society to the Department of Natural Resources. The state leased space in the old Owens China Company building. Once a thriving depression era pottery making fine dinnerware from rich local clay, the tile building was now a shell in which enterprising companies could construct freestanding state-of-the-art facilities. The DNR pioneered the concept with its GIS facility.

Corey, Dan and Michelle were eager to see how their map of The Great Trail would affect the correlation of the other clues. It was a triumph for the three of them. Dan discovered the GIS process. Michelle hoped her stone tree would lie on the edge of the Trail. Corey was waiting to see where the water samples would appear on the composite map. Their doubts in their ability to find the gold were waning.

"Where's Dr. Dorman?" asked Corey. "We've got to see him right away."

"He's not here," said Dr. Rossiter, Dorman's assistant. "He's still in Cleveland getting a picture from NASA."

"We found this map of The Great Trail," Dan said presenting the scroll to Rossiter. "We thought it might be important."

They unrolled the map. Corey began a detailed description about the relevance of the new find. Finally, Rossiter agreed to scan the map into the program.

"This will take most of the afternoon," Rossiter said. "Why don't you stop by in the morning? Dr. Dorman should be here by then."

* * *

"So, all the core samples show some wetlands properties," Ralph explained to Gunther on the other end of the telephone. "Well, we should have expected that based on Fernandez's earlier work."

"I think it's good you have Fernandez face Johnson with the results. He won't be happy . . . Oh, but he's going to let on like everything is OK, good idea. Maybe Johnson will slip up.

"You say there are a couple of oddities in a few of the samples which Fernandez is going to review. You don't suppose it's the gold do you?" Ralph and Gunther had a good laugh. They needed something to break the tension.

* * *

Corey watched as the light on the scanner went out, and the buzzer sounded. The message on the computer screen said, "Your document has been successfully scanned."

Dr. Rossiter looked at his watch. It was five-thirty and past time to go home. "I'm sorry Dr. Dorman isn't back. I'd have thought he'd be back here by now. He's gets to talking with his buddies at NASA and loses all track of time." He took the map from the scanner and rolled it up. "I'd really like to go home, but if I don't have this done for Dr. Dorman in the morning, he'll really be ticked."

He sat down to the computer and called up the data screen for the French gold clues. Corey watched in awe. He was in scientific heaven. Rossiter precisely entered the coordinates for the stone tree and the deer carving into the database. He exited the database and told the computer to compile the data. The message appeared on the screen. "Compiling . . . 75 minutes to completion."

"When this is finished, it will be pretty easy to start the correlation program." He looked at his watch. "Boy, my daughter has a soccer match in twenty minutes. She sure is going to be upset if I'm not there."

"I'm fairly familiar with computers," Corey said. "If you show me how, I could start it for you."

"That's a great idea. Dr. Dorman likes you, so I'm sure he won't mind. I'll write down the steps, and if you have any problems, here is a pager number. You call me and I'll come back after the match and straighten things out. I'll lock the door, so all you have to do is make sure it closes tight."

"Sounds great," said Corey. On another computer, Rossiter showed Corey the steps to start the next program. Corey wrote down each step precisely. Rossiter thanked him and left for the soccer match.

Corey slowly walked around the lab surveying each piece of equipment and wondering about its purpose. He checked out the titles of the books on the shelves, some of whose titles he couldn't even pronounce. He walked to the coffee machine and poured himself a cup. He was stuck in the lab at least another hour. After the GIS program complied a single map, he could run Dr. Dorman's program. It would run most of the night, but with the screen dimmed, it wouldn't hurt the computer. He could go home and Dr. Dorman would find the results when he came into the office in the morning.

Corey sat down, propped his feet on the desk and began reading a copy of the latest "Technology Today." He was home. If only Todd could see him now.

* * *

The whir of the computer and the drone of the air conditioning drowned out the sound of the spring crickets outside. The sunset was ablaze with the soft colors of spring. The air was crisp with the promise of summer.

Spring provides many promises - the promise of a new beginning, the promise of undiscovered treasures. It is a feeling that has permeated the air since the beginning of time. Johnson could feel it in the newly turned earth. Ralph and Martha could feel it in the pens of the newborn calves. Corey could feel it in the confines of the GIS lab. Henry could feel it in the notebooks of his ancestors he searched each evening looking for help to find the treasure. Huntsinger could feel it with every word he wrote in his deposition.

* * *

Todd lay bruised and broken in the underbrush. He tried to wake up, but couldn't. He fell back into a deep sleep and dreamed he could hear the British soldiers as they sat around their campfire reflecting about the skirmish a few days earlier. He saw a Native American scout as he roamed the woods looking for a suitable place to spend the night.

Ten miles from the site of the skirmish, hidden in deep underbrush, he saw Guardian come upon the inanimate form of a young brave apparently mauled by a wild animal. The scout rolled the boy over and found his shirt torn and chest scratched. His face was bloody and swollen, the result of a blow from a giant paw. His right forearm was swollen and bruised by the fall he took after the animal hurled him from his clutches. The boy was barely breathing and made no sound as the Indian touched each part of his body, checking for injuries.

Todd could tell the warrior knew better than to move the boy, so the wooded slope became camp for the night. He built a fire to warm the two of them. He used his shirt as a basket to ferry needles from a nearby stand of pine. This would be his mattress tonight. The young boy would benefit from the blanket the warrior normally used. He poured water from his leather canteen and washed the caked blood from the boy's face and chest. He fashioned a splint from branches and secured it to the deformed arm with rawhide lace.

When he was sure the boy was comfortable, he went down the hill into the valley and carefully uprooted several purple coneflowers. He carried them back to where the boy lay. One by one, he cut off and cleaned the roots. He meticulously sliced the roots and let the juices drop on the boy's wound. He gently rubbed in the balm, and then carefully covered the wounds with leaves from a nearby tulip poplar.

He added more wood to the fire so he would not be disturbed, then sat down next to his wounded comrade. He sat with arms folded and legs crossed - "Indian style." An onlooker would have described his visage as one of a person "meditating" or "communing with nature." His tribe called it "bambeday" - a consciousness of the divine. Todd heard the chant. He understood the words. Native Americans would have said that what was happening with the young boy was not an unfortunate "accident," but a disruption of the forces of Nature. He was wounded, not only in body, but also in spirit. It would take the healing powers of the plants as well as help from the spirits to make him whole again.

The dream continued as Guardian watched each shallow breath of the young boy absorb the incense of the hickory smoke, the aroma of the compassionate woods, and the fragrance of the loving warrior. Locked away beneath the superficial injuries, Todd began to feel the affectionate touch of his father soothing his broken heart when his hamster died. But piled upon the understanding were layers of scars brought on by years of neglect. The healing balm in his dream seemed to penetrate the bad memories, revealing a father who had made mistakes, but whose only solution was to run from them.

Nature's love enveloped Todd. His search was coming to an end. The seeds to the answer to his quest were beginning to sprout. In his dream, the flames of the fire grew smaller and smaller until they vanished into the glow of the coals. A thin trail of smoke ascended to the starry sky. The darkness of the forest encompassed the pair. The full moon rose to keep watch over the hillside.

* * *

There were no lights in the empty GIS lab. The computer finished its first task and Corey had sent it scurrying on to the next one. Computers are strange animals, drawing power from an unseen source. If programmed properly and asked the right questions, they are sources of unimaginable knowledge. The whir of the fan and the droning of the air conditioner drowned out the small ping announcing that deep within the computer, embedded in a silicon chip, lying on a strip of copper thinner than a human hair, encoded in ones and zeros, lay the resolution of a mystery for which generations had waited.

Chapter Twenty-Two

Henry Muselle's Journal
April 28
1:25 AM

Journal, I cannot sleep. It was almost nine before Howard and I got home with my car. I got undressed, showered and went right to bed. My mind raced as I reviewed the events of the day. I tossed and turned as I relived each activity. It was only when I got to the point that I sent Todd on his way that I realized I had not heard from him.

I went downstairs and found no messages on my machine. I checked every door to see if he might have left a note telling of his success. There was none. Now it is too late to call his home. I assume he's all right. He does tend to be a bit irresponsible.

As I fell back into a restless sleep, I was visited again by Guardian. He took me from his village a long distance to a large natural amphitheater. In its center was a huge council fire. The chiefs of Native American tribes from the beginning of time were sitting around the fire. As each chief stood and lamented the coming of the white man, the crowd of Indians seated on the hillside moaned and wailed in agreement. In the background I could hear the low chanting of one warrior as he beat out a funeral dirge on his drum. Guardian escorted me to the front row where two spots had been saved for us. As we sat down, Guardian pointed to a chief who had taken the white name, George Copway. He rose and spoke to the assembled multitude in his native tongue, but Guardian and I understood every word.

"I was born in Nature's wide domain! The trees were all that sheltered my infant limbs, the blue heavens all that covered me. I am one of Nature's children. I have always admired her. She shall be my glory: her features, her robes, and the wealth about her brow, the seasons, her stately oaks, and the evergreen - her hair, ringlets over the earth - all contribute to my enduring love of her.

"And wherever I see her, emotions of pleasure roll in my breast, and swell and burst like waves on the shores of the ocean, in prayer and praise to Him who has placed me in her hand. It is thought great to be born in palaces, surrounded with wealth - but to be born in Nature's wide domain is greater still!

"I would much more glory in this birthplace, with broad canopy of heaven above me, and the giant arms of the forest trees for my shelter, than to be born in palaces of marble, studded with pillars of gold! Nature will be nature still, while palaces shall decay and fall in ruins.

"Yes, Niagara will be Niagara a thousand years hence! The rainbow, a wreath over her brow, shall continue as long as the sun, and the flowing of the river - while the work of art, however carefully protected and preserved, shall fade and crumble into dust!"

The was great moaning and sobbing in the crowd.

Next, Chief Luther Standing Bear of the Ogala Sioux called the crowd to silence and expressed his sorrow.

"Nothing the great Mystery places in the land of the Indian pleases the white man, and nothing escaped his transforming hand. Wherever forests have not been mowed down, wherever the animal is recessed in their quiet protection, wherever the earth is not bereft of four-footed life - that to him is an "unbroken wilderness."

"But, because for the Lakota there was no wilderness, because nature was not dangerous but hospitable, not forbidding but friendly, Lakota philosophy was healthy - free from fear and dogmatism. And here I find the great distinction between the faith of the Indian and the white man. Indian faith sought the harmony of man with his surroundings; the other sought the dominance of surroundings.

"In sharing, in loving all and everything, one people naturally found a due portion of the thing they sought, while in faring, the other found need of conquest.

"For one man the world was full of beauty; for the other it was a place of sin and ugliness to be endured until he went to another world, there to be a creature of wings, half-man and half-bird.

"But the old Lakota was wise. He knew that man's heart, away from nature, becomes hard; he knew that the lack of respect for growing, living things soon led to lack of respect for humans, too. So he kept his children close to nature's softening influence."

The assemblage cried and beat the ground in agreement. Chief Seattle strolled before the dimming fire. He walked before the crowd as if he were looking for an individual to address. His eyes met mine. He walked toward me, his eyes glowing. He pulled me to my feet and called the other chiefs to gather around. He spoke to me as a loving father instructs his child.

"The sight of your cities pains the eyes of the red man. But perhaps it is because the red man is a savage and does not understand.

"There is no quiet place in the white man's cities, no place to hear the leaves of spring or the rustle of insects' wings. Perhaps it is because I am a savage and do not understand, but the clatter only seems to insult the ears.

"The Indian prefers the soft sound of the wind darting over the face of the pond, the smell of the wind itself cleansed by a midday rain, or scented with pinion pine. The air is precious to the red man, for all things share the same breath - the animals, the trees, the man. Like a man who has been dying for many days, a man in your city is numb to the stench."

I awoke and found myself weeping. I was soaking wet from perspiration. I am afraid we never learned from our native American brothers. I fear we are making the same mistakes today.

I must sleep. Today will be the day I have waited for. Today we will either find the gold or reveal the hoax. I have mixed feelings.

Chapter Twenty-Three

Friday, April 28
8:00 AM

Ralph was concerned with the progress of the investigation. Gunther arranged for him to be the silent third party on a conference call to Washington. That way, he could be an eyewitness to bureaucratic inefficiency. "Trust me," Gunther said to the person on the other end of the phone. "No one knows any better than I do how important it is to bring this matter to a quick conclusion." There was a pause and Ralph listened intently to the concerns of Gunther's superior.

"I know there are a lot of loose ends," he continued, "but from what my contacts are telling me, we may end up with a diversion."

Ralph knew Gunther's Regional Office was the stopping point for the blame in the road debacle. His solution to the problem was not sitting well in Washington. "I know you don't believe in the gold story. I'm telling you these kids have managed to drag some heavy hitters into this. They might be on to something." There was another tirade from the attorneys in Washington.

"I have the injunction in my pocket. All I need is the proof that Johnson violated a historical site. One of our groups called me and said they found a requisition authenticating the expedition. As soon as I have it in my hands, I'll present Mr. Johnson with his restraining order."

Ralph heard Washington complain about the delays. "I'm surprised I didn't get it last night," Gunther commented. "These kids were so excited I figured they'd bring it to my house."

Ralph listened as highly degreed career government employees decried the fact that the fate of a multi-million dollar road project was lying in the hands of high school science students. They wanted something documented by thousands of pages of testimony.

"On that other matter," Gunther said, "Huntsinger appears before the grand jury today. If I can get Johnson slowed down, Huntsinger will nail his coffin shut."

Ralph heard something hit the office door evidently a signal for his secretary to rescue him. "There's my intercom. I've got to go. Maybe it's the kids with the requisition. Yes, I'll keep you informed every step of the way. Good-bye." Ralph was not impressed.

* * *

The Grand Jury met in a special room designed much like a small auditorium. Three tiers of tables enabled the twenty-one members to look down on the witnesses. The prosecutor sat at a table on the floor in the front of the room. The witnesses sat in a comfortable office chair behind a desk of their own. Jurors took copious notes as the testimony began.

"Do you solemnly swear that the testimony you are about to give will be the truth, the whole truth and nothing but the truth, so help you God?"

"I do."

"Please be seated and state your name and occupation for the record."

"My name is George Michael Huntsinger. I am currently unemployed."

Huntsinger's words were transcribed by a court reporter. Unless they were subpoenaed for the criminal trial, his comments would remain secret. His heart pounded as he began down the path he had avoided for so long.

"Where were you employed, Mr. Huntsinger?"

"I was Vice-President of Johnson Construction. My employer was Mr. Fred Johnson."

* * *

"I don't care what that old fart of a farmer says." Johnson screamed into the telephone in his Johnson Center office. "You tell him I need to move my truck through his field to build that protective covering for his springs.

"You tell him I don't care if I mess up his cows' drinking water. He's going to move them anyway. They might as well do it now rather than later."

There was a commotion on the other end of the phone. Davis was talking to someone else in the room. Suddenly there was a new voice on the phone.

"Uh, yes sir . . . deputy," Johnson stammered. "I did get a little worked up. No, I didn't mean any harm by it. Certainly the man has a right to his property. No, if he says we can't then we won't. Sorry to trouble you, officer . . . Could I speak with my man again?"

Johnson swallowed hard and waited until he heard the officers leave his field office. His face turned beet red as he waited for Davis to return to the phone.

"Davis," he screamed, "what in the hell is the county sheriff doing in my field office? You weren't smoking pot again, were you?" There was a pregnant pause as Davis attempted to explain the social visit from the deputy sheriff.

"Well, you tell Deputy Offenberger that I don't like social calls from jack-booted thugs. If I want to talk to a cop, I'll visit him at the coffee shop. Don't you ever embarrass me like that again. You back our people off until the law clears out. Then you high tail it back here. I'm not gonna let that mud slinging farmer get the best of me."

* * *

"You see right here on the Saling property," Dr. Dorman pointed to the NASA satellite photograph. "There's a rectangular area that does not match the surrounding soil composition," he explained to Corey as Rossiter, Dan and Michelle looked on.

"Do you think it's the gold?" asked Michelle.

"We don't know. We sent the data through the computer a couple of times," Dr. Dorman said. "We magnified the area and analyzed the part of the spectrum where gold and silver might be. There were eight PhD's working on this and after ten hours the best we could conclude was a positive maybe."

"Do we really know any more than we did?" Dan said, tiring of the futile search.

"As a matter of fact, we do," Dr. Dorman said gleefully. "We know the exact latitude and longitude of the boundaries of this mysterious mass."

"Then we can enter that into the GIS and see if it matches our other data!" Corey exclaimed.

"Exactly!" Dr. Dorman concurred. "If this is the lost gold, as we suspect, it will correlate with our other findings." He walked to the computer and switched on the monitor. "Well, what's this?" he asked as the monitor faded on.

Correlation: 100%
Coverage Area: 1 Acre

The lab erupted in screams of jubilation. Even Dr. Dorman and Dr. Rossiter were dancing around the room. "We're down to a one acre area. Now we haven't confirmed it," Dr. Dorman cautioned, "but we're close. Let's put in the numbers from NASA and tighten up the deviation to see what happens."

"Isn't this great, Todd?" he said. It was the first time the group had noticed Todd's absence. It was not unusual for him to be tardy, but a quick check revealed no one had heard from him since he left with Mr. Muselle. Michelle decided it was time to begin a search for him, so she started on the phone, calling his most frequented haunts. The others turned their attention to the new data being entered into the computer.

* * *

Henry Muselle's Treasure

Todd awakened in the underbrush and brushed the leaves from his face. He felt the cut by his eye now covered with an oily substance. His eye nearly swollen shut, he rolled to one side and knocked the branches from his arm. He pushed himself up on his good arm and staggered to his feet. He attempted a step on his weak knee. He screamed in pain and collapsed in a pile of leaves.

8:30 AM

"Johnson reviewed Fernandez's draft of the Environmental Impact Statement," Huntsinger continued. "It identified seventy-five percent of the valley as wetlands with Ralph Saling's farm being nearly one hundred percent wetlands. He sent me to Fernandez's office with a copy of the Statement and a briefcase with $50,000. He told me to tell him there would be $100,000 more in a Costa Rican bank if he made a report that enabled the road to go through quickly and without a hitch."

"Do you know if Mr. Fernandez complied with Johnson's request?" the prosecutor asked.

"Yes sir. Two weeks later we received a revised report indicating there were minor wetlands on the Saling property and suggesting a method to insure their integrity."

The prosecutor began moving through the jury room. "Ladies and gentlemen, I am passing out to you a copy of the report to which Mr. Huntsinger is referring. I am also distributing a copy of the initial report, which Mr. Fernandez has so graciously provided us. Your job, as you know, is to return an indictment against Mr. Johnson, if you feel there is sufficient evidence that he stand trial. After you hear Mr. Huntsinger' complete testimony, we will call Mr. Fernandez."

"Mr. Huntsinger," he continued, "you have been granted immunity in this case. Were you a willing accomplice in this matter?"

"No sir," George replied. "I did what Fred asked me to do even though deep in my heart I felt it wasn't proper. There had been payoffs before, but none this large involving so major a project."

"Then why did you do it?"

"I was trapped. Fred was a friend. He gave me a good job, and as he became successful, he rewarded me well. If he paid off someone with $10,000, I could expect a twenty thousand dollar bonus. But he changed with this project. I don't know what it was, but it was more than simply building a road."

"How did he change?"

"He became more ruthless. There wasn't anything he wouldn't do to complete this project."

* * *

"Hello, Mr. Johnson? This is Enrico Fernandez."

"Well, Rico my good friend, it's been a long time since I've heard from you. Que pasa?" Johnson said, rocking confidently in his desk chair. "Do you have good news for me? I need good news today."

"Yes sir, I do. I have the results of the core sample that Mr. Gunther had you drill."

"Dear Mr. Gunther. Do you have that creep off my back?" Johnson swung around in his chair and put his feet on the desk.

"I think so."

Johnson didn't let him finish. "Do you know how much time this little drilling episode of yours cost me? You told me you had everything under control at the EPA! I paid you good money to keep those people out of my hair. What happened?"

"I have no control over my superiors," Fernandez said, trying to calm the savage beast. "I suggested that we do the core samples rather than a complete reevaluation of the area like he wanted to do. He could have closed down the road project for months."

Johnson was not impressed. "He knows better than to do that. I'd have more Congressmen down his back than he could shake a stick at. So tell me. What do the samples show?"

"We all know that they showed wetlands, but my report says they showed nothing. I've switched them with some other samples from a project a couple of years ago. No one will know the difference."

"That's my boy," Johnson said, much relieved. "I'll send an Easter present to mama and papa in Costa Rica."

"I'd appreciate that, sir," Fernandez replied. "You let me know if there is anything else I can do for you."

"Don't worry," Johnson said, "you know I will."

Johnson placed the phone gingerly in its cradle. He was confident his stooge was still obediently on the payroll.

* * *

Todd opened his eyes. The warm spring sun soothed his wounds. He couldn't tell if it was morning or afternoon. He forced himself to sit up. His arm throbbed. His head ached. He wasn't sure how he got there. Had he dreamed of terrifying truck rides and being watched by Indians? Nothing looked familiar. He forced himself to stand. Although sore, he was able to hobble a step or two on his knee.

He looked up the hill. All he could see was underbrush. He looked down the hill. In the distance off to his right, he could see a road. Maybe it passed near the bottom of the hill. He would start in that direction.

He noticed a long forked branch lying on the ground. He picked it up. *This will make a good walking stick*, he thought. He planted the stick and hopped with his good leg. He then dragged his sore leg down the hill. It would be a long walk to the road.

With each step he tried to figure out what had happened to him. He started at the beginning. His name was Todd. That was a good start. Todd Evans. At least he didn't have complete amnesia. With each painful step he worked his way through the family. That part of his memory seemed intact. There was also a new feeling about his father trying to work its way out. He wasn't sure what it was, but now was no time to fight against it. He could picture his house. That was very good. He remembered his address and his phone number. Thoughts were coming quickly now.

The tip of his stick caught a root and he went tumbling head over heels down the hill. His head hit, then his battered arm, finally his bad knee. Over and over he went, and as each injured part struck the ground he let out a scream. Finally, a gracious tree stuck out a branch and Todd grabbed it with his uninjured arm. Gravity pulled his legs on down the hill until his badly beaten body could stretch no more. He landed on the hard ground with a thud, which could have been heard throughout the valley.

As he pulled himself together and reassessed the damage, a thin piece of leather fell from around his neck. It was dark brown except for the ends, which were lighter in color. It looked like they had been attached to something. A pouch!

Suddenly, thoughts of Corey and the hunt for the gold came racing into his head. He remembered the paper he and Mr. Muselle found. He remembered the truck ride with Mr. Johnson. Finally, he remembered being pushed from the truck.

He felt for the pouch, but realized it was gone. He didn't know whether Johnson had it or it had been lost in the fall. What was important was that he find someone to tell about it. If he didn't have the memo, certainly there was something else in those trunks at the fort that could point to the expedition.

With all the strength he could muster, he pulled himself up and started down the hill again. He didn't notice the pain now. He had to get to the road. He had to get to Corey and Mr. Muselle. He had to tell them about the paper.

* * *

"Fred told me it would be over before I knew it," Huntsinger testified.

"So you're saying that Fred Johnson outlined for you in precise details how Howard Jackson's house would be destroyed," the prosecutor asked.

"Yes, he did."

There was a stirring in the jury room as the prosecutor's assistants handed out more paperwork. "You are receiving the report from the State Fire Marshall's office which describes in detail the fuse used to ignite the fire in Howard Jackson's basement. It's on page twelve, I believe. As you can see, Mr. Huntsinger did an excellent job of describing it for you."

"Mr. Huntsinger, you haven't seen the Fire Marshal's report, have you?"

"No I haven't."

"Tell me again why Mr. Johnson felt it so important to commit arson on poor Mr. Jackson. Was it a personal vendetta?"

"There is nothing personal in what Fred Johnson does when it comes to a project. He will do whatever it takes to complete it. People and property mean nothing to him." Huntsinger pointed to a jury member. "He'd burn your house if you were in the way." The jury member squirmed and jotted a note.

"Thank you for such graphic testimony, Mr. Huntsinger."

* * *

The clicking of the GIS computer suddenly stopped. The display on the screen read:

Correlation: **100%**
Coverage Area: **.99 Acre**

The screen went blank and then lit up with the display:

Correlation: 0%
Coverage Area: .99 Acre

The correlation number sped forward like the odometer on a racecar. When it reached 100%, the coverage area changed to .98 acre. The correlation started spinning again. Within a minute, the probability was 60%, but the change became much slower. Dr. Dorman had said if the correlation stayed at 100% and the coverage area reached .2 acre, the group could conclude that the gold lay beneath the mysterious area on the NASA photograph.

9:00 AM

Correlation: 25%
Coverage Area: .88 Acre

* * *

Ralph and Martha stood outside the house and watched the trucks loaded with steel pull down the hill and into the valley. Johnson's workers meticulously unloaded the girders and placed them where only a few days before, Ralph's cows had so peacefully grazed. A temporary fence kept the cattle out of harm's way.

Howard pulled into the drive in his red truck, got out and walked up to the house. "Have you heard from Todd, this morning?"

"No, we haven't," Ralph replied.

"Michelle called me. She said nobody's heard from him since he left Henry last night. I was supposed to pick him up on the road to Hanoverton, but I never saw him. Henry and I figured somebody else must have rescued him. We got so involved trying to get Henry's car running we both forgot all about him."

"He's a resourceful cuss. I'm sure he's all right, or somebody would have called."

"Henry said they found some sort of paper that would

solve all of our problems. Then we got to working on his car, and I never did get all the details. But Todd has it and he was supposed to get it to Gunther. You heard from him yet?"

"Yeah, but he said he didn't say anything about a paper."

The telephone rang. Martha handed the cordless phone to Ralph. "Are you enjoying the show, Mr. Saling?" Johnson's voice was heard above the roar of the trucks.

"Only if you consider watching your family's life work being destroyed – fun," was Ralph's reply.

"As you can see, my trucks are tearing up more of the right-of-way than we anticipated. I don't know if I can ever make it right. You see, Mr. Saling, I am willing to pay you handsomely to use that little stretch of property to gain access to our environmental cover," Johnson continued.

"I guess you're deaf as well as dumb, Mr. Johnson," Ralph said. "All the money in the world wouldn't convince me to let you use any more of my land. If you ever suggest it, I'll have my attorney sue you for harassment." He clicked the button on the phone and handed it back to Martha who put it in her purse.

"That guy will never learn," Howard said. "You'll have to physically block his way, or he'll figure out a method to get past you."

"We could always dig up the gold," Martha said.

"We're supposed to wait on Dr. Dorman's call with the location, so we don't tear up too much of the property," Ralph explained.

"We could look like we're digging," Howard said. "That way we'll keep old Johnson off guard."

"Good idea," said Ralph.

"I'll go get my backhoe," said Howard. "We'll act like we're going to start. That will get his goat."

"Better hurry," said Ralph, running across the field after a loose lamb. "Johnson's already getting mine."

* * *

"Let me get this straight, Mr. Huntsinger," the prosecutor continued. "There is no such thing as an 'environmental cover.'"

"That's right, sir. Fernandez and I made it up. It sounded good, and we could put together some crude drawings with enough technical jargon to sneak it past the inspectors."

"And your plan worked?" he asked.

"Like a dream. It was never questioned until Mr. Gunther reviewed the specifications."

"And what did he find?"

"Twelve foot girders," Huntsinger replied.

"Why is that significant?"

"This is a four lane highway which will be over sixty feet wide. Our platform would need steel cross members at least that long. We not only didn't specify heavy enough I-beams, we called for girders - wall supports - in our plan. Gunther caught the mistake in a heartbeat."

"And?" the prosecutor prodded.

"And that started him asking questions which ended up with me being here," Huntsinger concluded.

"Ladies and gentlemen, that concludes much of Mr. Huntsinger' testimony. I'm sure there is no doubt in your mind concerning the preponderance of evidence against Mr. Johnson. However, there is one other side of Mr. Johnson I would like Mr. Huntsinger to explain."

9:30 AM

Correlation: 100%
Coverage Area: .75 Acre

* * *

Todd was making steady progress. He learned, in his long journey, how to drag his bad leg after his good one. The noises of the cars on the road led him to believe he was approaching a major highway. The thick underbrush still obscured his view.

Each time he strained to bring his bad leg along side him, he hurt. It was almost the same hurt he felt when Michelle told him they were through. He only hoped that by delivering the news about the memo, she would give him another chance. There was no fooling around with this assignment. It was truly a life and death situation.

He took another step and his foot sank into mud above his ankle. He did not mind as he pulled his soggy appendage out of the muck. This meant he had reached the bottom. Now there should be a slight climb to the roadway.

He thought about Corey and how much he relied on him to make things right. Corey couldn't help him now. He was all alone. He had to succeed or Johnson would have the upper hand.

Step by step he grew stronger in his resolve. He didn't know how far he had walked, but it was certainly nearly a mile. A truck sped by and blew dirt through the weeds and into Todd's face. It was a welcome breeze.

Thoughts of Mr. Muselle raced through his mind like the passing traffic. Mr. Muselle's future, as well as his past, lay in Todd's hands. Todd's pain was nothing compared to the pain Henry would suffer if the paper were lost.

He took another step and for the first time could see the silhouette of cars speeding past. Another step and his shirt was grabbed by the thousand tiny barbs of a bramble bush. He tore himself free and lunged toward the thinning bushes. After a great struggle, he freed himself from the snare of the thicket and emerged onto the berm of the road.

What a sight he was! His shirt and pants were torn. His eye was bloodied and swollen. He leaned on his trusty stick and waved at an approaching car. The car moved to the inside of the highway and accelerated. He was too ghastly a sight for the driver. Car after car avoided him. One person slowed down enough to ask if he needed help. It was such a stupid question Todd told them no.

Finally, an old rattletrap of a truck, which looked in as good a condition as Todd, turned on its right turn signal and began to pull to the side of the road.

* * *

"Frankly sir, I was frightened for my life," Huntsinger continued. "It didn't matter to Fred whether or not Jackson was in his home. If Howard had died in the fire, Johnson would have figured there was one less person to worry about. He has the connections to have any kind of dirty work accomplished and no one can trace it back to him."

"How do you know this," the prosecutor inquired.

"Based on my Fifth Amendment right, sir, I'd rather not answer without consulting my attorney," he replied without hesitation. "But I will be more than happy to speak with you about it," he added with a wink.

"Do you feel he could personally commit such acts?"

"If he has his back up against the wall, I think he could," Huntsinger commented.

"Would he burglarize?" the prosecutor asked.

"Possibly."

"Commit arson?"

"Possibly."

"Commit Murder?"

"I think so."

The prosecutor leaned on the desk and looked Huntsinger in the eye. "Do you think his back is up against the wall?"

Never flinching, Huntsinger replied, "How far would you go if you were about to lose thirteen million dollars?"

* * *

The rickety truck pulled to a stop at the side of the road. Before Todd could hobble to the door and open it, the driver was out of the truck and around to give Todd a hand.

"Lord, son, what happened to you," he said, opening the door. "You look like you were run over by a train."

"Well not exactly," Todd said. He winced as he pulled his leg into the truck. It felt good to rest his battered arm on something solid. "Where am I?" he asked.

"You're on Route 43 just South of Waco," the driver replied. "Which hospital do you want to go to?"

"I can't go to the hospital," Todd said, "at least not yet."

"Boy, you need to see a physician."

"I have to go to Johnson Center. I have to get a message to the Director of the EPA."

"I'm gonna take you straight to the hospital. You're hurt too badly to be messing around," the driver objected.

Todd started to open the door. "You don't understand. I have to go to the EPA first. It's a matter of life and death. If you won't take me, I'll find someone who will," he said, starting to slide out of the truck.

"OK," the driver reluctantly agreed. "Johnson Center is on the way. I'll deliver your message, but you have to promise me that I can take you to the hospital."

"It's a deal," Todd said. He started to raise his hand to shake with the driver, but a stabbing pain clear to his shoulder forced a contrived wave.

* * *

Correlation: 100%
Coverage Area: .5 Acre

10:30 AM

Johnson was having a great deal of difficulty getting anything done. He made phone calls. He paced to the window to watch his trucks unloading materials. He looked in the files for something and forgot what he was looking for. He called his secretary and then forgot what he wanted.

He wanted to attack this "environmental cover" from two directions. Saling, for the first time, was blocking the easterly approach. Johnson was not used to being stopped, especially by a weasel like Saling. He opened his desk drawer. There laid the pouch he had taken from Todd. *At least I put an end to that threat. Imagine - gold being buried down there. If there was, I'd have heard about it before this,* he thought. He walked to the window and saw Howard drive up on his backhoe. *They're really going to start to dig!*

"Nooooooo!!!" he screamed, beating on the window. "They can't do this to me. I'm so close. No one is going to stop me now. Davis!! Bring the truck around, we're going to Saling's."

He walked to the desk, opened the bottom drawer and removed a gun and holster. He unsnapped the holster and pulled out a shiny .44 caliber semi-automatic pistol. He reached back into the drawer and pulled out two ammunition clips. One he slipped into the base of the gun and the other he placed in his back pocket.

"We'll put an end to this - one way or another!" He slammed the desk drawer and walked to the truck.

* * *

Correlation: **100%**
Coverage Area: **.45 Acre**

* * *

Henry pointed his newly restored car toward the Saling farm. Adorned with a new distributor, battery, alternator, generator, and timing chain, Henry had invested the trade-in value of his car into his car - again. It would take a treasure to get him out of debt.

Dr. Dorman had called to say that they would be "exploring the area once again to determine the feasibility of digging for the treasure." Why that man couldn't speak English was still a mystery to Henry.

He was really getting worried about Todd. He still hadn't called to tell him he had delivered the message to Gunther. Gunther hadn't called with any kind of news after receiving the memo. Henry even broke down and called Todd's mother. A new male voice answered and yelled to someone in the shower, "Who the hell's Todd?" This led to a quick check of local doctors and hospitals, which turned up nothing. Maybe Todd was on the lam from the new boyfriend. Maybe Todd would be at the Saling's starting to dig.

Suddenly, Henry was confronted by two horrible thoughts. One, the thought of fulfilling his deceased father's dream while at the same time losing Todd to the treasure hunt. He had become like a father to Todd through these many days. There had always been an attraction to the unruly, bright kid, but the revelations of the treasure and their shared vision made the mere thought of finding the treasure without him untenable.

With this thought surged the guilt of success. Why was he the one who after all these many generations was able to solve the riddle? Which brought him back to Todd, the precocious, unrelenting, overbearing child whose persistence was about to make them all very, very wealthy. That thought led him to the incomprehensible notion of Todd's demise. Fortunately, at that moment Henry arrived at the Saling farm.

* * *

Correlation: 100%
Coverage Area: .195 Acre

The special alarm sequence Dr. Dorman had programmed the computer to sound when it finally reached the target results went unheard. The group of scientists was so sure of their work that they had already left for the Saling farm.

Calls to alert the other interested parties, however, went unanswered. Gunther had left the office on unannounced business. The response of the male at Todd's house was, "Madge, who's this Todd everybody's calling about? You doin' somebody 'sides me?"

10:45 AM

Johnson's truck sped into Saling's lane. There was hardly room to park. Dr. Dorman's van was there. Fernandez's truck from the EPA was there. Henry's green car was parked next to the barn. Howard was there with the backhoe.

Johnson stepped from the truck, took the gun out of the holster and put the gun through his belt. He zipped his light jacket to cover the weapon. He closed the door of the truck, took a deep breath and walked toward the group standing in the field.

* * *

Henry felt that having Howard on a backhoe was worse than letting a bull loose in a china shop. Howard was heading right for a spot in between the flags that he and Todd had placed during their initial hunt. Ralph was following the tractor screaming and yelling that Howard was heading for the wrong place.

"Mr. Jackson," Corey yelled, "it's not there. The computer says the gold is thirty feet over this way."

"Get out of my way kid. I was looking for this gold long before you was a glimmer in your daddy's eye," Howard said raising the bucket of the backhoe high in the air. Corey ran ahead and positioned himself in front of the backhoe to finally stop Howard.

Henry saw Dan and Michelle placing flags he assumed were marking the boundaries of the mass discovered in the NASA photo as well as the location of the core sample. Suddenly, the war at the backhoe came to an abrupt halt as Dr. Dorman appeared in the field with a strange contraption strapped to his back. He had a lap top computer hanging from his front. He was wheeling along the ground a gizmo, which looked like the headboard of a twin bed.

"What in the world is that?" Howard exclaimed.

"That's Dr. Dorman's Ground Penetrating Radar system," replied Corey.

Henry Muselle's Treasure

"What's he going to do with it?" Ralph asked.

"Well," said Corey, thrust back into the scientist's role. "He will roll the thing in his hand along the ground. It sends radar waves, which are generated in the backpack into the ground. They travel about twenty feet down and return to the antenna. If they hit something on their trip, it will show up on the computer screen in front of Dr. Dorman."

Noting that Dr. Dorman was not walking near any of the flags, Howard wanted to know why Dorman was searching in the new area.

"First," Corey began, "the map from 1829 showed the four springs to be in a different location than they are now. As a matter of fact, the survey of 1797 showed them even more northerly than in 1829. So the center of the springs is much more north of the flag where you are about to dig."

Howard got down from the backhoe and the three of them began to walk toward Dr. Dorman's search area.

"Secondly," Corey continued, "the center of the springs in 1797 is almost exactly six hundred paces due south of the shovels using Todd's twenty-nine inch stride. He is closer to the size of an average Frenchman in 1755."

Dr. Dorman walked a few feet, stopped and entered data into the computer. He only talked to himself about the matter, but he seemed content with what he was finding.

"Third," the young scientist said, "when we entered the Great Trail Map into the GIS program, the stone tree and the deer carving were almost exactly where they were supposed to be. The springs in 1797 were to one side of the trail.

"All of these clues led us to an area about an acre in size as the possible location of the gold. The NASA photograph confirmed the location of a metallic mass in the center of our search area, and Dr. Dorman's probability program confirmed that this was the spot. It was only a coincidence that Mr. Johnson was forced to dig core samples, and according to Mr. Fernandez, one of them went right through the gold. Dr. Dorman wanted to use his radar system to confirm what every other technology has told us - the gold is here."

Henry watched Johnson listen intently to the last part of Corey's conversation. He did not like the way Johnson was looking.

"Ralph, old friend," Johnson began, unzipping his coat a little. "You and I need to have a talk."

"There's nothing I have to talk to you about, Mr. Johnson," Ralph said.

"Yeah, slimeball, butt out," countered Howard.

"Now gentlemen, let's be reasonable," he said, unzipping his coat a little farther. He reached into his shirt pocket. Henry moved closer, fearing what might be in the pocket. Johnson pulled out his checkbook. "Mr. Saling, if you start digging around for this gold, I'm afraid you'll ruin my access. I'm willing to pay you five hundred thousand dollars for the use of your right-of-way for one week."

"OK, I've got it," shouted Dr. Dorman from fifty feet away. "Howard, bring that backhoe over here. The kids have the area marked. We need to go down about sixteen feet."

Henry noticed Johnson was sweating profusely on this cool spring day. "All right, Mr. Saling two hundred thousand dollars a day. That's a million dollars for the use of your land for a week!"

Howard got on the backhoe and started toward Dr. Dorman. Ralph followed, ignoring Johnson's offers. Johnson ran after him, almost in tears. The zipper on Johnson's coat inched closer and closer to his waist. Henry thought he saw the sun reflect off something silver in Johnson's belt.

Out of the corner of his eye, Henry saw Joe Gunther's EPA truck pull into the field. Gunther walked across the field toward the men. Amid the mounting confusion Henry noticed a police car pull into the Saling farm.

"Mr. Johnson, how nice to see you," Gunther began. "You're going to save me a trip to your office. Ralph, you must be having a family reunion with all the cars I see."

"It's something like that," Ralph agreed.

"OK, Howard start digging here," Dr. Dorman called to the farmer. The giant bucket plunged deep into the soft earth, then pulled up, turned and dumped its cargo to one side. Over and

Henry Muselle's Treasure

over it returned to the hole creating an ever-growing crater.

"You know, Fred," Gunther continued over the roar of the backhoe. "Ralph and his friends have been investigating this tale of lost French gold."

"So I've heard," Johnson replied. Henry saw him resting his hand on what appeared to be the butt of a gun. What should he do? Was it really a gun or was he just imagining the worst? What if it was a gun? Henry couldn't imagine Johnson shooting anyone over this situation. He wasn't that desperate, was he? If he were going to shoot someone, who would it be? Ralph? Gunther? Howard? Henry's heart dropped to his stomach. Was it possible he was about to witness another death because of the treasure? He'd have to stop this, but how?

Gunther reached into his coat pocket. Henry winced. *No, not him, too.* He imagined an impending Old West style shootout. Gunther took out a piece of paper. "I have here an injunction I had hoped to serve you telling you to cease and desist because you are building a highway over a previously undiscovered historical site. Unfortunately, a key piece of historical information was inadvertently lost on the way to my office, so this injunction is no good . . . "

The backhoe strained with a large rock it uncovered on the side of the hole. Henry moved closer to the group looking for more weapons.

"Unless," he continued, "my friends should strike gold over there."

A police officer approached the gathering. At his side was a bruised, bandaged, and splinted young man. "Well, Todd," Gunther said, "how nice to see you again."

Todd reached in his back pocket and pulled out a battered piece of ancient paper. "Mr. Gunther, Mr. Muselle and I found this. I started to carry it in a pouch around my neck. After I called for help and left the farmhouse, I was afraid I'd lose it. So, I put it in my pocket. When they took my pants off at the hospital, it fell out."

"Well," Gunther asked, "what is it?"

"It is a paper written in 1755 ordering supplies for an

expedition to bring French gold from Fort Duquesne to Fort Detroit," Todd replied.

"You little son-of-a . . . " Johnson yelled, pulling the gun from its holster and pointing it at Todd's head. "This is all your fault. You and your gold!" Ralph took a step forward. Johnson turned and pointed the gun at Ralph's chest. "And you sniveling dirt farmer. You love the ground and you love springs and on and on and on. Maybe you'd like a little lead." Gunther took a step toward him; Johnson pointed the gun at him. "Stand back, you bureaucratic boob. We had a good thing going until you stuck your nose where it didn't belong. I could drop you where you stand and never think twice about it." Henry stepped forward and a twig snapped under his foot.

Johnson spun around and the gun pointed at Henry's nose. "Who are you?" he shouted. Out of instinct, like he was swatting at a fly, Henry's hand flew up hitting Johnson's wrist and knocked the gun out of his hand. The gun hit the ground and went off, the bullet ricocheting off the bulldozer track. Henry and Johnson looked at each other, stunned over the turn of events.

"I'll take that," said the officer, grabbing Johnson's hand.

"And you can take this," said Gunther slipping the injunction into Johnson's pocket.

The officer spun Johnson around and slapped a handcuff first on one wrist and then the other. "If you'll come with me, Mr. Johnson, I'd like to talk with you about assault, kidnapping and attempted murder."

"Davis," Johnson yelled, as the officer led him toward the cruiser. "Don't just stand there. Get me my attorney. Now!!!"

"Way to go Mr. Muselle," Todd screamed as he hobbled over and gave him a huge hug.

"That was quite a punch, Henry," Ralph said vigorously shaking his hand.

"Mr. Muselle, I don't think we've been introduced. I'm Joe Gunther from the EPA and I think I owe you my life," Gunther said hugging Henry from the side.

Henry was stupefied. He really hadn't done anything, but was now a hero. How quickly life's fate changes. How well his ancestors knew people interpret events from a point of view most advantageous to them. As one by one, the entourage praised him for his actions, he was amazed at the differences in the stories each one told him about what he had done.

"Whoa! Stop!! That's far enough!!!" Dr. Dorman yelled. He scurried into the hole nearly fifteen feet deep. Todd hurried as best he could to the edge of the pit. He was too bungled up to risk the excursion into the pit. Dan, however, was right at Dr. Dorman's side. Henry watched as Dr. Dorman got down on his hands and knees and carefully moved the dirt. Loose dirt gave way to grainy muck. "Deteriorated wood," he explained. With a little effort he was able to poke through the layer of wood. He bellowed when he scraped his hand on the hard metal on the other side. He wiggled his hand and with some effort knocked loose the material located under the ancient wood. With great fanfare he raised his hand, full of the treasure hunted by so many. He opened his palm to reveal a handful of coins - ancient French coins weathered by years of moisture and acids from the soil.

Henry called to him. "Let me see those." Dr. Dorman handed several coins to Henry. He looked at the figure of King Louis on the coin. He tried to make out the date and the inscription, but could only make out it was French. This had to be the treasure he and his family had sought.

"What do you think?" Ralph asked.

"Looks like what we've been hunting for," Henry said handing a coin to Ralph.

"Yep," Ralph says, "looks identical to the one I have at home."

Corey and Michelle jumped into the crater and helped Dr. Dorman wrestle the contents of the first box out of the hole.

"Here Todd, you need to see some of these," Henry said. He reached down picked up several coins and handed them to Todd. "You found your dream did you?"

"I think I did," said Todd as he examined the coins. Soon Ralph and Martha, Howard and Michelle, Corey and Henry, were in the pit on hands and knees uncovering their dreams.

* * *

The driver of Todd's rescue vehicle walked over to Todd, left out at the top of the mound. "If you hadn't been so persistent, they'd have never found it," he said. "Let them have the gold - for now. You've accomplished so much more."

Todd looked closely at the man. He hadn't paid any attention to him in the truck; he was too busy trying to deliver his message. Under the faded fedora, beneath the scraggly beard, hidden by flannel shirt and bibbed overalls was his father.

"Dad," he squealed squeezing him with as much strength as his crippled body could muster, "what are you doing here?"

"If you didn't notice, I picked you up along the highway. I didn't recognize you either until you gave your name at the hospital."

"But why didn't you tell me who you were when you drove me here?"

"Todd, this is your day. I've been reading about your exploits in the paper. I didn't want to do anything to take away from your success. I've messed up you life enough already."

"Not really, Dad. If you hadn't left, I wouldn't have become such good friends with Mr. Muselle. I would have messed up the science fair experiment. I wouldn't have helped find the treasure."

"Well, I 'm glad my screw-ups were so well received."

"By the way, why do you look like this? I thought you were a successful businessman in Cleveland?"

"Margaret left me. She found somebody new at one of my parties in Cleveland. She divorced me and took almost everything. I've been trying to figure out how to make it up to you and your mother. I borrowed this truck from my brother, have been living in a trailer outside of town and doing odd jobs to pay the rent and put groceries on the table. I was trying to find the best way to approach the two of you when I happen to pick you up by the side of the road. Lucky, huh?"

Todd hugged his dad again with the biggest bear hug he could muster. Through the bend in his dad's elbow he thought he saw Guardian standing on the edge of the gold hole, arms folded in stereotypical Indian style - smiling at him.

Chapter Twenty-Four

There was near chaos after the treasure was found. Dr. Dorman quickly got permission from Ralph to become the organizer of the search. The sheriff agreed to provide additional deputies to guard the find until a local security company could be contacted. Dr. Dorman called his academic friends on his cell phone for a complete analysis of the site.

What began as a private gathering soon drew throngs of onlookers from town. This was bigger news than Howard Jackson's fire. Anyone who was anybody in the area began arriving at the farm to take credit for his or her part in finding the gold. The mayor and council members from Minerva were there. Township trustees and county commissioners all arrived to stake their claim.

Dr. Dorman wanted the entire fortune uncovered before any of it was removed from the hole. This meant enlarging the hole with the backhoe then digging down to the level of the boxes.

Dr. Rice arrived to supervise the removal of the dirt without disturbing any thing of archeological significance to the area. Dr. Ragosin came to act as a historical adviser on the Pre-Revolutionary life in America. Carl came from the Minerva Savings to offer his vault for the storage of the treasure.

Everyone was amazed at the young scientists' ability to piece together the myriad of clues. Finally someone in the crowd asked the thirteen million dollar question - "Whose money is it?" They scanned the crowd for answers. There was one professional who had not chased the excitement - an attorney. Several persons ran for their cars. The situation would soon be remedied.

Todd and Henry stood on a mound of dirt overlooking the activity in the hole. Todd was in enough pain that he was satisfied to simply watch his friends doing all the manual labor. Henry was not sure whether the treasure proved what he hoped. It was still early in the search for any real conclusion; he was silently impressed with Todd's newfound maturity. Two weeks ago Todd would not have been content to let others hog the glory. He looked across the field Todd and he walked so many times. He could see the pendants waving in the breeze where they marked the original location. If we hadn't persisted, this search could have ended like all the rest. So many times Todd had wanted to dig, and he resisted. Looking back, it was almost miraculous how each clue revealed itself. It was as if, after a quarter of a millennium, the gold wanted to be found. There was a commotion in the hole. Dan had found the end of the boxes. Dr. Rice insisted that the area beyond the box had also been disturbed. They excavated beyond the length of another box until they hit the sand and clay of the undisturbed earth.

"It looks like there is one box missing," Dr. Dorman said.

"Maybe it simply disintegrated more than the others," Dr. Rice rationalized.

"Maybe someone came back and took it," reasoned Dan.

Henry watched intently as Dr. Rice began excavating the area, hoping to find remnants of a partially filled container. In the middle of the newly discovered area, about eight inches down, he came upon a badly decomposed tin box with a lead lining.

"This must have been used by the supply people to store important papers," Rice said. He opened it to find several documents. Two of them were sealed with wax. It was all Henry could take. He deserted his friends and scampered into the hole.

"May I see those papers?" Henry asked. Dr. Rice handed them to Dr. Ragosin for evaluation. Ragosin would not relinquish his acquisition. He broke the seal on the first letter. Although faded, the lead lining of the container had preserved the ancient penmanship. He read it to Henry. It described in vivid detail the events of the battle and then told of the markings used to identify the location of the gold. It was very specific as to the details of the placement of the triangular rock. The purpose of the letter was to authenticate the story the author was going to tell upon his return to Fort Duquesne. He was well aware of the potential outcry over losing the King's money. His signature was smeared and indecipherable.

"I wonder who wrote this?" Ragosin pondered.

"The 10th Frenchman." Henry snatched the other sealed envelope from the box and carefully removed the seal. It also detailed the battle, but its description of the clues did not mention the rock in the tree. Instead there was great detail about the carving of the deer in the tree. It also reflected the author's desire to thwart any misunderstanding of the intentions of the two survivors. The signature was not faded. It was big and bold, as brazen as John Hancock's on the Declaration of Independence. The letter was signed Henry Muselle.

A third document detailed the battle. It was evident that both authors contributed to the common letter after writing their individual epistles. It described the location of the shovels and the springs and referred the reader to the two sealed letters for the remaining markers.

"Isn't this remarkable?" Ragosin commented. "These men went to a great deal of trouble to make sure whoever recovered the gold did not blame them for its loss. It appears that they were going to relate this information to the proper authorities upon their return. Even as they wrote it, they anticipated a problem."

"There was a problem all right," Henry commented shaking my head in disbelief.

"And how would you know?" the scholarly Ragosin asked.

Henry explained his tale to the elder historian. "The men were court-martialed upon their return. They were accused of conspiring to rob the crown of the treasure. Things would probably have worked out if the Indians hadn't bragged about recovering the gold."

"Then you believe that there is a missing box?" Ragosin queried.

"I can't say for sure. I have a copy of the court-martial proceedings," Henry continued.

"You do?" Ragosin was obviously impressed. "How in the world did you find a copy after all these years?"

"I didn't find anything. Since 1755, these proceedings have been required reading for any Henry Muselle seeking to find the treasure. My great-something grandfather, the man who wrote that letter, wanted to make sure the family name was cleared - even if it took nine generations."

"Well, Mr. Muselle," Ragosin continued, "if you have these documents, I'm sure we can petition the French government to reconsider the court-martial and reverse the ruling. I would be more than happy to represent you in this matter. With my expertise, I'm sure . . . " One more person had found treasure in Ralph Saling's field.

* * *

Todd was being mobbed. A disgruntled parent whose child lost to the young scientists called Mrs. Talkington to tell her about the ruckus at the Saling farm. Mrs. T, anticipating Dr. Dorman's success, alerted the media. She told them that students under her direction, and with her extreme encouragement, were about to discover a lost treasure. That was all it took.

The news media descended en masse. Correspondents from the Leader and the Community News wanted exclusive interviews. The country music radio station was the first to grab him for live comments from the scene. The talk radio and all news stations soon followed them. Even the sports station covered the activity. The public radio station appeared, asking questions about the significance of the find and questioning the environmental impact of removing the gold after it had been a part of the substrata for so many years.

Henry Muselle's Treasure

Finally, the television stations from Cleveland arrived. They hated breaking news so far from home, and on a Friday night to boot. The news helicopter hovered overhead, while the satellite truck maneuvered the back roads from Minerva to facilitate the live shot on the five o'clock news. It was almost more than Todd could take.

Todd was having difficulty rationalizing his part in this mass of humanity. He had only been horsing around. He was simply showing off to impress his friends when he added the cyanide to the test tubes. From that one act, he changed the course of history for countless Minervians.

"Todd, what led you to search for the gold?" asked one reporter.

"Did you ever think you wouldn't find it?" asked another.

He was beginning to realize he accomplished what he set out to do. For the first time in his young life he had persevered. He worked through the problem clue by clue. He worked with other people, he listened and he stuck it out. He followed his dream. *His dream! It was Mr. Muselle's dream. He spent all those years preparing to search. He worked his way into the teaching position in Minerva. He shared his story with the kids. And yet, he eluded the media and let his students take the glory.* Todd repositioned himself on his crutch and realized his dream almost cost him his life.

"We've heard a report that you were held hostage by Fred Johnson of Johnson Construction. Is that true?" asked a television reporter.

"Well . . . "

"I was told, one of your teachers saw the incident, tackled Johnson and wrestled the gun away from him. Can you comment?" said another.

"It wasn't like that . . ." Suddenly, all he could imagine was being in Fred Johnson's huge hand, flying through the air and out into space. He shook his head to clear his mind and saw the hollow barrel of Johnson's 44 inches from his hand. He could still hear that hideous sneer as Johnson singled out his prey. He remembered the tone of voice changing and looking up to see the gun aimed right between Mr. Muselle's eyes.

He remembered seeing the punch, and the gun flying. He recalled the shot and the scuffle. Mr. Muselle had saved them. Instead of digging for gold, they might have been digging graves. Mr. Muselle was responsible for this party; after all, it was his treasure. Now the glory was not important. Todd was overwhelmed with the number of people whose lives had been touched and changed.

One of the reporters spotted Henry talking with Ragosin. "Hey, there's the teacher. Let's go talk to him." Like a swarm of bees racing to the hive, the press was after Henry.

Free at last, Todd and his dad pushed on toward the car when Michelle's contour standing in the shadow of the garage caught Todd's eye. When Todd and his dad passed the garage, Dan emerged. "There's someone here who wants to talk with you," he said.

Michelle, head bowed, had difficulty looking Todd in the eye. "I'm sorry I talked to you the way I did," she began, weakly. Todd limped his way to her and lifted her chin. "You're crying."

"Todd, I was so afraid something terrible had happened to you, and that I'd never get to see you again, and that you'd hate me forever . . . "

"Well, something not too great did happen to me, but everything turned out all right . . . Michelle, I'd like you to meet my dad."

Michelle's mouth dropped. She stammered and stuttered with a couple of awkward questions until Todd finally said, "I'll explain later, it'll be easier. Why don't you let us drop you off at home?"

"Good idea."

Michelle took Todd's good elbow and walked along next to him until they came to a small elm tree just a little taller than each of them. Todd aimed so that it would come between them. As the first branches brushed his arm and Michelle had to let go, he turned to her. "Is it true that if we hug a tree it will live longer?"

"That's what my mother said."

Todd extended his wounded appendage, which Michelle

gingerly took in her hand. He dropped his other crutch and balancing on one leg took her other hand. She gently pulled him through the loose leaves of the young tree until their lips amorously touched. As she let him lean back and gain his balance, she commented, "You'd better watch that. I could get used to it." With Michelle on one side and his dad on the other, Todd worked his way through the crowd and back to the truck.

The circus atmosphere at the farm continued for weeks. Skirmish after skirmish occurred as group after group attempted to seize control of the gold and its glory. The residents of the former Watertown attempted to return to normal as the media battled to make them celebrities. Scientists searching for answers to life's important questions struggled with treasure hunters who saw only the glitter of gold.

Occasionally, if one listened carefully, strange sounds resounded across the valley. From the east came the sound of men and horses. The rhythmic plodding of the horses and creaking of the leather straps struggling to contain the King's treasure punctuated idle conversation. From the West, the orderly sound of British soldiers resonated through the woods. The whoosh of wooden gunstocks chafed against their bright red uniforms. The staccato of brass cufflinks ricocheting off canteens and bayonets broke the calm. Some battles are timeless.

Chapter Twenty-Five

Saturday, April 29

The Minerva Jail was no Alcatraz, but then it was no Sunnybrook Farm either. The new facility was built to house prisoners for up to forty-eight hours while charges were brought and arraignments scheduled. The small cells had all the comforts of home, including stainless steel sinks, commodes and cots, but the video camera in the corner of each cell denied prisoners any real privacy. The police department tried to retain a homey and laid back atmosphere so prisoners felt more like a "guest of the village" rather than hardened criminals.

Attorney visits were not held with a barrier between counsel and client, but in the squad room at a small conference table. One needed not worry about escape, however, because electric locks on every portal secured the windowless confines.

Fred hired Bud Billips, a high-powered criminal attorney from Philadelphia to represent him. Bud successfully defended several "family" members back home. He was also instrumental in several "Godfathers" not being indicted and sent up the river. His work on the latter led to a convenient transfer of power that left him a dominant force in legitimizing "family" matters.

He had a staff of thirty attorneys working with him. In addition, to his Philadelphia office, he set up offices in various parts of the country to assist influential clients with their problems. Staff members moved as their clients' situations changed. They complained when they had to move from the San Fernando Valley to Maine. Their latest stint in Arkansas required the addition of several attorneys and the establishment of a crisis management office a block from the

White House. If anyone could get Fred Johnson off the hook, it was Bud Billips.

"I tell you this Todd kid was hitchhiking and out of the goodness of my heart, I stopped to give him a lift," Johnson began.

"Is that so?" Billips said, jotting a few notes.

"As a matter of fact, he jumped out in front of the truck, and forced me to stop," Fred embellished a bit. "What was I supposed to do?"

"I don't know," Billips said, without really reacting.

"I was trying to take him where he wanted to go. He was giving me directions on all these back roads. I had no idea where we were."

"Tell me about the pouch the police found in your truck, and how Todd was injured," Billips inquired.

"The urchin tried to rob me," Johnson said. "He got me on those back roads; and when he saw his opportunity, he grabbed for the steering wheel, trying to force us off the road. That's how my door got smashed. We slid off the road and into a tree. I was lucky we both weren't killed. Somehow the truck spun back on the road, and I was able to keep going."

"Did you hit him?" Billips asked.

"Sure I hit him. I didn't know what he was going to do to me."

"What about the pouch?"

"I guess it fell off during the struggle," Fred said.

"How did Todd leave the truck?"

"Well, he lunged at me this one time, and I pushed him away. I guess the impact with the tree busted the lock on the door because when Todd hit it, he fell out."

"Did you see if he got hurt?"

"Hurt? He jumped up as soon as he hit the ground and started throwing rocks at the truck."

"He sounds like a pretty nasty kid," Billips noted.

"He's the worst," said Johnson.

"Tell me, Fred," Billips said, relaxing a little and discontinuing his note taking, "how did that fire start at the Jackson house?"

"That no account George Huntsinger planned that whole thing," Johnson said. "He's been trouble since the day I hired him. I guess when you get me out of this; I'm going to have to fire him. Speaking about getting out, did you bring bail money?"

"As a matter of fact, I didn't," Billips said. Fred was confused. Billips always did what he was told.

Fred leaned across the table to lash out at Billips when he noticed that on Bud's pad were no notes, just a sketch - a very good pencil drawing - of Fred behind bars.

"You see, Fred, there have been some very important people watching you build this road. They've been monitoring some of your other projects," Billips continued.

"Somebody went to that new office building you're doing in Cadiz and found steel beams which were supposed to be shipped to this road project. Do you know how they got there?"

"I haven't a clue," Fred replied. He began to perspire and fidget in his chair.

"Fred, you're charged with attempted murder of a minor, and you've been indicted for conspiracy to defraud the government," Billips said rising from his chair. "Quite frankly, Fred, my people in Washington and Arkansas are up to their elbows in this kind of thing. Some of my other clients think it would be detrimental to our cause for me to be involved in something like this."

"What are you saying, Bud?" Fred asked. He was now up and pacing about the room. He looked out the window and contemplated smashing it to make an escape.

"What I am saying, Fred, is that I'm not going to take the case. Let's face it, you're just a little fish in a big pond, and someone has to get caught to keep the fishermen away from the big ones."

Fred lunged at the table where Billips was still seated, "You can't do that. Who'll defend me?"

"There's a nice young attorney here in town - fresh out of law school - just itching for a capital case. I've retained him for your counsel. Our friends think he has promise, so we'll help him with your defense - behind the scenes, of course."

"I'm a dead man," Fred said.

"Oh, don't be so glum," Billips said. "Prison food isn't so bad."

"At least I have the contacts made to get my revenge while I rot in here," Fred replied, regaining his composure.

"I almost forgot. There was a message on your machine this morning. Guido called and said to forget the hit on Huntsinger. He's under federal protection. You get those kinds of messages on your machine? Shame on you. You should be more careful."

Johnson hung his head.

Billips gathered his papers and started for the door. "I'm going to have to have a talk with Guido. The Don will not be happy about this. Oh, that reminds me, I have a message to you from the Don. He wants to know if you know what they do in prison to people convicted of molesting children?"

Fred did not respond. It was not true, but how could he prove it, especially in jail.

"Two," Billips yelled into the microphone to alert the dispatcher to open the door. A buzz and clunk indicated the door was open.

"Have a nice life, Fred," Billips said and closed the door.

Chapter Twenty-Six

A Month Later
Saturday, May 25

The security guard finished his coffee and went to relieve his associate standing watch over the gold hole. Although the treasure had been moved to the bank in Minerva, the academicians were still searching for artifacts, and local treasure hunters frequently tried to sneak in under the cover of darkness to snatch anything that was left behind.

A lot had changed in the last month, but the ritual of breakfast had not. The sound of construction vehicles rumbled outside. The noise of table saws, hammers and staple guns rattled the china in the cupboards. The disbursement of the treasure had not been determined, but the attorneys assured Ralph he would receive a significant portion. He took their assurance "to the bank", as they say. Carl was more than happy to lend Ralph the money to begin renovations on the farm.

There were three projects underway. A new gift shop with a large parking area was being built next to the road. A commercial kitchen was being added to the back of the farmhouse. The downstairs of the house would become a restaurant and the upstairs would contain a master suite for guests. The top of the barn would be transformed into additional rooms, retaining the feel of a barn yet providing the modern comforts guests would require. Ralph even envisioned rebuilding the privy behind the farmhouse to add a touch of rustic atmosphere to the place. The "Lost French Gold Bed and Breakfast" was becoming a reality.

All of this change meant Ralph and Martha would be homeless, so a major part of the construction was a suite of living quarters next to the new kitchen. Actually, there were two suites of rooms - one for Ralph and Martha and one for Edna who was moving back from the nursing home. Ralph's new found wealth would permit him to have a private duty nurse available for his mother as needed.

Howard came into the kitchen to conduct his Saturday morning harassment. "I can't believe all the building going on here," he said.

"And you didn't believe there was any gold, either," Edna responded.

"Edna, I was just teasing you," he replied. "You know with my family's interest in the gold, I had to have at least a curiosity about it. I just didn't want to seem too foolish gallivanting all over the countryside looking for it."

"It didn't take the gold to make you look foolish," she retorted.

"Have you folks seen this morning's newspaper?" he asked, trying to change the subject.

"No, we haven't," said Martha, finishing a serving of scrambled eggs.

"There's a big article about the kids who found the gold," he said.

"What's it say?" Ralph inquired.

"They took first place at the state science fair," Howard reported.

"Good, I knew they were concerned about this search fitting in with what they started," said Edna.

"Mrs. Talkington was awarded the Teacher of the Year Award by the district and the state science teachers association," he continued.

"You know, I never really liked her," Ralph said. "She was entirely too hard on those kids."

"She got a lot of glory for being an old witch," Edna said taking a bite of her home fries. "Martha, you could never cook in a nursing home," she said.

"Why not?"

"Your food has taste. Everything they served in the nursing home tasted the same - like warm cardboard."

They all had a good laugh as Martha served the rest of breakfast. Howard continued his report. Dan would spend the summer as an intern at The Department of Natural Resources. Corey would attend a young scholars camp at M.I.T. Michelle was asked to be an announcer on the excursion train. She helped write the script, which of course emphasized the lost gold and its recovery. Huntsinger would take over Johnson Construction assets and continue the road – in the right place. The shouting of one of the construction supervisors startled them.

"This was a good idea to turn this place into a bed and breakfast," Howard said.

"It was all Martha's idea," Ralph explained. "She will be the hostess for the farm, in addition to having a place to sell her crafts. She'll have a business to run which is what she always wanted. Mother's even going to help in the store."

"Don't believe that," Edna replied. "They're just keeping me around as a historical artifact."

"Now, Mother, you know that's not true," Ralph said.

"You didn't tell them you were converting the farm into an eighteenth century farm," Martha interjected.

"You say you're going to farm just like you did when you were a boy?" Howard asked.

"Leave me alone," Ralph said. "The funny thing is as I've been planning this new farm, I have an intense desire to devote a part of the farm as a dramatization of Native American life."

"Not me," said Howard, "I'm going to let the bushes grow up around the house and try to stay away from the tourists."

Todd threw the door of the kitchen open and announced, "Mr. Saling, I've finished your milking, and let the cows out to pasture."

"Look at your shoes," Martha exclaimed, pointing at the muddy tracks behind Todd, "won't you ever learn?"

"I'm sorry, Mrs. Saling," Todd said. He started toward the door when the sound of an approaching very out of tune car caught their attention. The green car pulled along side of the house and backfired.

"That's Mr. Muselle," Todd said. "He and I are going back to the fort in Hanoverton to look through their papers again. He's building his case to present to the French government."

"OK," Martha said. "You run along and we'll see you tomorrow."

Todd finished making his dirty trail across the kitchen floor as he exited.

"I've hired Todd to work around the place this summer," Ralph said. "I figured he was going to be here anyway, so I might as well get some use out of him."

"Good thinking," said Howard. "Has anyone decided who's going to get the money?"

"According to our attorneys, we will get the bulk of it," Ralph explained. "The French government has put in a claim as had the state and federal government. Then there's the problem of taxes."

"We're thinking about starting a charitable educational foundation in honor of the kids to protect some of the money."

"How in the world did this silly search get started?" Howard asked.

"I'm not sure," said Ralph. "As far as I can figure, it started as a simple science experiment . . . "

Chapter Twenty-Seven

Henry Muselle's Journal
May 29

I can't believe it's over. I can't believe we've found the treasure. No longer is Henry Muselle the coward who hid from the British ambush. Now, he is the hero who spent not only his lifetime, but also the lifetimes of nine of his descendants, searching for the truth of his story.

Journal, you have been good to my ancestors and me. You have provided us a place of refuge. You have been someone with whom we could share our deepest thoughts and fears. Now that the quest is over, there is no need for a written record of our activities. And yet, the acquisition of my share of the treasure will provide the funds for a plethora of new adventures. I may keep you to remind me of past missteps and blunders.

How exciting it will be to watch Todd, Corey, Dan and Michelle as they grow with their newfound fame and wealth. I will stay close to them and share the pitfalls of life as a reluctant celebrity.

Our search has been rewarded with Todd's mother and father reconciling. It will mean a new beginning for the three of them, but I am sure they will make the best of it. I just hope that my father knows of my success. I wish I could share it with him.

I am sure Ralph and Martha will be fine in their new enterprise. I must be careful, however, that

Edna does not snare me into becoming part of their attraction.

I think Howard likes the spotlight, although he will never admit it. He subtly mentioned that as Gen. John Morgan and his "Morgan's raiders" were fleeing Union troops during the Civil War, he came as far as Carroll County. Howard insists there is a document stating he wanted to find the lost French gold to finance the war effort in the South. I will only believe his tale if I see the proof. You know, Journal, how Howard is.

I have learned a great deal from this marvelous adventure. I am no longer afraid to be alone with my thoughts and my past. I am rededicated to my craft of teaching. I am excited to see, not only the changes I can make in my students, but also the changes they can bring about in me.

I now know why Guardian visited me so often. I am convinced he was a spirit sent to make sure that we protected his lands. We have so much to treasure in this valley. I am afraid that over the years the residents have forgotten or at least come to not appreciate its beauty and its value.

I had another dream last night in which Guardian appeared to me. He was on the edge of the mound on the other side of the hole where we found the gold. He was playing with a handful of French coins. I believe he returned to the site after a couple of days and retrieved just one box of the treasure. When the French threatened to abandon the Indians, he would flash several coins and tell the story of the ambush. He bragged about knowing the location of the treasure, and since the survivors would not reveal the remaining clues to their superiors, he was able to use his knowledge to keep the alliances with the French intact. After the British overran Fort Duquesne, the gold became insignificant.

The more the French heard of the Indian's tale,

the more pressure they put on the survivors to lead the army back to the gold. British harassment of Fort Duquesne, however, made frontier justice impractical. The commander sent my ancestor and his partner to Montreal for justice. He charged the pair with collusion and hoped the general staff could bring forth a confession. As a matter of honor, the pair refused to cooperate, and the matter came to an ugly resolution.

One small box taken to protect his people from an invading nation brought misery to generations of invaders. "The price of conquest," Guardian told me. He showed me a paper that I remembered seeing at Fort Hanover. It was by the Indian Chief Seattle speaking to Issac Stephens, Governor of Washington Territory in 1863. In my dream, I went over bits and pieces that I could remember. When I awakened, I found the copy I brought with me. I must record it in my Journal so I never forget his words.

> *Every part of this soil is sacred in the estimation of my people. Every hillside, every valley, every plain, and grove, has been hallowed by some sad or happy event in days long vanished.*
>
> *Even the rocks, which seem to be dumb and dead as they swelter in the sun along the silent shore, thrill with memories of stirring events connected with the lives of my people. And the very dust upon which you now stand responds more lovingly to their footsteps than to yours, because it is rich with the blood of our ancestors and our bare feet are conscious of the sympathetic touch.*
>
> *Our departed braves, fond mothers, glad, happy-hearted maidens, and even our little children who lived here and rejoiced here for a brief season, will love these somber solitudes, and at eventide they greet shadowy returning spirits.*

And when the last red man shall have perished, and the memory of my tribe shall have become a myth among the white men, these shores will swarm with the invisible dead of my tribe.

And when your children's children think themselves alone in the field, the store, the shop, upon the highway, or the silence of the pathless woods, they will not be alone.

In all the earth there is no place dedicated to solitude. At night, when the streets of your cities and villages are silent, and you think them deserted, they will throng with the returning hosts that once filled them and still love this beautiful land. The white man will never be alone.

I walked through Ralph Saling's valley this morning. I retraced the steps that led us to the treasure. As I reflected amidst the tranquility of Nature, I believe I found the purpose for this whole adventure.

In the solitude of the moment, with the curiosity of a child, we are presented all the answers - we just have to ask the right questions.

Henry Musselle

Printed in the United States
1035200002B/58-204